D1524321

LADS & LATTES

BOOK 1 OF THE HIGH SCHOOL CLOWNS & COFFEE GROUNDS SERIES

BY A.J. MACEY

Cover: Moonstruck Cover Design and Photography
Editing: Ms. Correct All's Editing and Proofreading Services
Formatting: Inked Inspiration Author Services

This book is dedicated to...

My daughter, Evelyn Rose.
Inspiration is everywhere.

The High School Clowns & Coffee Grounds Series is a WhyChoose/Reverse Harem trilogy featuring MFMM meaning the female main character doesn't have to choose between her love interests.

This book contains references involving PTSD, sexual assault recollections, abuse, underage drinking, and other themes that some readers may find triggering.

BLURB

Emma's to-do list:
1- dump Tyler
2- survive new school
3- rock senior year

My life was as perfect as a teenage girl could hope it would be: friends, boyfriend, straight-A student, loving parents, and all that jazz. Until my entire world comes crashing down. All right, that may be a bit dramatic, but come on, what sane person wants to move halfway across the country after their senior year has already started? That's not all that happened, but I digress. My entire world gets shaken up and suddenly I find myself in the middle of freaking nowhere Nebraska surrounded by three cute guys...

Reid, the clown of the group,
Kingston, the laidback, go with the flow kind of guy,
and Jesse, the closed off one you don't even want me to get started on.

Anyway, so here I am facing all sorts of challenges I never even thought of such as a creepy classmate, a mean Assistant Principal, and trouble with the law, but they've got my back.

We can totally handle our senior year and make it to graduation, right?

CONTENTS

PROLOGUE

We made it! We have officially graduated from high school.

It's hard to wrap my head around, you know? My entire life so far has been fairly predictable, up until this last fall, of course, but we'll get to that in a moment. I had always just been a normal student who went to classes, hung out with friends, did the usual 'teenager' thing like parties and spending time with my boyfriend, but that fateful weekend, it turned out, was to be the start of an entirely new life. I mean, *really* start, like a reboot.

That may be a bit dramatic, I'm still only 18 though, so I'm allowed to be dramatic for a little while longer. But it's true. We had our new (albeit a little rough) start, our ups and our downs, we even had a few close calls with the law, but we're here now. What the story holds for us after this day? Who knows, but we're excited to find out. Together.

You want to see how we made it? Keep reading.

If we can do it, so can you.

With love,
Emma

A.J. MACEY

CHAPTER 1
NINE MONTHS EARLIER

AUGUST 31ST

Today, ty dubbed my style 'homeless librarian chic' and all my friends laughed... I guess I must've missed the joke part.
#IGuess #FunnyFriday #Not

Waving to a few of my friends, I curved around the crowded group of dancers in the Peters' living room. The upbeat song filtering through the speakers was loud enough that the beat thrummed in my chest and, without thinking about it, I found myself swaying to the music. The modern kitchen with its marble counters, stainless steel appliances, and open concept to the breakfast nook was packed with more students. Kara's party was *the* place to be tonight. With her parents out of town on business again and the closest neighbors half a mile away, it was the perfect location for almost the entire senior class and half of the juniors to come drink and socialize.

I would be socializing too, if I could find Tyler.

After checking my phone for the fourth time I filled a plastic cup with whatever kind of beer was in the keg. *Where is he?* Focusing on trying to have fun until my boyfriend decided to show up, I sipped my drink and walked out the open back door.

"Emma!" Kara's bubbly voice shouted. "Over here!" She

waved me over, her frizzy blonde hair and summer tanned skin lit up by the bonfire.

"Hey." I sank into a forest green lawn chair, making sure to smooth my black tulle skirt before getting settled. Several greetings sounded around the group circling the smoky pit which I responded to, but my mind was only half paying attention. *I hope Ty's okay.* Kara's sympathetic facial expression caught my eye, pulling me out of my worrying.

"How are you doing?" She rested her hand on my forearm. Tilting my head in confusion, I couldn't understand why she had asked it like that. "You know"—she leaned into me, the smell of alcohol on her breath—"after your breakup."

"What?" My brows scrunched at her question. "Tyler and I didn't break up." Her eyes widened, and if it wasn't such a serious topic, I would have laughed at her comical expression.

"Oh." She tried to correct her surprise, but her smile turned into a grimace. "Nevermind, must have been mistaken." She shot up with a quick mumbled excuse and practically ran into the house. *Oookay, then.* After looking at my phone yet again, I decided to check inside to see if he was here. It wouldn't be the first time his phone was broken or dead. I had just stepped into the main hallway when I spotted his brown buzzcut curving into one of the side rooms. *Must be looking for me,* I reasoned, walking toward the door he had just entered.

Oh.

My.

God.

"Are you freaking kidding me?" I screeched. Tyler was in the process of shoving his tongue down the throat of a girl from my English class. The few minutes it had taken me to swerve around our classmates and get to the room was apparently enough time for my soon-to-be ex-boyfriend to shuck his pants and shove his hands up Laura's shirt. At the sound of my shrieking, they jumped apart.

"Emma, it's not what it looks like," Ty pleaded, stumbling to pull his jeans up his hips. I couldn't talk, not when my brain was still attempting to process what I had walked in on. Laura had yet to say anything, instead focusing on covering her chest despite the fact she was still wearing her shirt. Stumbling back out of the room, I didn't care that I was running into the other partygoers, I just wanted to get far away from him as fast as I could.

"Emma, wait!" my ex shouted behind me as I dropped the cup of beer on the lawn. Settling behind the wheel of my two-door Nissan, I peeled out of the line of cars. Tears poured down my face as I made my way home. They continued to do so when I fell into bed that night.

SEPTEMBER 1ST

Today, I will think about nothing to do with Turdtastic Tyler. #DouchebagExBoyfriend #StressfreeSaturday

"Emma, sweetheart," my dad called out from the hallway, my bedroom door muffling his voice. "Can you come downstairs, please? Your mother and I have some things to discuss with you." I sighed, wanting to lie in bed so I could mope and wallow in self-pity, but rolled out of bed anyway. I had gotten up earlier than usual this morning, washing the makeup that had smeared over my face in my bout of crying the night before. With no plans for the day, I'd ended up crawling back into bed over an hour ago.

Padding down the hall and carpeted stairs with my bare feet, I headed straight for our kitchen knowing my mom would be working at the table. My dad stood at the granite counter, his dark blue button-up tucked into his light gray slacks. His sleeves were rolled up to his elbows, and his black leather belt matched his dress shoes. Knowing his usual schedule for holiday weekends he had a large soiree to attend at the vineyard later this afternoon. My mom wore a pair of jeans and a loose t-shirt, hair in a low ponytail at the back of her head as she sat at the table. Only this time, instead of having papers and other marketing supplies laid out on the wooden surface, it was empty.

"What'd you guys want to talk to me about?" I asked, sitting in my usual chair across from my mom. Neither of them spoke for a moment, and the tension was growing thicker the longer the silence stretched.

"We're getting a divorce, sweetheart," my dad announced.

Say what, now? I sat there, stunned. My parents never argued or yelled at each other, and they had had a date night every week for as long as I could remember. *So, why are they getting a divorce?*

"All right." My words were hesitant and drawn out, hoping one of them would shout out 'just kidding' or 'gotcha.'

They didn't.

"I got a new job in Elk Ridge, Nebraska," my mom finally said. "We'll be moving Sunday. The movers will be picking things up later today."

"Wait, we?" I could have sworn I heard her wrong.

"Yes, Emma, *we*. You and I will be moving." She continued to talk, but I wasn't listening.

Moving.

To Nebraska.

"I need to get to the vineyard," my father murmured and, without another word, he walked out of the kitchen. The rumbling of his car sounded a few moments later.

"Emma?" My name brought me back to the present, my mom's brows raised at me in question. "Did you hear what I said?"

"Uh"—I tried to recall, but I couldn't—"movers today, we fly there next Sunday." She huffed giving me an exasperated look.

"Not next Sunday, tomorrow Sunday. Our flight leaves tomorrow evening. I have cars lined up for us, as well as a house we're going to rent. You'll be starting school on Tuesday." She had to be speaking in a foreign language because there was absolutely no way she'd just said we're moving halfway across the country tomorrow.

"Don't I get a say? Why are you even getting a divorce? It sounds like you've known about this for awhile if you have these things all lined up. Why am I just now finding out? Why didn't you tell me before now?" My voice was nearing a shout at the end of my questions. *I can't believe this.*

"Emma Brooke," she snapped, "do not raise your voice at me. I understand this is quite the change…"

"Quite the change?" I stood up, yelling. "We're moving out of state *tomorrow,* and I'm just supposed to agree?"

"I get that it's out of the blue, but my job starts on Tuesday so we need to be there before then." My mom tried to stay calm despite my outburst.

I ground my teeth. *What about my friends? Classes?*

"Why can't I stay here?" My voice was whiny. "It's my

senior year, Mom, classes just started the other week. I don't want to go to a new school in the middle of nowhere. I don't want to leave Dad either," I pleaded.

"I'm sorry, sweetie, but the decision has already been made." She stood. "Let's go work on packing up your stuff, all right?"

I couldn't believe this. Turning away from my mom, I sprinted up the stairs. The slamming of my bedroom door was loud in the silence of our broken home. I stood there, tears of anger and frustration pouring down my face as I glanced around my room.

My pictures filled with smiling faces of my closest friends stared back at me. My friends that I was about to leave behind, without any notice. Everything, my entire life, anything I had ever known or cared about was about to be ripped from me in a matter of hours. I received mere minutes to process not only my parents' divorce but a cross country move, a new school, and new people, while they've had… who knows how long. Days? Weeks? Months? They decided without me on everything and then at the last minute remembered I even freaking existed.

It's my life too, you know! I mentally screamed. *This is so unfair!!* Tears built, irritating my already red eyes. I swiped at my cheeks to try and wipe the wet tracks away. Taking in a shuddering breath, I shook myself out of my emotional breakdown and started angrily stuffing my belongings in a bag from my closet. There was nothing I could do regardless of how much it sucked. I was stuck.

Moving.

To Nebraska.

Could it get any worse?

SEPTEMBER 2ND

New state, new home, new everything. So fun.
#Sarcasm #FML #SundayFunday

Yes is the answer. It could get worse.

I sighed, staring at the ground far below from the plane window. Corn and farm land covered every inch of ground as far as the eye could see. Nebraska certainly wasn't like California. It was flat. Completely flat with no mountains or even rolling hills, just fields, the interstate, and tiny towns that shouldn't even be considered towns.

Awesome.

My mom and I hadn't spoken since the day before. I'd packed up my room alone before watching the movers fill the truck with all of my stuff. I knew I should talk to her, I mean it was *their marriage* that was falling apart, but I was still riding that anger at everything that had happened the last two days.

At least I won't have to see Tyler around school.

Holding on to that rapidly dimming silver lining we disembarked from the plane. The Omaha airport was small, only two terminals compared to the enormous LAX we had flown in from. The gates were filled with the quiet buzz of conversation, monotonous announcements filtering through the speakers, and the clopping of shoes echoing on the scuffed white tile.

An hour later, we pulled up to our new home. It was a split-level painted in a soft creamy off-white on the top half with a brick facade on the bottom. There was a two-car garage situated under two wide windows. Off the right of the driveway, there was a curved collection of cement steps leading to the front door. The grass was green and the fence surrounding the backyard had a gate to the right of the house. My mom parked in the driveway before getting out. She motioned for me to follow her when she reached the bottom of the cement stairs and I still hadn't exited the car. It was a nice looking house but I couldn't bring myself to be excited when all I could think about was the house I grew up in. Sighing, I slipped out of the front seat of my mom's new SUV and we walked up the steps to the front door together.

"Ready, honey?" My mom tried to look cheerful, but I knew her better. Her eyes didn't crinkle as they did when she was truly happy, and they were slightly puffy from the tears she had tried to hide from me. I nodded, looking at the foreign house briefly before glancing back to my mom's weary face and forced smile.

"Yeah, Mom, let's go." I tried to summon some excitement, hoping my smile didn't look like a grimace. If she wanted to pretend that this wasn't painful, then I guess I could too. Her hands trembled as she stuck the key in the lock, unintentionally letting her nerves show. Before turning the knob, she flashed me another quick, strained grin. Letting loose a deep breath, she opened the door to our new home.

As soon as I stepped over the threshold I was assaulted with the smell of fresh paint and new carpeting. Light cream carpeting lined both sets of stairs and a grayish-taupe tile was laid out in the small entryway. The walls were painted beige, a shade or two darker than our old house, making the white trim stand out against the walls. The living room was immediately off the top of the stairs and was open to a small breakfast area and galley kitchen. It wasn't furnished other than a stack of paper plates, pack of plastic silverware, and disposable cups. While the kitchen was small, it was updated with dark stone counters and warm-toned wood cabinets.

Venturing down the hall, I located a bathroom updated similarly to the space I had just left, only with a light countertop instead of the almost black that was in the kitchen. There was a master bedroom at the end of the hall with what looked to be an ensuite and a small walk-in closet. Across the hall from the bathroom was another bedroom, its large window looking out over the front yard. I absently noted that the carpet was soft and plush under my feet making my steps nearly silent in the empty house as I flitted from one room to the next.

"I figured if you wanted, this could be your room"—my mom stood in the open doorway glancing around—"or if you wanted, there's another bedroom downstairs in the basement. I actually think it's directly below this one if the windows on the front of the house line up." Her eyes were filled with hope laced with a silent plea to understand, to make the best of the situation. I bit back the irritated sigh I wanted to let loose and vowed to try because, really, what other choice did I have?

"I might take the one downstairs." I turned around and surveyed the room once more. I was thinking over the pros and cons of each space when I came up with an idea. "You could use this as your office?" My suggestion curved up sounding more like a question. My mom's eyes lit up.

"That's a great idea, Emma. Let's head down to the basement." I followed her back down the stairs at the front. The basement was well lit from the sliding glass door at the other end of the spacious room. The carpet, trim, and walls matched upstairs, and there were four doors off the bottom of the steps lining a small hallway.

The first was a matching bathroom to upstairs. Behind the second door was an unfinished utility room that held the water heater, furnace, and washer and dryer. The third, which was immediately to the left of the stairs, was the entrance to the two car garage. Finally, I reached the bedroom which was the door to the right of the staircase. It was identical to the room upstairs, only the window was a little shorter and directly above the grass.

"Yeah, I think I'll stay down here," I announced, stepping back into the main area. My mom nodded looking around.

"This would be a good place to put a couch and a TV for you, a place for your friends to come over. I'll order some furniture for rush delivery."

I bit back the retort I wanted to snap at the mention of friends. *All of my friends are back in California; who knows how it'll go here.* She opened her mouth to say something but closed it almost immediately after she seemed to think better of it. *Good.* I was rapidly approaching my 'fake it till you make it' limit at this point in this holiday weekend.

Nodding, I let my mom know I was tired before grabbing my two bags from the car. After a second trip to grab a blanket and pillow, I settled on the floor of my new room. I spent several hours staring at the ceiling, lost in thought, before eventually falling asleep.

SEPTEMBER 3RD - LABOR DAY

There are far, far better things ahead than any we leave behind. - C.S. Lewis
#PositiveThinking #MotivationMonday

The movers showed up right after eight in the morning. My body was sluggish as it struggled to adjust to the two-hour difference from the West Coast to the Midwest. I found myself standing in the kitchen, unmoving, exhaustion pressing down on me. My eyes glazed over staring at the front windows from my position of leaning on the counter without really seeing. My mom was eagerly directing the movers to specific areas of the house when they came in with different pieces of furniture and boxes. She certainly wasn't struggling this morning with lack of energy or jet lag.

The men who brought in our stuff moved quickly, and after a couple of hours, they were done. I wasted the time while they were assembling our furniture by checking my messages and social media accounts I'd avoided since the party. Multitudes of texts flooded my phone asking about what happened and if it was actually true that I'd moved. I felt my eyes burning with the urge to cry as I responded to my friends, specifically ignoring the apology texts and missed calls from Tyler. Changing quickly after the movers left, I threw on a pair of shorts and a band concert shirt. I made my way back out to the main living area of the basement and grabbed the sandals I had set by the door to the garage. Padding upstairs, I paused a few times to slip them on before I walked down the hall to where I heard my mom shuffling around.

"Mom." I ducked my head into her new office to see her situating files and papers into her filing cabinet and desk, organizing all of her marketing materials and work stuff. "I'm going to run to the store and grab some bedding and stuff for my room."

"All right honey, you have your phone?" I nodded. "Let

me know if you end up going to other places." I agreed once more and headed to the car my mom had gotten for me. It was a used, gray Honda Civic that was in good condition. I didn't much care about the kind of car I drove as long as it got me where I needed to go. Apparently though, that was too much to ask. *Ugh.*

Halfway to the store, I got a flat tire.

I thudded my forehead against the wheel of my car. The drive had been going pretty well up until that point. The house we had moved into was situated in a traditional suburban neighborhood with houses lining either side of the street. The yards were fairly spacious and almost all of the houses were two stories. Once I left the neighborhood though, is when I got my first dose of reality about the fact that I was no longer in California. A giant cornfield was across the divided highway.

Who needs that much corn?

After a little ways down the road, the flat fields started to give way to more homes and business as I neared the main city portion of Elk Ridge. Unfortunately, I didn't get there because now I was pulled over with at least a mile between the nearest business and me.

First, my boyfriend cheats on me.

Then, my parents get a divorce, and I get shipped to the middle of freaking nowhere.

Finally, I get stuck on the side of the road several miles from my house with a flat tire.

I took a deep breath, pushing away the urge to break down. *I can totally change a tire, right?* Groaning, I made sure I wasn't about to be run over by anyone and got out of the car. It was the passenger-side front tire that was flat, a large screw sticking up from the tread. I glared at the stupid thing, as if I expected it to fix itself.

It didn't.

I rounded the back of the car and popped open the trunk. After shifting around the floor mat, I found the spare tire and jack. I lugged them out, practically dropping them in a heap on the ground when a car pulled up behind me. Tucking my long, wavy burgundy-black hair out of my face I turned to see a tall guy around my age stepping out of his vehicle.

I'm about to get kidnapped.

Or murdered.

Awesome.

"Need some help?" The stranger's voice was a deeper baritone than I expected and was filled with an animated, happy tone. A pair of light wash jeans hugged his thighs and a plain, light-gray t-shirt hugged lean muscles that shifted as he walked. His hair was a dark brown that was curly and finger-combed away from his tanned olive skin. A wash of stubble coated his strong jaw, and as he neared I had to crane my neck up to look into his hazel eyes.

Jeez, he's tall.

"Yeah, that'd be great." I tried to sound normal as if him pulling over on the side of the road didn't just scare the crap out of me.

Or let him know that I think he's super cute.

He got to work, propping the jack under the car as I stood there awkwardly. I looked around me taking note of his car, a black Jeep Cherokee that was caked in mud on the bottom half. The dried dirt went as high as his windows, splattered across the shiny surface. His effervescent voice brought my eyes from scanning his car to him, his gaze filled with playfulness as he looked up to me from his crouched position. I purposely ignored the way his shirt was pulled tight over his back muscles.

"Haven't seen you around before."

"I just moved here," I supplied. He nodded absently making the curls bobble on top of his head.

"I'm Reid, what's your name?"

"Emma." I committed his name to memory, or at least tried to. I was pretty terrible at remembering people's names, but I figured he'd probably be going to the school I'd be starting at tomorrow, and it wouldn't hurt to know at least one person. "So," I started, looking around at the fields. "What does someone do for fun around here?" I tried to keep my voice from giving away that I really did not like it here so far, but I don't think I managed.

"A lot of girls go walk around the mall. When it's nice out, a lot of us go down to the river and float on inner tubes or go four-wheeling. The movies are big on the weekend." He paused to start tightening the nuts on the spare. When he was finished securing it, he stood wiping his hands on his jeans, the smears of dirt and grime dark against the light denim. "A lot of times, people just hang out with their friends."

"Thanks for your help." I waved to the flat he had just laid within the trunk of my car. "I hate to admit it, but I've never changed a tire, so I'm pretty sure I would have been stuck out here for a while trying to figure it out."

"No prob, Emma." He gave me a cheeky smile as he walked toward his Jeep. "I'll catch you later." I stood gaping after he drove off with a wink.

Well, that was certainly interesting.

Chapter 2

SEPTEMBER 4TH

In less than four days, I'm starting a new school a MONTH into my senior year... in the middle of freaking nowhere. #Ugh #IsItGraduationYet #TickedOffTuesday

Staring in the mirror of my bathroom, I took stock of my appearance before leaving for the first day. Loose, beachy waves flowed over my shoulders reaching mid-back. My natural black hair was tinted with a burgundy color I had done at the end of summer, having wanted to add something special to my hair. My brown eyes were rimmed with a line of black liner up top and mascara coated both top and bottom lashes. The inky eye makeup offset the plain and ordinary coloring of my irises—the rich brown pupil was encircled by a thin ring of darkened umber. A soft brick red chapstick coated my lips bringing some color to my slightly tanned face, along with the light dusting of blush I had thrown on.

I decided to put on a pair of black skinny jeans and my brown ankle boots. A white t-shirt hung loosely around my curves while a rust-colored scarf and olive utility anorak jacket topped off my outfit. I wanted to make an impression, but not be overly dressy. My friends back home were used to my fancy outfits of tulle skirts, blouses or button-ups, heeled booties, hats, or dresses, but being the new girl here, I didn't want to stick out too much.

The school was two stories and looked new with clean, tan stones and lots of tall windows. I had left my house a good forty-five minutes before school started at 8:10 AM to ensure I wouldn't be late, but the surprisingly decent amount of cars in the lot worried me until I noticed the sound of a marching band playing through the early morning humidity. At least back in California, it didn't feel like I was attempting to wade through a swimming pool.

Who lives in a place where it feels this freaking humid? Me, apparently.

The front walkway was wide and led to several sets of glass double doors. The front entrance opened into a large foyer. To the right of where I was standing sat the cafeteria; a second floor balcony up above overlooked the space and windows dotted the ceiling letting in natural light to illuminate the cavernous room. Three sets of double doors were on the far end of the cafeteria, revealing a large gymnasium. Two hallways going further down the right-hand side of the building sat on either side of the gym. To my left was a wide set of stairs and another hallway that was filled with tall lockers. I was surprised at the newness of the building. *Guess I should have done some research on this place instead of moping around.*

Hindsight is 20/20.

I made my way across the entryway to the door labeled 'Office.' A middle-aged woman sat behind the counter while an older looking gentleman stood near a filing cabinet pulling out several sheets of paper.

"Can I help you?" The woman's voice was friendly, her blue eyes focusing from her computer to me. I nodded as I stepped closer to the chest-high counter.

"My name's Emma Clark. It's my first day." Her face lit up in understanding as she grabbed a stack of papers and a hefty book.

"Yes, Principal Rudley informed me. Here's your schedule, it should line up with your previous school and the classes you were taking there." She handed me a sheet of paper with a list of classes, teachers, room numbers, and the times of when everything started. Her bright blue nail polish sparkled under the office lights. "This is a sheet for your teachers to sign. Here's your school map, rule book, academic calendar, and a sheet for your parent or guardian to fill out." I thanked her and made my way out to the cafeteria. There were a few more students sitting scattered around the tables than when I first arrived, most of which were reading or finishing up homework. Taking a seat at one of the tables off to the side, I pulled out a pen from my backpack and took a look at my senior year schedule.

Homeroom: 8:10 AM - 8:30 AM
Mr. Fergusen
Room 219
Period 1: 8:35 AM - 9:25 AM
American History
Miss Ester
Room 232
Period 2: 9:30 AM - 10:20 AM
AP English
Mr. Wright
Room 105
Period 3: 10:25 AM - 11:15 AM
Nutrition
Mrs. Sanders

Room 130
Period 4: 11:20 AM - 12:10 PM
Civics
Mr. Fergusen
Room 219
Lunch: 12:10 PM - 1:00 PM
Cafeteria
Period 5: 1:05 PM - 1:55 PM
Trigonometry
Mrs. Hazel
Room 112
Period 6: 2:00 PM - 2:50 PM
AP Chemistry
Mr. Davids
Science Lab 3
Period 7: 2:55 PM - 3:45 PM
Dance
Mrs. Petra
Theatre Studio

Not too bad.
At least it's not a typical gym class.

I shuddered thinking about how we had to run laps and play sports that I was terrible at back at my old school. Over the next little while I marked down the paths on my map that I would need to take and tried to orient myself when the first bell rang.

Startled out of my own little world, I looked up to see hundreds of kids filling the cafeteria and front walkway, the conversations melding together into one large cluster of noise. Lots of eyes were wandering in my direction as I made my way up the stairs, but I focused on glancing between my map and the overhead signs and ignored the wayward stares. Thankfully, my homeroom was easy to find right at the end of one of the interior hallways.

"Ah, you must be our new student!" my teacher bellowed out. His belly strained against his button-up, and his pants were belted tight underneath the round mass. His dark brunette hair was graying and matched the goatee on his olive face. I stepped up to his desk and handed him one of the sheets the secretary had given me. He signed it quickly, bending over his desk and giving me a chance to glance around the room. The walls were covered in history posters, maps, and a timeline of important dates in American history. The whiteboard was mostly clear except a small portion on the end that held a 'Quote of the Day' that read "With the new day comes new strength and new thoughts. -Eleanor Roosevelt."

"Everyone, I would like to introduce Arbor Ridge High School's newest student, Emma," he boastfully announced to the filled classroom. All eyes landed on me if they hadn't been already. Giving a small, awkward wave, I turned back to Mr. Fergusen and took my paper back. A slight tingle of a blush crept across my cheeks at the unwanted attention of the other students. "If you would, take a seat please, next to Jesse over there."

Mr. Fergusen pointed to the spot on the end of the second row next to a student who I assumed was Jesse. His full lips were downturned in a scowl, his skin the color of dark chocolate, and his black hair was short against his scalp. He was clean shaven, and his ears held a square diamond stud in each lobe. I sank into the chair next to him, keeping my eyes on my own desk. His attitude was very much put-off that I had been seated next to him.

Get in line, buddy.

I don't want to be here, either.

Homeroom went by quickly, the other students just talking amongst themselves after Mr. Fergusen took roll. When the bell rang, I stood and slung my bag over my shoulder. My eyes darted between hall signs and the markings I had made on my map as I headed toward American History. Thankfully, it was right along the main corridor and down one of the next interior hallways. My teacher, Miss Ester, was a short woman with a curvy figure clad in a navy skirt and yellow blouse. Her red hair was cut in a long bob, and the straight tresses brushed the tops of her shoulders.

"Miss Ester? My name's Emma, and I'm new," I murmured not wanting to pull any more attention than I already was. I didn't like being the center of attention, and being the new student in a school, especially senior year after the year had started, was the very definition of the epicenter of attention and gossip.

"Yes, the office informed me you would be starting today." She handed me a thick textbook and a syllabus. "We're currently covering the American Revolution, and there will be a test at the end of next week. I suggest either gathering the class notes from another student, or..."

"I can help her, Miss E," a familiar effervescent voice behind me offered happily. A tanned arm slid around my shoulders, and the scent of Old Spice deodorant filled my nose. Reid focused a broad smile at our teacher. "Emma and I go way back. Don't we?" I choked back a retort and just nodded, not trusting whatever could come out of my mouth if I attempted to speak. Miss Ester glanced between the two of us with an eyebrow raised and a skeptical 'mhm' before shoo-ing us to get settled. Reid steered me over toward one of the two-person desks and sank into the seat on the left. When I made no move to sit, he tugged on my jacket until I flopped into the cold metal chair.

"Fancy seeing you here," he started. Another cheeky smile appeared as he leaned forward on our desk and looked at me. "What's your schedule look like?"

"Why would you need to know?" I smarted, pulling a notebook and pen out to take notes.

"Well," he dragged out, "I was going to see if I could help in any of your other classes, but if that's how it's going to be..." He trailed off shrugging one shoulder. I pursed my lips knowing I should accept his help, but after the last several days of being let down by everyone, I wasn't sure I wanted to rely on somebody.

He did change my tire out of the goodness of his heart though.

He seemed to be watching me flit through my back and forth mental argument, his lips twitching when he saw me make my decision. Digging out my schedule, I passed it over to him with a huff. After flashing me a cocksure smile, he examined my schedule. We didn't talk through the rest of class as Miss Ester lectured about different things I had already covered in my last school. I took notes anyway, figuring it wouldn't hurt to have a refresher since there was a test next week. The bell rang signifying the end of class. Stuffing everything back into my bag, I reached for my schedule, but Reid pulled it out of my reach before I could take it back.

"Reid!" I snapped exasperatedly. I just wanted to make it through the rest of the day, and I couldn't do that without knowing where to go. He hooked his arm over my shoulder once more and dragged me along into the crowded hallways. "What are you doing?" I whined. I had to lean into his muscled chest to avoid running into people, purposely ignoring how warm or solid his body felt against me.

"Walking you to"—he paused glancing down at my schedule—"AP English." Navigating the hallway under his arm was difficult at my 5'5" height when he was easily 6', but somehow we managed. He high-fived people he knew or gave a wave with a warm smile as we walked. Reid seemed to know almost everyone in the school, including the teachers. Girls threw flirty smiles at him as he walked by and batted their eyelashes at him while guys did their usual bro-macho passing greetings of 'sup' or 'hey dude.' I forced myself to pay attention to where we were walking despite having eyes watching me under his arm or that I felt my phone vibrate in my back pocket. I wanted to be able to find my way tomorrow when I did this on my own because I knew this wouldn't become an everyday thing.

"Hey, Reid," a smooth greeting sounded from the opposite side of him. The melodic tone of the man's voice reminded me of a finely tuned guitar, and I immediately felt my breath catch when I saw who the voice belonged to. He was tall, taller than Reid by an inch or two, with golden blond hair that was combed away from his face like Reid's, only his was mostly straight instead of curly. His warm tan skin tone reminded me of the guys back home, and his handsome face was framed by a short beard. His body was lean and clothed in a denim chambray button-up and khakis, and cognac colored boots adorned his feet. His saturated coffee brown eyes glanced at me curiously from where I was tucked under Reid's arm.

"Kingston, I want you to meet the new girl." Reid tugged me forward so I was standing directly in front of his friend. Two large hands rested on my shoulders as Reid held me steadfast between them, his breath shifting my hair slightly as he introduced me. "Emma, this is one of my best buddies, Kingston. He's in your AP English class."

"Hi," I squeaked. Smashing my lips together, I focused on keeping my heart from pitter-pattering out of my chest at their combined attentions.

"Hey." He gave me a soft smile, but before either of them could say more, the warning bell rang signifying class would be starting shortly. Reid shifted me once again and squeezed me to his muscled torso in a brief side hug before taking off down the hall. Dark, curly hair flopped on top of his head as he swerved around the other students on his way to make it to class on time. When I turned back toward the classroom, Kingston was holding it open for me to enter. His hand came to rest on my lower back when I passed, and he walked me up to our teacher who was standing by his desk.

"Mr. Wright, this is Emma. The new student." Kingston took the lead introducing me to the tall, lanky man before me. Mr. Wright's head was shaved in a buzzcut and a pair of sharp green eyes focused on me at Kingston's words.

"Ms. Clark"—Mr. Wright handed me a copy of *Crime and Punishment* by Fyodor Dostoevsky—"we're currently reading this. An essay based on the topic assigned on your syllabus will be due Friday, but since you are arriving late I will give you until next Wednesday." I took the materials he handed me and waited patiently while he signed my paper from the office. Kingston's hand stayed on my back, the warmth of his touch nearly burning my skin with how much focus I was putting on it.

In a similar fashion to what Reid had done, his 'best buddy' led me to a desk and proceeded to have me sit next to him. I focused on pulling my materials out of my bag, feeling Kingston's gaze on me every so often from his leaned back, relaxed position in his chair, but I didn't look at him because if I did, I'd probably embarrass myself.

And trust me, no one wants to see that.

To distract from the urge to look over at him, I busied myself with my usual routine before classes. Nibbling on my lip, I doodled quickly in the top corner of my blank notebook page. The little inked character was frowning back at me as I made the usual speech bubble next to the little drawing writing "two classes down, five to go."

A small musical chuckle pulled me out of my focus and I glanced over at Kingston. His gaze drifted from my doodle to my face; the hint of laughter filled his eyes making the coffee brown irises stand out. I immediately tensed, embarrassed that he had noticed my ritual.

So naturally, I had to immediately embarrass myself further.

"Did you know Johnny Cash was also an artist?" I asked hurriedly, my voice pitched up in my urge to redirect his focus. I nodded absently as I talked, barely waiting for him to shake his head. "Mhm. His painting, *Flight*, was highly sought after but he was too busy with music to produce much art. Yup!"

So much for not embarrassing myself.

"That's very interesting, Emma," he commented with a tiny smile. Internally groaning, I gave him a forced and awkward grin in return thankful that the teacher started talking essentially saving me from embarrassing myself more.

I couldn't bring myself to look over at Kingston for the rest of class and when the bell rang, I shot out of my chair and practically ran out of the room, frazzled not only from that interaction with Kingston but from all of the attention I had been receiving. Getting lost in the crowd of students, I walked several hallways over to my nutrition class. The class passed the same as all the others; Mrs. Sanders signed my papers, handed me my materials, and let me know what information was being covered. Thankfully, this class didn't have any homework giving me a slight reprieve on my expanding to-do list. I spent most of the class only half listening since I had taken a health and nutrition class last year in California, splitting my time between taking notes and texting Kara and my other friends under the desk.

They were hunting for information like sharks that smelled blood in the water. While they asked about Tyler and the breakup, they were more focused on my move. I fielded the inquiries as best I could and asked how things were there to try and redirect their nosy questions, but the bell rang before I could check their responses. Ignoring Tyler's messages that were still coming in every hour since the party, I shoved my phone into my back pocket. Weaving around my fellow students, I made my way back upstairs to the classroom I was in earlier for homeroom since Mr. Fergusen was also my Civics teacher. I had just taken a seat when the familiar scent of Old Spice surrounded me.

"You're in my spot," Reid teased, "but I'll forgive you seeing as how you're new and everything." I glared over at him. My fuse was growing shorter the longer the day went on, and it wasn't even noon. I had yet to hear from my dad since before I left for the airport, Tyler's incessant messaging was wearing on me, and my agitation at every little thing was multiplying. I knew he was trying to make conversation and joke around, but I really didn't want to keep being reminded that I was new.

Or that my boyfriend had cheated on me.

Or that my parents were no longer together.

Or finally, that I was in the middle of the country while my entire life was back in Cali.

"I'll sit somewhere else tomorrow," I muttered, turning my eyes quickly to my empty notebook page as they filled with tears. The compounding events over the weekend were finally taking their emotional toll, my chest constricting tightly at the thought of everything.

"Hey"—he tilted his head down to look at my face—"I was just kidding. You can sit wherever you want. Well, as long as it's next to me." I couldn't help it, but a strangled laugh bubbled out of me at his addition to his statement. "Aha! There's that smile." I looked over at him. His amused eyes were bright and a wide smile highlighted white teeth against his warm skin tone. Feeling a blush creep up my neck and cheeks, I gave him a small smirk before turning my attention to the teacher as he started class.

"Come on, Emma." Reid's head jerked toward the door of the classroom as I finished packing up my stuff. My resistance to his attention melted away as he started toward the cafeteria, and I decided to follow him, not wanting to sit alone at lunchtime. Since getting lost in the rush of students was a realistic possibility, I held onto Reid. His black backpack was hanging off one shoulder allowing me to grab ahold of the back of his shirt. The light green material was soft under my fingertips and warm from his skin.

We ran through the serving area quickly as I made sure to get enough to quell my hunger-a chicken sandwich, some fries, and a banana. Grabbing a bottle of water on my way through the checkout process, I continued to trail after Reid to a table near one of the gym doors. When we reached the table I noticed two other bags tossed on the top, but no one was sitting there.

"They're grabbing food," he answered, having understood my confused expression. "You've already met one of them."

"Kingston?" I surmised sitting next to Reid.

"Look at you"—he nudged my elbow—"you'll be one of us in no time." I chuckled and took a bite of my sandwich. When Kingston and whoever the other bag belonged to walked back to the table, I looked up, my skin prickling when I saw who the other student was.

Jesse. The guy who didn't want to sit next to me in homeroom.

Don't worry though, he didn't lose his attitude in the few hours between homeroom and lunch. His scowl was still firmly in place when he saw me at their table.

Awesome.

"Jesse, meet…" Reid started to introduce me.

"Emma. Yeah, I know," Jesse cut him off, his voice disinterested and short. Kingston looked at his friend discreetly out of the corner of his eye, his brows furrowing ever so slightly at his gruff attitude.

"Oh, when did you guys meet?" Reid didn't seem fazed by Jesse's interruption, his next question directed at me. "Why didn't you mention you knew Jesse?" His words held a playful note, an eyebrow raised questioningly at me.

"I didn't know you were friends. So, how am I supposed to know when to mention I meet someone?" I pointed out taking another bite. I was determined not to let Jesse's irritating attitude get to me.

"She's got you there." Kingston smiled at Reid before going back to his food. He seemed content to just hang out at the table, not concerned that I was new or that I was sitting with them.

"Where'd you move from anyway?" Reid's question was muffled behind his hand as he chewed an overly large bite of hamburger.

"California," I answered as I finished my sandwich and started in on my fries.

"Senior?" Reid continued his questions. I nodded, feeling my phone start to vibrate in the steady pattern of a call. Pulling it out, I saw Tyler's name flash on the screen before I ignored the call and laid it on the table. "What brought you to The Good Life?"

"The what?" I asked confused. *What the heck is that?*

"The Good Life, it's one of the slogans used for Nebraska," Reid supplied. I barely restrained the urge to roll my eyes. Being in the middle of nowhere was not 'The Good Life.'

Not to me, anyway.

"My mom got a new job"—I swallowed back the surge of emotion as I spoke—"and my parents were getting divorced, so apparently I had to tag along on this cross-country adventure." Reid nodded, but before he could ask another question my phone started to ring yet again. I picked it up to ignore the call when Reid plucked my phone from my fingers and answered it.

"Yellow," he dragged out the playful greeting despite my shocked face.

He seriously just answered my phone.

I mean, who does that?

"Emma is right here"—he paused and glanced over at me—"and I'm Reid." I shook myself out of my stupor and snatched my phone from him.

"What do you want, Tyler?" I rubbed my forehead before propping my elbows on the table and shoving my tray away.

"Who the hell was that? Why haven't you been answering my texts? Did you seriously move because of me?" he rattled off, his questions growing increasingly angry and full of disbelief.

"Obviously my new boyfriend Tyler, because it's my first day at a new school and I have no problems shoving my tongue down some random person's throat like you. Seriously? He's just a friend of mine. I haven't answered because I don't want to talk to you and no, I did not move away because of you," I drawled out, not wanting to deal with this. *This is just what I wanted to deal with today. Not.*

"I miss you, babe," he pleaded. "When are you coming home?"

"I don't know when I'm visiting, and even if I was, I wouldn't see you." I sighed, my arm dropping to the table. Purposely ignoring the curious gazes of my tablemates, I stared at the far wall of the cafeteria.

"Why? I said I was sorry. It was a mistake, Emma. You're the only one I want. Can we please get back together?"

I ground my teeth at his incessant begging. *Does he not understand what the word "no" means?*

"No. We're not getting back together." I saw the guys' eyebrows raise at my harsh and irritable tone. "I freaking walked in on you about to screw someone from my English class! Not just no, but hell no." I hung up, dropped my phone on the table, and covered my face. I groaned miserably when I heard the phone start to go off again, but it was immediately cut off. Looking down in confusion, I saw Reid had ignored the call.

"Well," he started. *At least he has the decency to look a little bad.* "That was not what I was expecting." I continued to glare at him as his tanned, stubble-covered cheeks began to turn red. "Sorry."

"Don't do it again unless I say it's okay." I gave in, tired of being angry. I turned off my cell and shoved it in my bag.

"So, friend, huh?" he teased, essentially breaking the tension around the table. Kingston laughed and shook his head while I couldn't hide the smile that spread across my face. Jesse though... he still looked peeved.

"I guess," I teased back, "you didn't exactly give me a choice on tagging along throughout the day. "

"That's what us midwesterners are known for, don't you know?" Reid spouted playfully. "We're all about the friendliness. Forget about southern hospitality, they don't have anything on us." I rolled my eyes at his exaggeration but couldn't stop the tiny curl to my lip.

"Well, it's certainly not like I was expecting here that's for sure," I joked back. "You guys actually drive cars to school, not tractors or horses." No joke, Kara actually spouted that to me yesterday saying it was something she had heard they did here. Reid and Kingston burst out laughing; apparently even Jesse thought it was funny because his lip twitched just a bit before smoothing over into his irritated frown.

"And you're not blonde haired and super tan from spending all your time surfing or laying out on the beach," Reid shot back with cocky smile. "Do you always believe what you hear?" I scoffed, my eyes narrowing on him.

"Of course not," I huffed. "I also never said I was the one who said tha..." I trailed off when I saw him trying hide a laugh behind a hand realizing he was joking. "Ha ha," I hummed flatly, "very funny." At that he couldn't hold it in.

"I'm glad you're not like that otherwise you'd fall in your own valley girl stereotype there, Cali girl." I glared at him playfully trying not to think about the warm tingles that filled me.

"What other classes do you have?" Kingston asked. His laid back demeanor emanated from across the table calming my spiraling thoughts about Reid and his nickname for me. I breathed a sigh of relief at the change of topic, although Kingston's gaze focusing on my face didn't help the little wiggle of butterflies in my stomach.

"Uh"—I dug in my bag and pulled out the wrinkled paper—"trig, AP chem, and dance."

"Who's your teacher for trig?" Kingston's smooth voice had little butterflies taking off in my stomach while Reid's vivid eyes, which were trained on my face intently, had me blushing.

"Mrs. Hazel." I tilted my head to read the paper that was upside down as I had started to tuck it back in my bag.

"Me too." Kingston smiled, and I'm pretty sure I felt my heart stutter painfully in my chest. "I'll walk you." They started to stand and gather their bags, the clock showing a couple of minutes before the warning bell would go off. I took my time tossing my tray to calm my racing heart.

Two insanely attractive guys who want to be friends?

Well, technically three, but only two seem content to keep me around.

I'm so screwed.

CHAPTER 3

SEPTEMBER 4TH

First, a guy I don't even know is snippy with me and then Turdastic Tyler calls ruining a perfectly good lunch. #ISuckAtMakingFriends #DouchebagExBoyfriend #TickedOffTuesday

The next class passed quickly with Kingston sitting next to me in trig. The easy smile that he kept throwing me made my cheeks burn. Jesse was in my AP chem class. Pretty sure he didn't want me to sit next to him, but Kingston walked me into the lab and deposited me next to his friend. I kept my eyes forward on the notes Mr. Davids was writing on the whiteboard, but I felt animosity flowing off him in harsh waves. As soon as the bell rang, Jesse hopped up like his stool was on fire and took off out the lab door. I sighed, unsure of what I'd done to him to make him hate me so much, but I decided that was on him.

Since I didn't know I needed a change of clothes, Mrs. Petra allowed me to sit to the side and observe the dance class today. I ended up zoning out for most of the class, the day and my stubborn jet lag having taxed my limited energy. When the final bell rang, I sagged under the weight of everything in my backpack since my to-do list had grown to ridiculous lengths with the amount of homework and studying I had to catch up on.

Nearing my car, I spotted Kingston and Reid a few spaces down leaning against Reid's Jeep. I tossed my bag in the backseat, but before I could get settled behind the wheel, they were standing by my car. Jesse had appeared as well, but he was sulking over by the Jeep looking aggravated that he had to wait for them to talk to me.

"Hey there," Reid greeted cheerfully, and Kingston just gave me a small smile. "What are you doing tonight?"

"Homework, and probably unpacking," I supplied. Their brows furrowed.

"You haven't unpacked yet?" Kingston asked. I tilted my head at them in confusion. *Of course I haven't, I just got here*, I thought to myself.

"No, when I say I just moved here, I mean literally. As in we packed the truck on Saturday, flew in Sunday, and the movers unloaded the truck yesterday." Their brows went from drawn down in puzzlement to up their forehead in shock in a split second flat.

"Oh, I didn't realize you had just gotten to town yesterday or I would have invited you over to our Labor Day party we had." Reid grimaced, but I waved his worry away. *Although, he looked pretty cute when he made that face*. I pushed the wayward thought away as he continued talking. "Do you want some help unpacking?"

"I don't think there's much, just some clothes and miscellaneous stuff," I answered shrugging half-heartedly. Although, I did enjoy spending time with them throughout the day, and I knew I needed notes from Reid for our history class. With those thoughts in mind, I solidified my decision. "Do you guys want to come over and study? We've got a large area in the basement we could work in, and I'm pretty sure my mom said some furniture was being delivered this morning."

"Yeah, let me go tell Jesse." Reid hitched his thumb toward his friend whose scowl grew when he noticed the motion. Leaving me and Kingston alone, he headed over to inform Jesse of our plans.

"He doesn't seem to like me," I noted quietly as I eyed Jesse's angry expression and harsh stare. I had tried to not let it bother me, but for some reason I couldn't understand, it did. *I haven't done anything to him*, I thought ruefully. Granted, I probably could have tried to say hi or something, but I didn't think I'd been rude or mean.

"That's not you, Emma. Jesse is just a bit more wary of people than you're probably used to," Kingston murmured, watching his two friends argue back and forth with a tiny downturned curl of his lips. I pretended not to see the arms waving in my direction as they talked about me. "He'll come around," Kingston assured. I nodded, unsure on whether or not to believe him.

Reid had followed me to the house, parking his Jeep on the street out front as I pulled into my spot in the driveway. Hopping out, I went to the front door and unlocked it not having remembered the code for the garage. I held the door open for them to enter, and their eyes darted around curiously. Except for Jesse who just looked annoyed to be there.

"You can drop your bags downstairs. Do you guys want anything to drink or eat? I think I have some food, but if not, we could always order something," I offered, following them into the house. Locking the door, I joined them down the short staircase and looked at the new furniture my mom had gotten. The main space held a large sectional in a dark gray fabric, a white wooden coffee table, and a rustic styled entertainment center with a brand new TV. There was also a small, round dining table and chairs by the back door and a desk against the wall, the sun from outside splaying over the white-washed wood top.

"We can help get it," Reid offered after setting his bag at the table. I nodded, dropping my own bag and taking off my jacket since the sun filtering in the room made it warm enough not to need it. They followed me back to the stairs, but before I headed up I opened my door and tossed my coat in a heap on my unmade bed.

"Nice room," Reid exclaimed. His bright voice came from right above me as he looked over my shoulder, his gaze darting around my room. "Looks like more than just some clothes to put away." His eyes focused on the large stack of moving boxes piled against the wall. Rolling my eyes, I nudged him back out of the doorway.

"I said clothes *and* miscellaneous stuff," I countered turning toward the steps, but he paused and walked deeper into my room. When I followed him in, I noticed him holding my favorite bear. He turned to me with a wry smile on his face.

"And who is this? I didn't peg you for the stuffed animal type," he said holding him out to me. I grabbed him from his hands and hugged him close to my chest.

"Don't mock, Mr. Fritz. My grandpa gave him to me the birthday before he died. He makes me feel safe," I mumbled looking down at the bear's tattered ear and matted fur. Silence reigned long enough for me to look back up at him; his eyes were downcast and he nibbled on his lip seemingly lost in thought before glancing at me.

"I'm sorry, Emma," he murmured before giving me a shy smile, "I have a bear too. Mr. Jangles. Although he's a little more jangled than bear at this point. I should probably get rid of him, but I can't bring myself to." I couldn't stop the grin that curled my lips at his sweet story. Setting Mr. Fritz back on my bed, I walked over to Reid and grabbed his hand. He glanced down and intertwined our fingers before looking down at me.

"It's okay, Reid. It'll be our little secret." I tugged his hand lightly as I started toward the door before he could say another word. "Let's get some stuff to eat and drink and get down to homework. My list of assignments is unbelievably long," I told Kingston and Jesse who were pulling out classwork and textbooks near the table. Reid squeezed my hand before letting go and starting up the stairs. The other two fell in step behind me as we walked to the upstairs level.

"What do you have to do?" Kingston's smooth and melodious voice danced over to me as we waded through the living room that had been furnished with our family's fairly new couch and furniture that we had in California. The large TV rested on a rustic, farmhouse style stand similar to the one downstairs. The piece of furniture matched the coffee table and the end tables were similar in style, but stained and off-white cream paired well with the muted gray-brown fabric couch. The bright-colored curtains, throw pillows, and patterned rug stood out against all of the neutral colors as I walked into the kitchen.

"I have that test on Friday in history, an essay on *Crime and Punishment* in AP English, my giant list of trig problems, then a chapter for civics, and a chapter for AP chem," I rattled off while bending down to look in the fridge. "All right, we have water, some soda, milk, juice, and yeah…" I trailed off looking around the food my mom picked up Sunday in an attempt to see all the beverages.

"First of all, I'll take a water," Reid said from behind me, his light wash jeans showing in the corner of my eyesight. "Second, you're in the Midwest now, so it's pop not soda." I blinked in confusion.

"I'll take a pop," Kingston added before I could question Reid. I glanced to the right at Jesse over the top of the refrigerator door. He stood stoic, his lean muscled arms crossed tightly over his chest as he looked around the kitchen and dining area. When he realized I was staring at him, he answered.

"Water," he muttered disinterestedly before looking toward the back door by the dining table which led out to a small deck.

"Water for you two." I handed out the bottles to Reid and Jesse before handing the cold can to Kingston and making sure to grab my own. "*Soda*," I emphasized, "for you." Reid groaned behind me as Kingston's laidback smile curled his lips.

"We'll get you broken in in no time, Cali girl." Reid's arm slithered over my shoulder directing me toward the stairs. "Let's go get that pile of stuff you have to do done." I grumbled under my breath as we made our way back to the basement taking up residence around the four person table. Kingston sank into the chair across from me, Reid to my left, with Jesse to my right. We worked in companionable silence for a while before Kingston randomly huffed and gave Reid a look.

"Reid," Kingston lectured, "stop bumping my arm." Reid just chuckled. My brows dipped down until I realized Reid was left handed, his elbow purposely shifting to hit Kingston who was right-handed.

"I'm not doing anything," he claimed innocently although

he was clearly moving his arm.

"You're hungry for pizza, aren't you?" Kingston sighed, dropping his pen on his notebook to pull out his phone. Reid nodded enthusiastically in response. Jesse rolled his eyes and turned back to his homework. "You hungry, Emma?" I hadn't given it much thought having been focused on trigonometry, but at the mention of pizza my stomach rumbled slightly.

"I could eat, but you don't have to order it, I can do it," I tried to explain. *I mean, this is my house and they are guests.* But Kingston and Reid waved me off as Jesse eyed me suspiciously. I rolled my eyes at them before going back to my homework.

"What do you want on your pizza?" Kingston angled his phone away from his face as he directed his question at me.

"Just whatever works," I mumbled, finishing up the last problem I had for trig. Kingston got up and stepped out to the patio, the closed glass door muting his voice. After double checking the problem, I tucked the pages away in my notebook and switched it out for my Civics textbook. Kingston returned as I started taking notes.

"It'll be here in a half hour to 45 minutes," he mentioned, sitting back in his seat. I was thankful that the chapter I had to read for class was short and I had finished it in twenty minutes. I was debating what to work on next when Reid's pen tapped my arm.

"You want to copy the history notes?" He held up his notebook with a flashy wave of his hand making me chuckle.

"Yeah that'd be great." I tried to grab them, but he pulled the spiral bound pages out of my reach. I gaped at him while he just smiled brightly at me.

"What're the magic words?" he taunted as I pulled my arm back.

"Please?" I tried, but of course that wasn't it. "May I please have the notes?" I tried again.

I should have just chosen to read all the material.

"It's 'Reid is the awesomest for allowing me to use his notes because I decided to be a rebel and start school late,'" he recited in faux-prestige.

Definitely should have just read the material.

"Dude, just give her the notes," Jesse grumbled, his soft command filled with irritation as he glared at Reid. A blush crept up my neck and cheeks at his sharp tone, feeling like I had been reprimanded for horsing around. The silence was tense as Reid and Kingston stared at their friend.

"Fine, spoilsport." Reid played off Jesse's outburst before handing the notebook to me. "Here you go, Emma." I flashed him a grateful smile before taking it from his outstretched hand. His handwriting was small, slightly messy, but still legible. The doorbell ringing broke up the study group we were having shortly after. Kingston and Reid went to the front door telling me I didn't have to help. Rolling my eyes yet again, I huffed but agreed. Their talking with the delivery driver was quiet, and the awkwardness between Jesse and me was creeping its way to uncomfortable levels.

"So," I started, figuring I might as well try to talk to him since it seemed like I'd be sticking around for a while. "How long have you known those two?" He glanced up at me briefly before looking down at what looked to be calculus.

"Since pre-school," he answered, his words and tone short like he didn't actually want to talk to me.

Well, that's just too dang bad.

"That's pretty cool," I continued, "that's how it was for most of my friends back in Cali." I tried to smile, but at that thought, a rush of raw emotions flooded my chest. Glancing down at Reid's notebook, a stupid, unwanted tear dripped onto the page.

"I'm sorry." Jesse's eyes were on me, for once not filled with contempt as he spoke. "That must be hard." I pushed back the tears, having shed enough since last Friday. Trying to play it off, I shrugged.

"Not much I can do about it," I murmured. Before we could talk anymore, Reid bounded into the room, his curls bouncing on top of his head.

"I come bearing pizza!" he half-sang, half-shouted in excitement. His arms were full of three large pizza boxes, Kingston joined us with a small stack of paper plates and napkins. Jesse and I moved all the papers and textbooks off the surface so there would be room.

"We have hamburger"—Reid pointed to the first box as he set it down on the table before then pointing to the other two—"cheese, and meat lovers." I scrunched my brows.

Just hamburger pizza?
What kind of crazy place is this?

"What?" Reid must have noticed my face cause he directed his question at me. "Do you not like any of those?" I shook my head.

"It isn't that, I've just never heard of only hamburger on a pizza." I took a slice of it as well as a slice of cheese since the three boys went directly into the meat lovers. They all stopped and gaped at me.

"Say what now?" Reid gasped dramatically. "What kind of crazy place did you come from? Hamburger pizza is a staple."

Me, come from a crazy place?

They're clearly from the crazy place.

"California, where pizza is normal," I teased, taking a bite of the odd piece. *Not bad.* I hummed when I realized all three of them were watching me. I stopped my movement as I was about to take another bite, the slice right outside my open mouth. "What?"

"Well…" Reid dragged out the word, his hand rolled in the air for me to elaborate on whatever he was trying to ask of me.

"How is it?" Kingston clarified, digging into his own slice. Jesse remained silent, but he watched me out of the corner of his eye.

"It's pretty good, I'm just used to it being on a pizza with pepperoni or an all meat pizza," I responded taking another bite.

"All right, you're allowed to stay." Reid emphasized his dramatic statement with a single nod at the end.

"You don't hate hamburger pizza," Kingston explained teasingly at my scrunched up facial expression. "Meaning you aren't too much of a lost cause." I rolled my eyes for what seemed like the tenth time this afternoon and went back to eating, not dignifying their ridiculousness with a response.

A couple hours later, we had finished up homework, the boys had gone home, and now I was staring at the large pile of boxes against the wall.

Maybe I should have taken up their offer to help.

I sighed, opening the first box, and was greeted with a large pile of neatly folded clothes. It might have been weird, but I took great pride in my clothing and outfits so I always made sure to fold them or hang them immediately after cleaning. As I unloaded the box into my closet and dresser, my phone dinged with a text message.

Mom: I'll be home in a little while, business dinner running a bit long.
Emma: No worries, just unpacking. Love you.

I plugged my phone in and dropped it on my nightstand, the light from my lamp softly illuminating my new room. Sinking onto my new light pink sheets, I glanced around and took it all in. My bed frame was an upholstered gray with buttons tufted into the headboard, my new comforter was white with a simple black geometric pattern. The nightstands were also white with two drawers and crystal pulls; a matching set of lamps with pink shades sat on top as well as a picture of my friends and me from back in California. The walls were painted the same gray-beige as the rest of the house with white trim, both of which coordinated nicely with my white 6-drawer dresser that matched the nightstands.

My room didn't have a television, only a mirror on top of my dresser that was book ended by jewelry and makeup stands that would soon prettily display my items. *Once I get them unpacked, that is.* My closet was a standard size and only held half a dozen items since all of my underwear, socks, bras, and bottoms were folded in my dresser. I knew I had about two more boxes of tops, skirts, and dresses I needed to unload as well as a box with my jackets, scarves, hats, and other accessories.

I have too much stuff.

Huffing, I stood back up off my queen sized bed and

opened the next box of clothing. By the time I got my clothing and makeup unpacked, it was getting late. Looking at the remaining four boxes that held my accessories, books, movies, and other random stuff I had collected over the years, I decided I'd tackle those another day. I changed into my pajamas, a pair of soft shorts and a matching button-up flannel shirt before slipping into my bed, making sure to set my alarm. I had several unread texts from a multitude of people that I ignored before shutting out the light. It took me a long time to finally fall asleep despite being exhausted.

The morning is going to be fun… not.

Chapter 4

SEPTEMBER 5TH

Reid made a joke at lunch and soda came out my nose.
Thankfully it was just us, but he still laughed at me.
#Embarrassing #WhyAmILikeThis #WeirdnessWednesday

The smell of spaghetti and garlic bread permeated the house when I got home, my mom's figure shuffling around in the galley kitchen. I dropped my bag down on the couch before heading upstairs. I hadn't realized how long I'd been at the library scouring sources for my AP English essay until I glanced at the clock that read almost six in the evening.

"Hey, honey." She smiled over at me from the stove, her arm stirring the large amount of pasta she had just added to the pot. "How was school?" I grabbed a soda, or pop if you're *Nebraskan* which Reid had emphasized again today, and sank into the wooden chair at the table.

"It was good, same as yesterday," I answered. The day had flown by just as it had the day before, Reid and Kingston walking me from one class to the next while Jesse ignored me. Although, it seemed he wasn't nearly as irritable today so that was a positive.

Baby steps.

"That's wonderful. How are classes?" Her question was

distracted as she moved her attention from the noodles to the sauce. "What are you taking? You were passed out by the time I got home last night, so I wasn't able to interrogate you yesterday," she teased.

"All of the same classes I was in in Cali, only difference is I have a dance class instead of a traditional gym class, and I have to take another nutrition class." The hiss and fizz of the soda can opening filled the space as I finished talking. Taking a long drink, I continued. "All my teachers seem good so far, haven't had any issues and none of them seem super strict which is nice."

"Making any friends?" She smiled over at me. Her dark circles were prominent, but her smile and happiness were genuine and had me smiling back at her.

"A couple of guys, one was the guy who changed my tire the other day," I explained.

"No girls?" She sounded surprised and slightly concerned. My brows furrowed at her tone. She never had issues before when we were in Cali if I was friends with guys or not.

"Not yet, it's only been two days and I've been trying to catch up on schoolwork," I reasoned, hoping to put her strange reaction at ease. "I'm probably going to be stopping by the coffee shop over near school tomorrow, maybe I'll meet up with some girls there."

"That sounds good." Her shoulders dropped in relief as she went back to preparing dinner. We ate with companionable conversation about her job, and the topic of Reid, Kingston, and Jesse didn't come up again.

SEPTEMBER 6TH

Reid and Kingston kept me from being run over in the hallways yesterday...
this school is way too crowded.
#WatchWhereYoureGoing #ThankfulThursday

The front walkway was crowded with other students heading into the building for school to start. I was just inside the glass doors when Reid's curly head popped up above the students who had already settled in the cafeteria, his arms waving animatedly in the air to get my attention. Chuckling, I curved around the cluster of tables between them and me and stepped up to the table.

"Good morning, Cali girl," Reid chimed with a cocksure smile. Kingston gave his typical laidback smile and a single wave while Jesse just ignored me, intent to focus on the textbook that was open on the table. The other half of the round table held a small group of students I didn't recognize who were talking amongst themselves. Two were girls wearing their hair in messy ponytails and headbands, their outfits made up of athletic shorts, a cross country race t-shirt, and running shoes. The other three were guys, two of which were in basketball shorts and similar shirts while the last boy was in a pair of jeans and a plain black shirt.

"Morning," I greeted, my word nearly swallowed up in the loud chatter of students. Reid waved a hand out toward the other half of the table.

"Let me introduce you." His waving hand caught the attention of the others before swinging it in my direction. "This is Emma. Emma this is Zoey and Aubrey." He gestured to the two girls who waved at me. Returning the wave, Reid continued on to the boy in jeans and ending with the two boys in shorts. "Brayden, Carter, and Jason."

They gave their greetings and waves that I returned before they went back to their conversations. Trying to commit their names to memory, I picked out identifying things about each of them to try and make it easier. Zoey had black hair that was slightly wavy and brushed her shoulders in her high ponytail while Aubrey had long, straight, chestnut brown hair that reached to her mid-back. They were both pale, but Aubrey was a shade fairer than Zoey. Carter had blond hair that was shaggy and brushing down his forehead in a mop of wavy curls. Brayden had coffee colored skin with short cropped tight curls, and Jason had olive skin and black hair that wasn't long, but wasn't necessarily short either.

The bell pulled my attention from my inner musings to remember their names over to the shifting mass of students. Kingston broke off from us with Zoey, Carter, and Jason while Aubrey and Reid turned down another hall. Jesse, Brayden, and I headed up the stairs in the large crowd.

"How're you liking Arbor Ridge so far?" Brayden's voice was warm and friendly. Jesse remained silent on the other side of me as he walked near, but not next to me. I shrugged.

"It's high school, not much different than back home," I answered, "although Nebraska is quite a change. Lots of corn." I ignored Jesse's scoff, or was it an attempt at a laugh?

Does he even know how to laugh?
Or smile?
Who knows.

"Yeah, there's a lot of that here, but there's some fun stuff to do too." Brayden's smile was bright as he pointed farther down the hall. "My class is that way, I'll catch you later. Bye, Jesse." He waved toward my sullen partner before continuing down the main corridor, walking out of my eyesight in the next section of dark blue lockers. Jesse and I didn't talk through homeroom, both of us going our separate ways as soon as the bell rang. I sighed, guessing my attempts at being friendly didn't work.

Oh well...

The little bell above the door to the small coffee shop, Coffee Grounds, dinged as I entered. The smell of freshly brewed coffee filled the air as I looked around. The counter ran along the wall across from me, the wall covered in black chalkboards that were filled with menus and prices while the counter held coffee machines and syrups. The wall that the door was on held bright windows and a wood bar top, with stools running from the corner to the door. In the center of the room were metal and wood tables, chairs, and comfy leather lounge chairs and fabric poufs. It was cozy, and there were several teenagers from the high school scattered around the room, but none that I recognized or knew the names of.

"What can I get you?" the woman on the other side of the counter asked me cheerfully. She couldn't be much older than me with straight, shoulder length red hair and bangs that hung straight across her forehead, tastefully brushing her brows.

"Just a caramel latte please," I ordered, and her friendly smile had me smiling in response. Her skin held a small tan and her Coffee Grounds t-shirt hung around her thin frame as her bootcut jeans were a dark wash almost black in color.

"You new around here? I don't think I've seen you before," she asked making polite conversation as she started brewing my order. I made sure to look at her name tag, Lyla, and commit it to memory.

"Yeah, my mom and I just moved over Labor Day weekend." She nodded as she packed the espresso in the brew cup.

"Rad. You going to Arbor Ridge?" Her head tilted toward my backpack on my shoulder, and I nodded.

"Yeah, it's my senior year." My eyes landed on a 'Now Hiring' sign sitting on the counter. Lyla must have noticed me looking.

"You looking for a job? You could do part-time here after school couple days a week and for a few hours on the weekend"—she started pumping the syrup in the cup—"I'm Lyla, by the way. I work here full time."

"Emma, and I hadn't thought about, but I'll take an application," I reasoned, figuring it wouldn't hurt to have a job with some extra money. I could have it to save which would be nice especially with college next year. Lyla nodded happily before handing me a two-page stapled application and my drink. With a quick thanks, I sank into one of the chairs at a table away from the other students.

Do I want a job? Not really.

Would the extra money be nice? Yes, definitely.

Will it help with resume later in life? Absolutely.

With those answers in mind, I filled out the application. Since the year I'd turned fifteen, I'd worked part time each summer and taken on a counselor job at the summer camp near my house. I'd always taken the academic year off from both so I could focus on school. Now that college was approaching though, focusing on building a work portion of my resume would be a good idea. At the thought of college I felt my chest seize. I had always planned on going to the college near where I grew up, but now that I was here it would be very expensive with the out-of-state tuition rates.

Breathe, don't panic.

Maybe I could go to college here in Nebraska.

That idea didn't sound much better, but it would be a good option so I made a note to look into the universities around here and set up visitations and tours. I pushed the anxiety-inducing topic of college away in favor of sipping of my drink and focusing on homework, but my phone buzzing repeatedly caught my attention.

> **Unknown Number**: Hey, Cali girl.
> **Unknown Number**: Can you guess who this is?
> **Unknown Number**: Bet you can't.
> **Unknown Number**: But if you do, I'll bring you a cookie tomorrow.
> **Emma**: Hi Reid. How'd you get my number? I like chocolate chip cookies, BTW.

I made sure to save his number under his name before he texted back, his response in one message instead of a long string of them.

> **Reid**: How did you know?? I may or may not have copied it down when you were getting lunch today. Chocolate chip cookie, got it.
> **Emma**: You're literally the only one who calls me Cali girl. Also, you're excitable like a child. How was practice?

Reid had been carrying around a lacrosse stick today which had caught my attention, so he had explained he played on the team and they had practices Thursdays after school and Tuesdays before school.

Reid: Not bad, just practice for the game tomorrow at Millmer East High School. What are you doing?
Emma: Just at that coffee shop, but I'm about to head home for dinner and to do homework.

I realized it was getting to the time my mom would be getting home, and she was typically a stickler about eating dinner together, so I started packing up my stuff making sure to drop off the application at the counter. Reid and I continued to text for the majority of the night after my mom and I had eaten, his virtual company helping make homework a little less torturous.

SEPTEMBER 7TH

Read a funny joke this morning-
"Hedgehogs, eh? Why can't they just share the hedge?"
#TerribleJoke #YesILaughed #FunnyFriday

I had just taken a seat in nutrition when the girl in front of me turned in her chair to look at me with a prying eye. The girl in front of her, as well as the girl to her left also turned, three sets of nosy gazes staring directly at me. The girl in front of me had dark blonde hair that was super curly and held back with a black bow headband, her skin sporting a sun-kissed tan and her shirt one of the popular TV shows currently on air. The other two girls were carbon copy twins, both with dark chocolate hair that was pulled over one shoulder. They had bright green eyes and pale skin with lots of freckles. Even their clothes matched, so the only reason I could tell them apart was one had her hair over her left shoulder and the other draped in front of her right.

"You're the new girl, Emily," the one in front of me started, her voice melodic and sweet.

"Emma," I corrected, trying to be polite, but their intense eyes were putting me on edge. She nodded as if that's what she had meant to say.

"I'm Ashley and that's Iris and Ivy." I gave a polite 'nice to meet you' that they didn't return. The twins had yet to speak, content to just watch me.

"Can I help you?" I asked after they didn't say anything. Ashley leaned forward, her elbows leaning on my desk.

"We've seen you hanging around Reid Hughes and Kingston Bell." She raised a brow at me. I didn't see where the conversation was going or what I was supposed to say so I nodded. "Are you dating either of them?"

"Uh, no." I chuckled at the ridiculousness of her question, not that I hadn't noticed how attractive the three of them were. "Reid, Kingston, Jesse, and I are just friends."

"Jesse?" one of the twins finally questioned. I wasn't sure which one it was other than it was the one with her hair over her left shoulder. "You're friends with Jesse Parker?" I nodded, leaving out the fact we weren't necessarily *friends* friends.

They don't need to know that though.

"So Reid and Kingston are single?" Ashley took over the questioning which was feeling more and more like an interrogation by the minute.

"I haven't seen them with any other girls, but I don't

know for sure." I shrugged, not feeling comfortable discussing their personal lives behind their backs. Ashley's smile was presumptuous and smug as Mrs. Sanders called class to start, her curly hair flaring out when she turned back around.

Well, that was different.

"I'll only be gone for a couple hours. My boss and I are meeting with a new client we signed on with for their next project for dinner"—my mom's voice echoed out of her master bathroom—"will you be all right here by yourself?" I flopped back on her bed feeling my hair fan out around me in a blackened halo.

"Yes, Mom." I tried to keep the attitude out of my response, but even I could hear it in my voice. "I'm just going to study and probably relax. Maybe finish unpacking." I heard her shuffling makeup or products around in one of her drawers.

"That would be good. Before you head downstairs can you tell me which necklace would look better with that dress and heels?" she asked. I turned my head to the side and propped up onto my elbow so I could fully take in the outfit she had picked out for tonight. It was a simple black sheath dress and a pair of shiny nude-colored heels with a conservative height of around two inches.

I eyed the two necklaces she had laid out: one was a single strand of shiny pearls and the other was a simple gold necklace with three different length strands. Tilting my head back and forth, I focused on one option then the other before finally deciding.

"The pearls, they go with the shoes better and have more of a visual impact," I told her before shifting to sit up.

"I'm going to head downstairs and get some homework done."

"All right, honey," she called out, "you have fun." I heaved off the quilt that covered her new queen mattress and headed down the hall before clopping downstairs. I sank onto the corner of the sectional with a huff and set my backpack onto the chaise portion to pull out my history book to read the chapter due on Monday. The TV show I had turned on earlier had shifted into an episode I had seen multiple times before requiring me not to have to pay attention to it, I just liked having the noise on in the background. After a little while of reading, the doorbell rang.

"I've got it." My mom's voice filtered down the stairs as she walked the small handful to the entryway landing. I turned back to my homework uninterested with the visitor. "Hello, boys. Can I help you?"

"Yes, we were wondering if Emma was here?" Reid's exuberant words reached my ears making me dip my head down enough to see up the stairs. All I could see was a pair of light wash jeans and one of his tanned arms clothed in a light green t-shirt, with my mom's slim figure blocking the rest of the door frame.

"Yes, she is, come on in." She stepped out of the way, and I saw Reid followed closely by Kingston who was dressed in his usual khakis, boots, and button-up, although this one was a dark blue plaid instead of a solid color. My eyebrows shot up when I saw Jesse in his dark wash jeans and a gray shirt step into the entryway.

"We were hoping to hang out for a while, but she hasn't been answering her texts or phone." At his reminder, I dug my phone out of my bag seeing double digits for text messages and no less than six calls. Grimacing, I felt bad

I had ignored their messages, I had just gotten tired of my friends from back home fishing for gossip and Tyler's incessant requests to get back together.

"Emma, honey? Your friends are here." She dipped her head down, and I was able to get a look at her fully ready to go. Her black hair was down and curled, her face done up in classy and sophisticated makeup. Her tanned figure was clad in the dress she had laid out and she wore the pearl necklace I had suggested. Seeing that she took my suggestion had me smiling just a little. "You up for company?" Reid's head tilted as he bent over to see down the stairs, his hand waving enthusiastically.

"Hi, Cali girl!" he greeted cheerfully, and my mom cracked a small smile at the nickname. I nodded at my mom before speaking.

"Yeah, that's Reid, Kingston, and Jesse by the way," I hollered up the stairs, too comfortable in my spot on the couch to go introduce them properly. My mom and Reid both straightened and faced each other, Reid's hand going out to shake.

"It's nice to meet you, Ms. Clark, I'm Reid." His introduction was very gentlemanly as my mom shook his hand.

"Please, just call me Erin." I saw her turn to the left.

"Kingston, pleasure to meet you," Kingston introduced himself, his smooth and melodious voice making my toes curl.

"Jesse, ma'am." A shiver rolled down my spine and my jaw dropped at Jesse's honeyed, polite, and quite honestly, gentle voice. It was completely different than the disinterested and short tone he always used with me.

Well, how rude.

"Very nice to meet you, boys. I'm actually heading out

for a business dinner so be good," she lectured before bending down again. "Emma Brooke, you behave yourself, and if I find out you've been doing something you shouldn't I'll skin you alive, understood?" My face burned in embarrassment, my muscles tensing under her harsh warning.

Treating me like I'm selling myself on the corner or something.

I'm a virgin for Christ's sake!

"Oh, my god, Mom! Yes, understood. Please just go before you embarrass me any further," I groaned, my bright red face pressed into the couch cushion so my frantic words were slightly muffled.

"Good, see you later, honey!" The door closed immediately after her farewell followed quickly by Reid running down the stairs and all of the boys' snickering. Shifting my beet red face, I peeked my eyes over the top of the plush couch to gaze at them as they reached the basement, happy that the dark cushion hid my overly pink cheeks.

"Emma Brooke," Reid teased, his head tilting to the side as he glanced off lost in thought. "I like it." I pushed away from the couch cushion to sit back up fully when I felt the flushing tingles recede.

"What are you working on?" Kingston questioned, leaning over the back of the couch to look at the book splayed out in my lap. Reid gasped in horror at my textbook before snatching it away from me.

"Reid!" I snapped. The jerk just shook his head hiding the book behind his back before grabbing my book bag off the couch as well. "Well, I *was* working on history," I answered Kingston in an irritated tone.

"It's Friday night. There is no doing homework on Friday

night. What kind of crazy person does homework on Fridays?" Reid huffed, the last question mumbled at no one in particular. "What else were you planning on doing tonight?"

"Probably nothing, just watch a movie or something," I answered, getting up to take my stuff to my room, but Reid stepped away from me and shook his head sharply, his curls rustling on top of his head at the motion.

"I'll carry it. Got to make sure you aren't going to try and sneak it back out here." He followed me to my room after I realized there was no use fighting him.

"Just put it on my bed." A portion of me was grateful for actually having the motivation to make my bed this morning. He stopped and eyed the boxes with a raised brow.

"I thought you were going to unpack the other day?" He pointed at the remaining boxes.

"I had gotten half of it done, but I couldn't bring myself to finish. Too tired." He clapped loudly once before sticking his head out of the door.

"All right, before we do anything we're helping Emma unpack," he announced to Kingston and Jesse. Both of them got up without an argument and walked to my room, their eyes darting around the space eagerly.

"You don't have to do that," I protested, but Reid waved me off.

"Don't be silly, of course we do," he urged, taking the first box and placing it in the middle of the floor.

"It's really no issue, Emma." Kingston gave me a conspiratorial smile before stepping over to the box that Reid had opened. I glanced at Jesse who didn't look pleased, but he didn't argue as he took a seat on the end of my bed, his eyes on the box with curiosity.

"Fine!" I threw my hands up. "You guys win. Let's unpack. I just don't understand why it has to be done tonight."

"Because once you're unpacked, you're officially one of us," Reid chirped as he dug out a large stack of books. "Besides, you can't leave once you're unpacked, and then you'll be ours forever!" He faked an evil laugh, his hands coming up with gusto after Kingston took the stack. I rolled my eyes, but started directing them where to put things.

"Books will go on my bookshelf." I pointed to the new tall bookshelf my mom had ordered that was sitting in the corner. Kingston was looking through the titles as he lined them up on the shelf. Jesse continued to just sulk on the comforter as Reid handed a stack of books to me.

"Any particular order?" Kingston asked, taking the books from my arms, his smile lighting up his handsome face. I shook my head, overcome with the fact I had three very cute guys in my room going through my stuff.

I hope there's nothing embarrassing in these boxes.

"Nope," I squeaked before clearing my throat. "I'll go through and organize them later." Focusing on taking books from Reid to hand off to Kingston, I felt the blush of embarrassment start to fade from my cheeks.

"All right," Reid chirped, "one box down and on to the next!" He pointed in the air as he practically shouted the statement. His antics made me chuckle, he was such a clown sometimes.

Sometimes?

Try all the time.

"Where do you want these, Emma?" Reid's voice pulled me back to the present. It was my movies and CD's as well as my CD player. "Why on Earth do you have CDs? What are you? From the 80's?" I scoffed and pulled the player out and set it up on my dresser.

"No, I just like CDs." I shrugged putting one of my more recent purchases in, letting Panic! At the Disco fill the room. "The movies can go out in the entertainment unit." Reid started dancing to the music as he and Kingston took the movies to the basement living room. I quickly unpacked the CDs and lined them up on the bottom shelf of my bookshelf. Within a few minutes, the two had returned to the room and opened the third box.

"Ooo," Reid cooed, placing one of my floppy summer hats on his curly head and wrapping a flowy scarf around his neck. "These are pretty." He struck a pose, his hand going behind his head while he jutted out a hip, his right hand on the extended hip. "How do I look?" he asked in a girly voice and batted his eyelashes. Picking my phone up quickly, I snapped a photo. I tried to keep my giggling under control, but when I saw the picture I burst out laughing.

"Oh, my god, you look…" I couldn't finished the sentence with how hard I was laughing. Kingston's warm, smooth palm cupped my hand as he steadied the phone enough to look at it. He laughed, the heat of his hand surrounding my fingers making me flush.

"You look like a pretty princess, Reid," he teased, but before either of us knew what was happening, Reid had stuffed hats on our heads and draped scarves over our shoulders. Even Jesse wore a hat, although his was a baseball cap and a plain black scarf while ours were patterned and our hats were girly.

"There, now we all look like pretty princesses," Reid said triumphantly. "Although, Emma's the prettiest." I blushed even harder under his compliment. "We need a picture!"

he shouted, corralling all of us on the bed to squish us in the frame on my phone. "Say Go Big Red!" I made a face, but smiled right before he took the photo. All of us were smiling save for Jesse who just glared at the camera with pursed lips. Despite the ridiculous accessories and Jesse's irritation, the photo was really good.

I might print that out and put it on my nightstand.

"All right, back to unpacking." Reid shuffled off the bed noisily before going back to the box. His head tilted making the bill of the sun hat flop. "What's this?" He pulled out a black leather album. "Oh, pictures of Emma's life!"

"It's just my photo album," I offered as he sank back onto the bed. Crawling up behind him, I propped my arms on his shoulders so I could look over his torso to see it. I purposely ignored the feeling of his lean muscles rippling under my arms as he turned the pages. Kingston sat to the right with Jesse on the left who I noticed was looking at it despite his attitude.

The book started out with me as a little girl and all the trips my dad, mom, and I would take including Disney World, amusement parks, and the San Diego zoo. It had photos of the vineyard when my dad had purchased it with his business partner, Todd Hamilton, and photos of their opening party.

"What's this?" Reid asked me softly, pointing to the place I spent almost all of my life at.

"That's the vineyard my dad owns, this was the party when they opened officially," I explained, pointing to Todd. "That's his business partner." They hummed and nodded before flipping to the next few pages which were filled with elementary and middle school, friends, and birthday parties. My heart squeezed at all the memories contained within the pages of the album.

"Aw, look at little Emma," Reid teased good heartedly at one picture from my sixth birthday. "So cute." I blushed as he smiled at me over his shoulder, his stubble roughly brushing my arm.

"Shush." I poked his cheek until he was facing the album and not me, knowing my face was bright pink. He continued to flip through, Kingston smiling at the photos while Jesse was content to stay quiet, his eyes darting around the different pages soaking in the glossy colored photographs. We'd reached the high school photos including homecoming and prom pictures, Tyler's arm tossed around my shoulder in several of them.

"This is Tyler?" Kingston asked, waving at the tall guy standing with me. I made a face and yanked the photos out of their sleeves. "What are you doing?" His coffee eyes centered on my face as he furrowed his brows. I piled them up in a stack and ripped it down the middle chucking the halves with Tyler on them over my shoulder.

"Wow." Reid chuckled, his body turned on the bed so he could see me. "He really did mess up, huh? I thought you were joking on the phone the other day. So, you're not forgiving him?" I looked at him like he was insane.

"I walked in on him with his pants around his ankles and his hands up another girl's shirt, what do you think?" Even Jesse had the decency to grimace.

"Well, he's an idiot," Kingston supplied sweetly, and his charming smile once again had me blushing. Reid's furious nodding had the near permanent flush turning from pink to red.

"Thanks, guys." I smiled. "I think I'll put this photo in there." I took my phone and pulled up the picture of us, holding the phone in front of one of the slots as I leaned over Reid. "What do you think?"

"Perfect," Reid offered as Kingston nodded, Jesse remained silent, but didn't argue. "We'll take more. So many more in fact you'll have to buy another album just for your life in Nebraska. Also, remind us to take you to the Henry Doorly Zoo in downtown Omaha because it's way better than any other zoo." He poked me lightly in the arm at the statement. I rolled my eyes, but made a mental note to do that because spending more time with them?

Count me in.

CHAPTER 5

SEPTEMBER 10TH

Knocked out all my homework yesterday! Heck yeah, take that long to-do list!
#GetItDone #MotivationMonday

"Hey, Emma." Zoey waved from down the parking lot aisle, her SUV parked four spots over from mine. "How's it going?" She jogged over, her signature ponytail bouncing with her quick strides. She was in her usual athletic attire, but instead of a cross-country or sports shirt she wore an Arbor Ridge class shirt.

"Not bad, it's Monday though." I smiled over at her while shifting my bag strap on my shoulder and adjusted my burgundy scarf. My outfit was what I had been sticking with since moving; skinny jeans cuffed right above my ankle booties, a loose plain shirt, a jacket, and a scarf. Unlike my old school, Arbor Ridge kept their classrooms freezing so I couldn't wear my skirts or dresses without fear of turning into a popsicle. Today, I was rocking a light washed, pre-destroyed denim jacket and black skinny jeans, my lipstick matching my scarf.

"Truth, I hate Mondays." She walked to my left as we entered the mass of students filing towards the doors. "How was your weekend? Do anything fun?" I smiled remembering our Friday night and the long conversations through the weekend with Reid and Kingston in a group chat they had added me to.

"It was good. Reid, Kingston, and Jesse stopped by for a while on Friday, and I just spent Saturday and Sunday working on school work so now I'm all caught up." I looked to her. "What about you?"

"It was good, we had a cross country practice yesterday. Other than that, I was just a lazy log and watched TV all weekend." She laughed. "Well, I did homework, but you know what I mean."

I nodded, my cheeks starting to hurt from the amount of smiling my tired face was doing. I liked Zoey, she was nice and fun and didn't seem to be honing in on my relationship with the boys unlike all of my other friends after we had posted that photo on Facebook Friday night.

"Hey." Kingston's voice flowed over me as he joined us on the way to the table. "How are you, Emma?" he questioned after Zoey had sunk into her seat next to Aubrey. Glancing up at Kingston through my lashes, I saw he was smiling down at me. His dark green button-up brushed my arm with how close he was standing.

"Tired, but not too bad. I got caught up on all my homework though," I responded, feeling the signature weight of Reid's arm curl over my shoulder. Squeezing, he tugged me into his muscled torso for a hug.

"Good morning, Cali girl," he muttered tiredly as he nearly squeezed me to death, leaving me gasping for air as soon as he let go. I playfully smacked him in the stomach.

"Way to nearly kill me there," I teased. Jesse was yet again focusing on the textbook that was sprawled out in front of him, purposely ignoring us. "Is it Friday yet?" I whined as the bell rang, and the swarm of students all moved at once. Reid and Kingston chuckled before breaking off toward their respective homerooms leaving me, Brayden, and Jesse together.

"Hey, Emma." Brayden smiled at me before turning his attention to the broody boy next to me. "Hey, Jesse." Jesse gave a slight nod before turning his attention back to where he was walking effectively ending any other conversation.

"Hi. How was your weekend?" I asked quickly, a passing student going the opposite direction walking right between us making me crowd into Jesse's space. The smell of mint and pine filled my nose, and a warm hand caught me before I could trip.

"You all right?" Jesse's question was so quiet I almost couldn't hear him over the hallway crowd, his tone honeyed and not short like usual. I nodded, blushing at his attentions.

This was so not *like Jesse.*

"I'll catch you two later!" Brayden smirked at us with an odd expression I couldn't put my finger on before he continued down the hall. Pulling away, I gave Jesse a small smile before heading into the room. Jesse was back to his scowling, irritated self by the time he sank into his seat next to me.

That didn't last long.

Nutrition was passing slowly, my eyes glazing over as Mrs. Sanders droned on and on about the importance of food safety before finally allowing us to talk amongst ourselves until the bell. Packing away my notebook and pen, I pulled out my phone and had several texts from Reid and Kingston.

Reid: We up for homework group tonight? I think that should be a tradition*!*
Kingston: I'm down. We could do it on more days than just Monday too, you know.
Jesse: K.
Emma: My house again*?*

Before they had a chance to respond, a girly cough brought my attention away from my phone. Ashley and the twins were watching me with hungry gazes, the facial expressions similar to how Kara looked before going into the latest gossip around the student body.

"Are you dating Jesse Parker?" she questioned. No 'hello' or 'how's it going' beforehand, just right into the prying.

Rude.

"No," I huffed, "we're just friends." I contained the eye roll that wanted so desperately to escape.

Why couldn't they just leave me alone?

"I heard you two were cuddling in the hallway earlier," one of the twins, Ivy I think, spouted.

Whichever one with the hair over her left shoulder.

I'm just going to refer to them as Left Twin and Right Twin.

"I almost got knocked over by a passing student, Jesse just happened to be there and I ran into him," I explained, "no cuddling happened." Not that I would necessarily complain about cuddling with Jesse, if he wasn't so short with me.

"That's probably best," Ashley snarked with a mean girl smile. "He's not exactly the best guy to hang around." I furrowed my brows. He might not be the most social guy, but he wasn't bad by any means.

"He's gotten in trouble with the law before for fighting, and he's skipped school a lot too," Right Twin added at my confused look. "He's dangerous and a bad influence." My brows shot up. Fighting? Skipping school? They nodded, but before they could spout anymore crap about Jesse, the bell rang.

I made my way to Civics lost in thought. I really didn't know anything about Jesse, but I didn't think they were right in saying he was a 'bad guy.' They just seemed like girls who thrived on gossip and stirring up trouble. Pushing away their words, I sank into my normal seat and pulled out my class materials. Reid came bolting into the room right before the bell rang, sinking into his seat next to me as he panted. Mr. Fergusen started lecturing right after he sat down. I eyed him out of the corner of my eye; he shuffled around in his bag before yanking out a large notebook and uncapped pen. He flashed me a smile before tuning into the lecture.

The class passed by quickly, and Mr. Fergusen was quickly becoming one of my top teachers of all time with how energetic and engaging he was. My skin tingled every so often as Reid's gaze flickered over to me at random intervals. I kept my eyes firmly on my paper or on the notes the teacher was writing up on the board even though I wanted to look at him. Finally, after ignoring him for at least a half hour, a little piece of paper appeared on my half of the desk.

Heard you and Jesse were making out in the hall this morning.

I clenched my jaw scribbling back a response explaining what happened, my irritation growing with each ridiculous addition to the rumor. When Mr. Fergusen wasn't looking, I dropped the paper on Reid's notebook. A few moments later, it reappeared.

I didn't think you two would be, just wanted to let you know.

I nodded slightly, so he knew I understood before stuffing the paper in my bag, I didn't want to get in trouble within my first month at the school for passing notes. The bell rang a little while later, surprising me, my brain having shoved the rumor about me and Jesse out of my mind. Reid's arm wrapped around me, my face heating as the other students eyed us with curiosity, a few with open hostility.

"Come on, Cali girl. Lunch time." He shook me slightly, wanting me to hurry, but I was uncomfortable with the attention and wanted to wait until almost everyone had filtered out. "Emma," he whined playfully nudging me towards the door.

"All right, all right, let's go." I finally gave in, walking to the cafeteria tucked under his arm. Crossing my arms over my chest, I found myself curling into his warm body before pulling back to grab food.

"Hey, Emma." Kingston's golden blond head appeared in my eyesight as he lined up to grab fries next to me. "How's it going?" I shrugged, something about Kingston made it hard to keep the fake facade going. All three of them somehow made me want to show them all my emotions, not just the 'fake it till you make it' persona I'd been sporting since Labor Day, but Kingston seemed the one of the group who would listen without some intense reaction.

"Typical day," I responded, not bothering to keep my tone cheery as I pulled a set of fries off the warming shelf. "I'm sure you've heard the latest rumors going around." He gave me a sympathetic smile, his hand going to my lower back to rub soothing circles into the tense muscles.

"Yeah, but I like to think I know Jesse and you better than that," he murmured in an attempt to calm me. "I don't put much stock into what people say anyways." Smiling slightly, I glanced up at him. He really was the picture perfect version of someone who just goes with the flow, not taking anything too seriously. It was a nice change from my Cali friends who took every little thing and made it way bigger than it was.

"Did you know that a single strand of spaghetti is known as 'spaghetto'?" I spouted randomly to silence the string of thoughts that were attempting to spiral into negative territory at the thought of my friends back home. Kingston glanced over with a single brow raised, a small grin on his face despite him obviously being confused. I dipped my head toward his tray, specifically his bowl of spaghetti.

"Ah," he smiled fully as an odd light sparkled in his eyes, "I did not know that." I flashed a bright smile before turning to walk out of the crowded kitchen. He followed closely as we made our way toward the four person table we had claimed as our own. Jesse's gaze was on the table while Reid had just taken a seat across from him.

"I haven't had a chance to check my phone since earlier, but we're studying at my house tonight?" I questioned, Kingston taking his usual seat next to Jesse directly across from me. They both nodded, opting for non-verbal communication since their mouths were full.

"Yeah, you totally just left us hanging in that conversation, Emma," Reid teased as soon as he was able to talk. I chuckled despite my somewhat dour mood.

"I was being pestered by some girls in my nutrition class for gossip," I informed them. "They're like vultures." Jesse's dark eyes glanced up at me, but when I looked at him, he turned his attention back to his food.

"What did they want to know?" Reid propped his elbows on the table with his chin in his hands. His hazel eyes focused on me, the ring of green haloing the honey brown center as they lit up with humor.

"Well, today, I'm sure you can guess. Last week they wanted to know if you two had girlfriends and if we were dating." I stuffed a fry in my mouth as I answered him. Kingston's brows furrowed slightly while Reid's shot up his face.

"Who was asking about us? And us who?" He glanced around the table, this time Jesse's full attention on the conversation.

"You and Kingston." I tilted my head toward him before glancing at Jesse. "They were asking about you today and if we were cuddling this morning in the hall."

"And you said?" he prompted, making this his second real conversation with me since I met him. His question was quiet as he watched me with rapt attention. My heart pitter-pattered in my chest at his attention, the three sets of intense gazes focused on my face making the little butterflies soar.

"That I got ran over and you stopped me from falling," I murmured. His shoulders relaxed as he nodded and just like that, the moment was broken as he went back to ignoring me.

Well, that didn't last long.

"Who was asking?" Kingston prodded, his voice curious. I shrugged, realizing I didn't know much about them since they had always been so focused on me.

"I don't know their last names, but Ashley and the twins Ivy and Iris." Understanding washed over their faces as I spoke

"Yeah, Ashley Green and Ivy and Iris Vine are the gossips of the school," Reid explained finally going back to eating.

"Green, Ivy, Iris, Vine? What's with the nature theme?" I questioned, finishing off my food, no longer hungry after my sandwich and half of my fries.

"They're cousins, the moms are all big into gardening. Been a family tradition for generations," Kingston told me grabbing my tray after I had pushed it away. He waved away any protests as he carried them to the trash and return cart. Grabbing my bag, Kingston walked me to our trig class, and eyes glanced at us the entire way.

That's going to get annoying.

Buttoning my jeans, I cuffed the ankles before sliding on my boots. My hair was no longer down but pulled back in a ponytail after dance class today since we were working on turns and I had gotten tired of my hair smacking me in the face. I was slow in terms of changing, and most of the girls were already standing out in the hall waiting out the last few minutes until the final bell. I had just grabbed my backpack out of the assigned locker when my phone started to ring.

"Hello," I greeted, not recognizing the number of who was calling.

"Is this Emma Clark?" a female voice asked politely. My brows drew down as I paused in my walking.

"Yes. May I ask who's calling?" I kept my tone friendly, trying to keep the confusion out of my question. The unwanted attention throughout the day had put me on edge.

"It's Lyla from Coffee Grounds," she explained. "The manager wanted me to call and get an interview set up for the part-time gig over here at the shop." I felt my tension melt away as I smiled even though she couldn't see me.

"Oh, awesome. Is there any particular time you'd like to schedule for? I'm pretty much open everyday after school this week." I found myself mindlessly pacing as I talked.

"Would tomorrow after school work?" I gave a quick affirmative before checking if there was anything I needed to bring or anything specific I should wear. "Nothing fancy, whatever you wear to school is fine, we're pretty relaxed here with dress code. As for anything you need to bring, just your ID so Rick knows it's actually you. That's the store manager by the way, Rick Dawlson. He's cool, so don't be nervous. I'll be here when you come in, so you can leave your bag behind the counter or in the employee area if you want."

"Awesome, thanks so much. I'll see you tomorrow!" After a quick farewell, I did a little excited dance about the possibility of getting job experience even if it was just from a part-time coffee shop.

Got to start somewhere!

I finally exited the locker room, the halls mostly empty except for students heading toward clubs or practices as I went out to the lot. The weather was warm, but not hot in the cloudy overcast, the last of the summer heat clinging to the city. Cars were filing out of the lot quickly in a rush to get home or wherever it was that the other students wanted to be. Reid had been parking in the same spot every day since I arrived, and it was easy to recognize his Jeep with its trademark coating of mud. My Honda looked brand new in comparison to his dirty vehicle in its spot next to it. Reid's curly head popped out of the open driver's side window to look at me.

"What took so long, slow poke?"

I chuckled while unlocking my car before tossing my bag in the back seat. "I'll tell you when we get to the house." I sank into the fabric seat, the drive home passing quickly once we were out of the traffic surrounding the school. Reid parked in his usual spot in front of the house as I typed in the code to the garage, too lazy to go up to the front door. Reid's stomping footsteps came barrelling into the basement living room, his arms wrapping around me tightly.

"So..." He drew out the word, his arms squeezing me. I tapped his arms lightly, unable to breathe under the pressure.

"Got a job interview," I huffed, sucking wind into my deprived lungs when he finally loosened. "Part time gig at Coffee Grounds."

"Oh, nice!" He squeezed me again, and a squeak escaped me before he let go completely. "They don't typically hire too many students, but if they're giving you an interview, they'll hire you."

"Awesome, I'm excited but nervous," I explained as we all sat down at our usual seats. Now that it had been a bit since the call, nerves and worries filled me at the thought of an interview. It had been a couple of years since I had done one, my summer jobs secured each year without needing to go through the process each time.

"You'll do great," Kingston said, easing my nerves slightly with his melodious voice. His confident smile lit up his face as he started on his work. Reid quickly agreed, his attention turning to Jesse who wasn't paying attention to the conversation. A thud sounded under the table.

"Ow! What?" He glared at Reid who was sitting with the perfect look of innocence, his hazel eyes darting to me quickly before returning to Jesse. Jesse sighed before glancing at me. "You'll be fine," he offered. His attempt at a smile was appreciated despite it having to be forced through violent means. I smiled at him.

"Thanks, Jesse." My tone was friendly, determined to change his disinterested and irritated attitude toward me.

Kill them with kindness and all that jazz.

"You're welcome," he mumbled softly before returning to his work, his full lips no longer curled in a scowl. Reid and Kingston shared a conspiratorial smile before focusing on their own homework.

These three will be the death of me.

SEPTEMBER 11TH

Nothing like your alarm not going off so you have to rush in the morning like a chicken with its head chopped off.
#WhereIsTheCaffeine #TickedOffTuesday

"Hey, Emma!" Lyla waved enthusiastically as I walked into the coffee shop. Smiling, I made my way over to where she held open the half-door separating the customer area from behind the bar. "You want to leave your bag with me? I'll keep it safe." Nodding, I placed the bag in her outstretched hands before watching her stow it safely in an open cabinet area beneath the register. A man who I would guess was in his early thirties stepped out from behind the 'Employee Only' door, his red hair almost the same color as Lyla's. The red mop was wavy and brushing the top of his ears, and warm brown eyes landed on me as his hand came out to shake.

"You must be Emma!" he exclaimed cheerfully. "I'm Rick, the store manager. If you want to come on back, we can start your interview." I smiled and dipped my head in acknowledgment. Lyla flashed a double thumbs-up as I walked back making me chuckle.

"We'll just be back here." He stepped through one of the several open doors in the hallway. "No need to be in the back office, it's overrun with papers anyways." The room was filled with several small tables and chairs, and a refrigerator sat tucked into the corner. Lining the far wall was a counter that matched the ones out front topped by a microwave and toaster. "This is the employee break room. The open door on the left hand side of the hall is the storage room, and the door on the right is the office"—he pointed to two doors on the wall inside the break room—"those are the employee bathrooms, and there's lockers in there for your stuff if you're coming from school or what have you." I followed his lead and sat in the chair across from him, my application on the table in front of him.

He outlined the basic flow of customers as he scanned the pages I had filled out last week. "We don't typically get very busy, usually lunch rush which you wouldn't have to worry about with school and then after school with the rush of students. The weekends are busy in the mornings, but the afternoons are more relaxed." Flipping through a few pieces of paper I didn't recognize, although the last one looked like a shift schedule, he continued talking instead of asking any actual 'interview type' questions.

"You'd be working with Lyla most likely since she works the afternoon and evening shifts during the week and then during the mornings on Saturday and Sunday. Think you'd be able to handle that?" I nodded giving a friendly smile. This was not what I was expecting from an interview, but Lyla had said this was a pretty relaxed place.

"I'll probably have you start with three to four hour shifts during the weekdays and five or six hours on the weekends since you've already had some experience working in the customer service and serving industry with your previous summer job at the cafe." He nodded, seemingly more talking to himself than to me. "We're pretty relaxed here, but we don't hire very often because we prefer loyal workers rather than workers who will only be around for a couple of months, so if you would be willing to work twice during the week and once on the weekend, we can schedule you consistently for the rest of the school year. Summer hours would adjust, and if you stick around after summer, we can work around your college classes." I felt my excitement bubble up, glad that my previous work history spoke for itself and my old bosses spoke highly of me.

"That would be perfect." Although I was practically giddy, I kept my tone even. "I haven't decided on college yet, but when I do I'll let you know." He nodded happily and stuck his hand out for me to shake.

"Well then, Emma Clark, welcome to Coffee Grounds."

CHAPTER 6

Aubrey brought up before school today that when you say 'forward' or 'back', your mouth moves the same way.
#HolyCrap #IGapedLikeAFish #FunnyFriday

Emma," Mr. Fergusen called as I entered homeroom. Jesse glanced between us but continued to his seat. I strode over to the teacher and he held out an office slip. "You're scheduled to meet with your career counselor later this morning during your third period." I took the slip and scanned the information scrawled in pretty cursive.

10:25 AM, Counselor Office, Ms. Rogers, Reasoning: Career and College planning.

"All right, thank you." I dipped my head before heading to my seat. Jesse read the note I had just laid on the desk. When he caught me watching him with a small smile, he sat up straight and turned back to the textbook that he seemed to always be reading. "Where's the counselor's office?" I asked Jesse quickly after realizing I had no idea where I was supposed to go.

"It's in the door to the left of the main office," he offered quietly, his voice catching the attention of several people around us all of who glanced at us with surprise. He hunkered down away from the attention, not looking back up until I rested my hand lightly on his arm.

"Thanks." Smiling, I pulled my hand back. The warmth from his skin radiated through my fingers and down my arm, making those butterflies flutter as I turned away from him.

The bell had rung, and the hallways emptied as I stepped through the wooden door with the long, skinny window that showed a small lobby area. There was a student working at the front desk, her schoolwork splayed on the laminate top. Her bright blue eyes looked up at me before she hit a button on the phone, and a muffled buzz sounded down the hall that twisted off from the left side of the counter. A rotund woman with graying hair that was cut in a trendy pixie style came down the hall. Red cat's-eye glasses were perched on her thin nose with a silver shiny chain connecting the ends. Her outfit was a pair of black pinstripe slacks and a red blouse that flattered her curvy figure.

"You must be Emma!" she exclaimed warmly before waving me down the hall. "I'm Ms. Rogers, you can call me Mimi if you want. I'm assuming you were told why you were called down today?"

"Career and college planning," I answered, glancing around her spacious office. Her desk jutted out into the room from the left wall, while a white, furry office chair was sandwiched between the desk and the far wall. A short bookshelf was flush against the right wall, with a large bulletin board above it. Lots of flyers and motivational quotes were tacked to the cork in a rainbow of colors while a small two-person table and comfy looking chairs sat directly to the right of the door in the front corner.

"Very good," she praised, taking a seat in the chair that faced the now closed door leaving me to sit in the chair facing her. "Have you given any thought to college or what you would like to do?"

"I had planned on going to college in California, but now it would be really expensive with out-of-state tuition rates, so I was going to look into the universities here," I explained, shifting my bag off my back and onto the carpet at my feet. Her pen effortlessly flowed across her note page in the same pretty cursive from earlier.

"There are several options depending on what you are looking for. The University of Nebraska system has three separate city campuses, Lincoln, Omaha, and Kearney. We're right between Lincoln and Omaha's campuses, but there is also a community college if you would prefer to go through the general education courses that way before transferring. I will advise that sometimes credits don't transfer despite them essentially being the same content. There's also Creighton, which is more expensive, as well as several other state and private colleges throughout Nebraska," she explained, pulling out several brochures.

"The Lincoln and Omaha ones sound the most promising," I muttered, busy examining the colorful pamphlets she had spread out on the table between us. She nodded and slid the two trifolded papers for the universities over to me. Their colors were the same with red, black, and white with the only differences being the name and logo.

"They offer similar degrees. The Lincoln campus is big in sports especially college football, volleyball, and basketball while Omaha is known for their hockey team," she explained before looking at me. "Do you have an idea of what you want to study?"

"I was thinking business. My mom works in marketing, and my dad owns and runs a vineyard." My heart squeezed in my chest at the mention of my dad since I'd heard nothing from him aside from two very brief texts. "I don't have an idea of what specifically, but I think in broad topic conversation business would be a good decision for me."

"That would be good, Omaha's campus would be good for business. They have multiple concentrations, and their business department is well known, but so is UNL's, so it's more which campus you would prefer, the cost, and where you would rather be in terms of location," she continued, effortlessly explaining all the ins and outs of college planning. I listened intently as she talked about different requirements for the schools, the costs between the two, as well as the campus and surrounding areas. She asked if I wanted her to set up a tour, but I told her I would handle it this weekend because I would need to talk to my mom first.

Maybe the guys would go with me.

I made a mental note to ask them what their plans were and if they'd want to go with me. Not sure Jesse would be up for it, but I was pretty certain Reid and Kingston would be down. The bell rang for the next class out in the main lobby of the counselor's office. Making sure I wouldn't be counted tardy, Ms. Rogers wrote me a late slip and sent me on my way. Ashley, Ivy, and Iris were eyeing me with suspicion as I passed them in the hall on my way to Civics, but I darted out of the way quickly enough for them not to be able to corner me and interrogate me about why I wasn't in nutrition.

Thank goodness it's Friday.

"Emma Brooke," Reid started, his tone demanding. "We're going out tonight to celebrate and that's final." I groaned, my head falling back as I pouted. The sun blinded me as it peeked out from behind the cloud and ended my dramatics early.

"Fine, fine," I agreed. Reid had cornered me in Civics saying we were all going to go out and get dinner to celebrate me getting a job, but all I wanted to do tonight was lounge about. My brain had been preoccupied with college, reminding me constantly that I needed to register to take a practice ACT test for next week.

"Good." He clapped while Kingston looked happy that we were all going out while Jesse, as per usual, was content to just tag along despite looking as if he'd rather be anywhere else.

I'm going to get him to like me.

Even if it kills me.

"Where are we going?" I sank into my seat, turning my car on as I waited for him to answer.

"We'll drive you, so let's go drop your car off." He gave me a sneaky smile which made me wary. Kingston chuckled before getting into the Jeep with Jesse. I rolled my eyes, but obliged Reid anyway, realizing I would never win at these playful arguments.

When we reached my house, Kingston got out of the passenger seat and slid into the back leaving the door open for me. I gave a small thanks and climbed up into the seat, the cool breeze of the air conditioning brushing against my skin. A rock station was playing from the speakers as Reid drove us through the neighborhood and back out onto the divided highway. I watched the corn fields flow into soybean fields, the flat land divided into squares over the plane in front of me.

After two more songs had played through the radio, we reached a portion of town I hadn't been to yet, with businesses lining either side of the major street. Reid took the first turn and drove up the hill, following the winding road toward a large building. I tilted my head in confusion but stayed silent. Thunder Cat Alley Bowling and Arcade read the large neon sign above the front door, a graphic of a bowling ball hitting pins behind the bright lights.

"We're going bowling?" I asked, my excitement growing. I hadn't gone bowling in ages. Reid nodded before parking and immediately hopping from the car. Kingston had gotten out when I was unbuckling, his tanned arm pulling open the door for me before I could do it myself.

"We figured you should see one of the main places to go to around town," he reasoned, his smooth voice making me blush as he whispered in my ear. His hand migrated to my lower back, and the warmth occupied all of my attention as we walked to the door that Reid was holding open.

The smell of fried food, pizza, and grease accompanied the sounds of pins falling down, happy laughter, and dinging of the arcade games. My eyes bounced between the bright, colorful lights, and the galaxy swirled carpet taking in the abundance of color before landing on the different sections of the building. The large space split into three main areas, each filled with a different type of activity. The section closest to the door was the arcade.

It was well-stocked with newer looking machines as well as vintage games like Pac-Man and Asteroid. The second space in the middle of the building was a food court area with pizza, burgers, fries, and ice cream. Finally, there were two halves of a bowling alley with a long double-sided bar in the middle with a shoe rental off to the side.

"Wow," I exhaled, mesmerized by the place. "This is awesome." I came out of my dazzled stupor, excitement flooding my system. "What are we doing first?" I clapped my hands together.

"You're like a female version of Reid right now," Kingston teased, his hand still on my back. Speaking of Reid, his arm snaked around my shoulders and pulled me toward the shoe rental.

"We'll get a lane and eat while we bowl. We can play some arcade games later after the young kids get a chance to play." He watched the elementary and middle school aged kids bounce animatedly from one game to the next. "Wouldn't want to ruin their good time." I smiled at his reasoning, liking that he was so considerate. Turning my attention back to what we were doing, I got my shoes and headed toward the lane number, the boys refusing to let me pay for any of it despite being able to. Jesse followed behind me, quiet and looking much more relaxed than usual.

"You guys do this a lot?" I asked him as we sat on the couches at the end of our lane while Kingston and Reid finished up paying.

"Yeah, when it's colder out, we typically go here or to the movies. Unless we don't want to spend money, then we'll just hang at one of their houses," Jesse answered. I was hooked on his honeyed voice as he continued. "When it's nicer, we go out to the lake and do some grilling out and camping." He looked at me, and I think he finally realized he had said more than two gruff words to me in one sitting because he immediately clammed up, focusing solely on his shoes.

"Sounds awesome," I responded getting used to his odd behavior. "I'm looking forward to it." Despite busying myself with my own shoes, I saw him smile ever so slightly out of the corner of my eye.

Aha! Success.

"Emma, you're going first!" Reid announced, sitting at the computer to input our names. "Go get a ball." I finished tying the bowling shoe and tucked my ankle booties under the couch with my small crossbody purse. Scouring the neon bowling balls, I went with a nine pound one, mainly because it was pink and light enough for me to carry.

"Aw, such an Emma color," Reid teased, so I stuck my tongue out at him and walked up to the lane. Taking a deep breath, I walked forward and launched the ball down the lane.

"Yay!" I squealed happily when almost all of the pins fell down. "I normally suck at bowling," I explained, waiting for the ball to come back through the return. As I did, I eyed the boys. Reid was laughing, his curls bouncing around on his head as his shoulders shook with mirth. Kingston was leaned back, lounging on the couch across from where my stuff was. His tanned forearms were on display since he always rolled his shirts up to his elbow, and his right leg was crossed with his ankle resting on his khaki covered thigh. Jesse was the opposite of Kingston, leaning forward with his elbows braced on his legs, but he had a very tiny curl to his lips that showed he actually was enjoying our outing.

I missed my second shot, but I was still happy with the

fact I hit the pins at all. As I sank back onto the couch next to Jesse, Reid stepped up to the ball return. His green ball shot down the lane at a dizzying speed before knocking all the pins down in a strike. My jaw dropped because he looked like he had barely put any effort into it. Kingston chuckled at my expression as he switched positions with Reid.

"I've been bowling for years. I was on a league for a long time," Reid explained with a cocky smile. "Did you know it's called a Golden Turkey when you get nine strikes in a row?"

Huh, the more you know.

"I know that now," I admitted. He nodded happily and turned to watch Kingston bowl. He did similarly to me but was able to make a spare while Jesse hit five the first frame and four the second frame.

After our first game, in which I ended up losing because Reid and Kingston were really good at bowling and Jesse was decent all while I was not, we left our street shoes at our lane to grab food in pairs. Kingston and Jesse went first as Reid plopped down next to me. His arm landed over my shoulders, the smell of Old Spice filling my nose as he tugged me over to him.

"I'm glad we went out tonight." He smiled down at me, his dark stubble a bit longer than usual on his strong jaw. "This is fun." I chuckled but agreed.

"Oh, hello, Reid," a tinkling feminine voice rang out from my right at the end of the couch. A petite girl who looked about our age walked the rest of the way around the couch, her bowling shoes quiet against the wood flooring. She wore a pair of black shorts and a mint blue tank top. Platinum blonde hair was piled in a messy bun high on the back of her head, and dark brown eyes darted between us as as a sickly sweet smile stayed plastered on her face. Something about her instantly put me on edge, but I just wasn't sure if it was her in particular or the fact that Reid's happy smile melted into a flat mask.

"Veronica," he responded coolly. Keeping my face neutral, I tried to look up at him under my lashes. He must have seen the motion because he squeezed me lightly in a reassuring hug until my left shoulder blade was resting against his muscled chest.

"I didn't expect to see you here with… " She hesitated as she looked at me expectantly.

"Emma," I added quietly. The sensation of Reid's thundering heart against my back had me anxious.

"Ah." She added a sweet smile, but it didn't reach her eyes before turning back to Reid who continued to clutch onto me like a life preserver. "Where are Kingston and Jesse?"

"Right here," Kingston answered, but his laidback attitude was gone. In its wake were anger and tension, and his body was rigid as he stared down the petite girl. I thought the way Jesse responded to me was bad, but the way he was staring at Veronica made me feel like I was his best friend.

Ice was warmer than his look.

"It's nice to see all of you," she cooed, trying to sweet talk them before turning back toward Reid. "Is this your girlfriend?"

"Yup," he responded with a happy smile before pressing a quick kiss on the top of my head. My heart pounded within my chest while I kept a faked smug smile plastered on my face, because whoever this was, they were all trying very hard to get her to go away.

"Ah." She raised a brow and looked down her nose at me

in a very Ashley fashion. "I guess I'll let you guys get back to your *date*." Her footsteps were quiet as she strutted away.

"Fuck that bitch," Jesse growled, glaring over his shoulder at her retreating figure. My brows shot up at his words.

"Wow, that makes me feel like you love me then if that's how you treat people you hate," I teased with a nervous chuckle, my arms trembling after the impromptu stand-off. He huffed out a single laugh before sitting next to Kingston on the couch.

"Sorry about that, Cali girl." Reid squeezed me against him, his words remorseful as he hugged me. "That's my ex-girlfriend." I nodded.

"I guess that makes us even after the phone call thing," I murmured breathlessly, essentially breaking the tension as they all laughed. "It's all right. I get it." I turned to him as he stood up. "Jerk ex-boyfriend who constantly bothers me, remember?" He nodded, his effervescent smile returning.

"I'll go get us food, be right back." He ruffled my hair lightly as he practically ran to the food line before I could protest. Sighing, I fixed my hair.

"We don't like her," Kingston added after he finished a bite of his pizza. I thinned my lips to keep a smile from popping through.

"You don't say, I never would have been able to tell," I teased, earning a dramatic eye roll in response. "Can I ask what happened?"

"She was with Reid, but then she tried to split all of us up by telling lies to each of us," he explained. "We got into a big fight about it, but we talked when she wasn't around and figured out what had happened. When he found out she was like that, he kicked her to the curb."

"That's just stupid," I supplied as Reid returned and handed me a slice of hamburger pizza and a soda.

"That she is, but now you're officially my fake girlfriend whenever she's around, so she'll leave me alone now." He smiled, overly proud of his plan. I chuckled and took a bite but didn't argue. A portion of me liked the idea of being Reid's girlfriend, real or fake.

A very large portion.

But I couldn't deny that I felt the same about Kingston. Jesse, well, he was debatable, but I was still determined to get him to like me, so who knew when it came to him. Our conversation moved away from Veronica and jerk exes and back toward whether we wanted to play another game before going to play the arcade games. With a quick unanimous decision we reset the pins for one more game. I ended up in third place because Reid had spent the entire game trying to only hit the pins that Kingston had picked out, meaning he ended up with a score of 16. Granted, I was actually trying, and my score wasn't much better at 49, but it wasn't last place.

Cleaning up the lane, we returned our bowling shoes and headed toward the cleared out arcade games. The giant clock on the wall read almost eight in the evening, and the crowd around the building slowly filtered from young kids to teenagers and adults. Kingston's hand rested against my lower back, his thumb rubbing slowly against my white shirt making it brush against my skin. Shivers wanted to escape at the touch, but I kept them contained. Unfortunately, I couldn't contain the goosebumps or the blush that had crept up my cheeks.

"What do you want to play first?" Kingston bent down, his breath tickling the side of my face with his words. I looked around and when I glanced to the left, his bearded jaw was rough against my scalp with how close his face was. To keep my sanity, I picked the first game I saw.

"Pac-Man." I pointed at the iconic game before shuffling over to it. Kingston's forearm rested on the top portion of the machine as he watched me put in the tokens Reid had gotten me earlier. I couldn't help but smile at the iconic maze, ghosts, and the little yellow orb of the main character when they appeared on the screen. I made it through several levels before eventually dying.

"Aw," Reid teased coming up behind me as I groaned. "Poor Cali girl. You going to play again?" He pointed at the machine with a token between his fingers. Moving out of the way, I stepped up to the side over to the next machine, a new one I didn't recognize.

I realized I had no idea what I was doing when I started and found myself totally stuck on how to start. "How do you play this?" Kingston stepped up behind me. His arms wrapped around me, his smooth hands grabbing mine so he could manipulate the joystick and hit the buttons.

"It's similar to Donkey Kong and Mario where you're just attempting to get to the end without hitting any of the stuff," he murmured, and my heart beat rapidly as my breath hitched. With a glance to the side, I noticed Reid was watching us as he waited for the game to start. When he caught me looking, he gave me a smile and winked before turning back to the game, unconcerned that his 'best buddy' had me wrapped in his arms.

Does that mean he doesn't like me like that?

Oh, stop. You have more important things to worry about. Like your new job and college.

I turned my attention back to the game, the little character running the direction Kingston pointed the stick and jumping or ducking when he hit the specific buttons. He chuckled as I purposely pushed the stick in the wrong direction and hit the opposite button.

"We're supposed to be working together here, Emma." He continued to laugh, the warm, musical sound making me want to giggle at his attentions. After I had calmed down in my playful fighting through a few more rounds, our three lives were up. "Let me know if there are any other games you haven't played," he murmured in my ear before heading over to Reid who was waving animatedly at him over at a two player shooting game. Jesse was hovering next to the wide screen, his arms crossed as he watched them start. I recognized the game from the movie theater that had been right down the road from my house. Having spent a lot of time there most weekends, I got really good at the zombie shooting game and could feel the excitement building to play.

"Ah, man," Reid huffed when they finally died, his hazel eyes focusing on me and Jesse. "You two want to play?" I nodded calmly despite wanting to squeal in with excitement. Jesse agreed and took the red gun from Kingston as I took the blue gun from Reid. "Don't forget, Cali girl, you want to shoot the dead ones," Reid teased next to me as the game's countdown started. I nodded, but inside I was smirking.

Jesse was good at this game. His reflexes were decent as he took care of some of the zombies, but having played this game so many times I was able to know where they would come crawling out from. I started to giggle to myself when I saw Reid stand up straight, his arms falling to the side as his jaw dropped.

"Wow," I heard Kingston whisper from the other side of Jesse, joining him in glancing between me and the screen with confusion. Once the boss was defeated they all looked at me, and I had to fight the urge to rub it in since I was supposed to 'shoot the dead ones.' I held the gun up and pretended to blow at the end of the barrel.

"Holy crap! Emma Brooke has some arcading skills!" Reid exclaimed, wrapping me in his arms until my back was flush against his chest and his arms around my chest. "How'd you learn to play like that?" I felt his stubble rub against my scalp as he propped his chin on my head.

"There was one of these at the movie theater near my house in Cali." I chuckled at Kingston's still stunned facial expression and Jesse's surprise. "Played it a lot." I shrugged, Reid's arms moving in time with my shifting shoulders.

"I'm thoroughly impressed," Kingston responded, finally coming to from his surprise. "Want to head out and go binge on snacks and a movie at Emma's?" A round of yeses went up around the group, and we eagerly headed out, my face hurting from how much I had been smiling. I had to make a mental note to print out the multitude of photos we had taken tonight for my album.

Maybe Nebraska isn't so bad after all.

Well... we'll see.

CHAPTER 7

It's been exactly 8 days since I last heard from my dad.
#WhatAmI #ChoppedLiver #TickedOffTuesday

The bell above the door dinged as I walked through the shop's entrance. Lyla's red hair was bright in front of me as she wiped the counter against the wall, making extra care to not knock any of the large machines. I had my bag slung over my shoulder to put in the locker room and headed around behind the counter. Lyla lit up when she saw me, her smile bright.

"Hey," she greeted cheerfully, "your work shirt is in the back if you want to go put it on. There's two of them, so you'll always have an extra. I typically keep my spares in the locker in case I spill on myself." I nodded and headed back, my head darting around the hall as I made my way back to the breakroom. Rick was working in the office surrounded by piles of paper. The click of typing was the only noise back here other than my shuffling footsteps. I continued on my way back to the locker room since Rick was so engrossed in his work.

The Coffee Grounds shirt was a dark color, but I couldn't tell if it was black or blue in the fluorescent light. The front held the shop's circular logo, Coffee Grounds in white typography with "Hand Crafted" and "Best Coffee" above and below the title within the two golden, circular rings. Slipping off my current shirt, I pulled the soft cotton shirt over my head. I pulled out my slip-on Toms from my backpack, not wanting to work for several hours on my feet in my slightly heeled ankle booties. Once I had changed my shoes and shirt, I locked my bag in the locker, putting my phone on silent in my back pocket in case I needed it. Taking a deep, calming breath, I went back out to the counter.

"Ready?" Lyla chirped happily. "I'll just be explaining all the equipment today as well as the register. We'll work on making drinks on Thursday, but the best thing to learn is the menu and the register." She pulled out a stapled stack of paper, photos of different drinks that accompanied explanations of what they were and how they were traditionally made. "I think this should help if you want to look over it before Thursday. You don't have to have everything memorized, but it's easier to make if you know the basics ahead of time."

"Awesome." I nodded while flipping through the packet. The most common drinks like lattes, cappuccinos, and mochas were on the first page followed by more complex drinks as well as the different flavorings we had and how they could be used. "I'll look at this when we're done going through the stuff behind the counter."

Lyla was a great teacher. She explained things quickly and efficiently but not to the point I couldn't understand. There was a lot of information, and she never made me feel dumb, like when I mixed up what one thing did when in actuality it was something else. After about an hour of running through the machines and where everything was kept behind the counter, she started explaining the register. It was a similar system to the one we had at the cafe I had worked at during the summers, the only differences were the category names which included drinks, syrups, and extras, and the actual buttons which didn't include food except for the small selection of baked goods behind the glass enclosure to the left of the counter.

The stream of people coming into the shop was slow but steady, allowing me to observe Lyla a few times before attempting to use the system under her watchful eye. I had about fifteen minutes before the end of my shift before someone I recognized came in. The familiar hazel eyes sparkled as they located me behind the register.

"Hello, ma'am," Reid teased, "I'm looking for this new hire who's about this tall and is really awesome at the shooting zombies arcade game." He held his hand up to how tall I was before making little finger guns making me laugh.

"Hey, Reid," I chuckled. "What can I get for you?" My heart was full, and my stomach filled with fluttering butterflies, knowing he'd made the effort to stop by after lacrosse practice just to see me.

"Hm," he hummed looking at the menu with rapt attention. "Can I just get a small latte?" I started entering it in, my confidence having grown over the last two and a half hours of using the machine.

"Just plain or do you want a flavor?" I pointed to the syrups. "We have vanilla, caramel, peppermint, pumpkin, hazelnut, toffee, raspberry, and a sweetener."

"Pumpkin, I like to get my basic on during the fall." He flashed me a wide smile that made me chuckle again.

Or was I giggling?

Oh, well.

"That'll be three dollars," I took the five he held out for me and quickly made change, Lyla moving swiftly behind the counter making his drink.

"You off soon?" he asked as he waited. Nodding, I looked at the clock.

"Yeah, ten minutes. You want to hang out, don't you?" My lips curled up at his excitement. "Are Kingston and Jesse going to join?" He nodded and pointed out the windows where they were climbing out of a new Chevy Impala. My brows shot up not realizing Kingston had a car since he was always riding with Reid.

"Hey, Emma," Kingston greeted sweetly while Jesse attempted a friendly smile. Honestly, it was clearly forced, but at least he was trying.

"You two want anything?" I asked. Kingston looked over at the drink Lyla had just handed Reid and pointed. "You want a pumpkin latte?" He shrugged, looking lost, but nodded his head anyway.

"No, thank you," Jesse said quietly, following Reid to a table in the far corner. I slightly shook my head as I entered the information and made Kingston's change.

"How's your first day?" His smooth voice washed over me.

"It was good, I really liked it." I looked over to Lyla and hitched a thumb. "She's a good teacher."

"Of course I am, I'm awesome," she teased throwing me a playful smile. "Besides, teaching runs in the family. You might know my older sister, Leena Ester."

"She's my history teacher," I told her, surprised at how small the world suddenly felt. She nodded as she handed the drink to Kingston, his long legs carrying him over to our friends quickly. "Crazy how small the world feels sometimes," I mumbled as she came over to me.

"Yeah, trust me I know. Rick"—she waved a hand to the employee area—"that's my cousin. So," she changed the topic quickly, "they're cute. You like any of them?" I felt my face flare, and she gave me a knowing smile. "Yeah, I figured. Which one?"

"All of them," I coughed under my breath so they couldn't hear me. Lyla was asking her questions quietly, but I was still worried.

"Ah"—she nodded—"yeah I can see why. You did good." She nudged my arm and left the conversation at that, much to my surprise. I liked Lyla before for her warm and welcoming behavior despite me being new to the city, but now I liked her even more since she didn't pester me for details on the boys. Rick's head popped out of the door right before the end of my shift.

"Everything good out here?" We nodded in response. "Awesome. Emma, you're good to head on home, we'll see you on Thursday." With that, he headed back to his office, Lyla shaking her head at him as he ducked away.

"He tends to get sucked into the paperwork portion of the businessing, leaving me to actually run the front," she explained with a warm smile. After she had revealed they were cousins, I could see the resemblance with the same hair color, eye color, and build. "Here's my cell number by the way, if you ever want to hang out sometime." Lyla scribbled on a notepad, tearing off the sheet when she was finished.

"Definitely, I'll text you when I get home so you have my number." I left my first day of work feeling accomplished and accepted. The guys had been including me in all of their activities and conversations, and making friends hadn't been nearly as hard as I originally thought. Being surrounded by people who made me feel good, who helped me laugh despite having my life in upheaval for the last two weeks, was definitely a blessing.

So far so good here in Nebraska.
Never thought I'd say that.

SEPTEMBER 29TH

At least the practice test is over. Now I can focus on fun things, like my friends!
#IgnoreTheTestAnxiety #CalmingThoughts
#StressFreeSaturday

Rick waved at me as I headed into the locker room. I was already dressed in my work outfit, so I just needed to drop off my purse. My head was pounding with a headache, and the sharp thuds within my skull had me gritting my teeth. I wasn't sure if it was because I hadn't eaten much today or if it was from the practice ACT test I had taken this morning. I never seemed to do well on tests, I panicked and overthought everything and despite this morning only being a practice, I felt my heart racing.

I pushed the worries down and focused on getting ready for work, but my mind drifted to other thoughts. The last week had moved at lightning speed in a blur of classes, studying, and work. I had barely seen my mom since we moved; the house only felt homey when Reid, Kingston, and Jesse were there to keep away the loneliness. That last boy was still being stubborn toward interacting with me, but I think I was wearing him down ever so slowly. I had even caught him smothering a smile at something I had said when we walked to class. At least I think it was a smile, it could have been a grimace, but I decided to take it as a smile.

Baby steps.

The crowd in the shop was fairly busy since it was early Saturday afternoon. People who worked nearby would come in for a quick lunch break and to refuel before heading back to their jobs. Lyla was scheduled to get off at the same time as me today, so I would be finally meeting the other employee. Taking up my usual position behind the register, I started to take orders. Lyla would help me with the machines after the lunch rush was over.

The headache didn't ease as the shift went on, the only reprieve the lull in customers allowing me to zone out for a little while. It was nearing six in the evening when several familiar faces came into the shop, only this time it was faces I didn't particularly want to see. Ivy and Iris were wearing matching olive green dresses, the tops were v-neck with tank straps, and the skirts ending nearing their knees. Ashley was in a dark blue strapless dress with crystals lining the bodice and a floofy skirt that reached a little past mid-thigh. I kept my face polite, but my body thrummed with tension at their nosy gazes.

"Hello, Emily," Ashley started. Keeping a sigh inside, I corrected her.

"Emma. What can I get you?" They rattled their orders and paid without further snark or interrogation, but that didn't last long.

"You're not going to homecoming?" Ashley's brow raised, her heels clicking on the shop floor tile as she walked out of the way of the register. Ivy and Iris followed behind her as they always did, each standing behind their respective shoulders.

"Nope." I popped the p of the word and prayed another customer would come in so I wouldn't have to be questioned by the school gossips.

"None of your boys asked you to the dance?" Left Twin asked, the words laced with snotty intonation.

"I had work scheduled, so… " I trailed off with a shrug letting them believe they didn't ask because the schedule had already been written, not the other way around. A ding from the bell cut off anything they were about to say.

"Cali girl!" Reid practically shouted his sentimental nickname for me. Kingston trailed behind him, but Jesse was oddly absent. Both were in their typical outfits and not in fancy suits or dress clothes, meaning I was right in thinking they weren't going to the dance. I tried to not let it bother me that we hadn't brought up the dance in any of our numerous conversations over the last week. "How's my Emma's shift going?"

"Not bad." My smile was genuine despite the slight sting of the previous thought. Ashley tittered slightly as she turned to them.

"Not going to the dance, Reid? Kingston?" Her words were innocent enough, but I knew better and apparently so did my boys.

"Nah"—Reid smiled toward me—"we'd rather come see Emma. Can't do that at a dance that she isn't at, now can we?" A blush flourished on my cheeks. Lyla gave me a sly smile from the other side of the girls as she placed the cups on the pick-up counter. Ashley's statement was cut off once more as Lyla informed them that their orders were finished. Thankfully, they left after getting their drinks, leaving the shop filled with only Lyla, Reid, Kingston, and myself. Well, Rick was still here, but he was doing inventory in the stock room. Remembering Reid and Kingston hadn't been properly introduced to Lyla, I waved a hand toward her.

"Guys, this is Lyla. She's Miss Ester's younger sister."

"For real?" Reid questioned, his hand coming over the counter. "Nice to meet you, I'm Reid."

"Kingston." His tanned arm followed suit and shook Lyla's hand. She nodded her head respectfully before pulling her hand back.

"Jesse would be here too, but he got caught up in some work stuff," Reid explained to me in between sips of the drink Lyla had just handed him. "But we figured we'd come stop by and see you before going to pick him up to take him home."

"That's good." My hip rested against the counter as I crossed my arms snuggly over my chest. "So what's the real reason you guys didn't go to the dance?"

"Didn't really want to," Reid explained, looking to Kingston who nodded in agreement. "The only girl we'd want to take had to work, like a responsible adult," he teased, but both Kingston's and his eyes sparkled with an honesty that made my breath catch.

"Well, next time there's a dance," Lyla said as she started wiping the counters down as she talked, "just tell me, and I'll make sure she isn't working so you all can go." She directed her statement at Reid and Kingston who smiled as if they would do just that.

Don't I get a say?

Not that I'd complain about going to the dance with either of them.

"We'll do that." Kingston surprised me by being the one to respond when I'd thought Reid would crack a joke about it instead. Lyla nodded before taking the dirty rag back into the employees' area to drop it in the laundry cart. I raised a brow at them when we were alone.

"What is this 'we' stuff? I couldn't go with both of you

to a dance," I challenged, playing it down, but my heart seized at the thought of having to pick between the three of them.

Wait, did I just say three of them?

I guess Jesse weaseled his way in the 'Emma's crushes' department.

"Why not?" Reid asked, his tone serious, probably for the first time ever, as he looked at me. "We do everything as a group, so why couldn't the four of us go together?" I smiled at the fact that I wasn't the only one who was considering Jesse as a part of this crazy idea.

"Well." I pursed my lips in thought as I stared at them. "Next time there's a dance, ask me and we'll see. How about that?"

"Deal." Reid's hazel eyes lit up at my compromise making my heart go from constricted with worry to pitter-pattering its way into my throat. Kingston's laidback smile curled his lips as he nodded in agreement. The ding of the bell saved me from having to try and fill the silence with conversation after their admission of wanting to share me as a date. "We'll see you tomorrow, Cali girl. Text us when you're off, we need to go grab Jesse." Reid gave me a wink, and Kingston waved as they left me alone with the customer and my crazy thoughts. Hopefully the sharing conversation wouldn't make it too complicated between us.

I suck at complicated.

Clocking out, I left work before Lyla as she was relaying what needed to be done to Cara, the other Coffee Grounds employee. The air outside was comfortably warm as I walked to my car and drove home despite the darkening sky. The windows were rolled down so the nice weather could brush across my face. The music from the radio kept my attention away from the thoughts of dances and boys until they were pushed into the back of my mind.

The house was empty when I got home, my mom working on an event set-up for her client. I didn't try to understand her schedule since it was so busy here. Back home it had been relatively normal because the company they worked with was large but not enormous or taking multiple contracts like her new one does. I ground my teeth together at the oppressive silence, growing increasingly more irritated. The longer I listened to the empty house the more I was reminded how broken our family was.

No, I still didn't know why my parents divorced.

Or why I had to move to the middle of nowhere

Or why my parents seemed to have completely forgotten I existed.

Why even bother to push? To try and force an answer to a question they seemed determined to ignore? It's not like it really mattered anyway now. We were here, in Nebraska, and there was nothing I could do. All I could do now was focus on those who were actually making this new life into some sort of home.

With that, I shook myself out of my stupor and walked into the kitchen content to focus on something other than the thoughts of my broken family. Searching through the cabinets, I decided to just make a peanut butter and jelly sandwich not wanting to cook or clean the dishes. I had just taken a bite when my phone buzzed.

Reid: Would it be frowned upon if I put my headphones in while my parents lectured about college?

Emma: Probs, I've been meaning to ask, are you planning on going to UNO or UNL?

Reid: Yeah most likely one of them, I considered community college for a while but decided against it. Why?

Kingston: UNL most likely, they have a pre-law program.

My brows went up, I hadn't expected laid back Kingston to consider being a lawyer. Jesse hadn't responded, but I knew he had read the messages.

Emma: I was going to set up a visit or tour or whatever. Wanna come with me?

Reid: Hell yeah! We can make a day trip out of it, get lunch and walk around the areas near campus.

Kingston: I'm down.

Jesse: Fine.

I let them know I'd get it all set up after I finished eating. They all had stipulations on when they wanted the tour to be, so it wouldn't be until after Thanksgiving to give Reid a chance to finish up his fall season of lacrosse. Scarfing down the rest of my sandwich, I was already feeling better from the practice ACT test after my shift at work, but after eating I felt more like my normal myself.

Emailing the advisors at both universities, I opened the communications for setting up the tours. Once that was done, I spent a little bit cleaning my room before collapsing onto my bed in exhaustion. I was asleep within moments, my dreams filled with visions of dancing away the night in the arms of my boys.

Chapter 8

OCTOBER 7TH

No words for this.
#WhatDoIDoNow #FML #SundayFunday

I sat staring once again at the piece of paper that had come in the mail yesterday. The large 19 in the corner taunted me as I glared at the page. I knew it was just practice, and I knew my anxiety had a lot to do with the low scoring, but I couldn't bring myself to believe I got a 19 on my ACT.

No, technically it wasn't terrible.

But to me, it was awful.

I wasn't a bad student, averaging A's most of the time. Heck, I was even an honor roll student and had been since freshman year of high school, so I didn't understand how I could do so poorly. The stressful topic of college just got so much worse.

What the heck am I going to do?

OCTOBER 8TH

Success is not final, failure is not fatal: it is the courage to continue that counts. -Winston Churchill
#PracticeMakesPerfect #ItllBeOkay #MotivationMonday

That dark cloud that had descended over me for the last 24 hours was still going strong when I left for school that morning. My mood was grim as I kept my arms crossed over my chest to hold my jacket closed, trying my best to keep the slight chill in the air out. None of my friends were in the parking lot this morning as I walked into the school, and the sound of everyone talking within the crowded cafeteria grated on my already dismal morning. I took my time as I made my way over to the table, not in the proper mindset to make meaningless chit chat with people. The bell ringing surprised me before I made it to the table, my slow going attitude today making me arrive a bit later than normal. Forgoing waiting for the boys, knowing Jesse wouldn't want to be near me anyway, I went to my class.

I felt my curiosity burn when Jesse never walked in, the seat to my right empty throughout the twenty minute homeroom. Without realizing it, my eyes darted around the halls for Jesse's familiar scowl and square diamond stud earrings, but I couldn't find them by the time I reached history. Reid was already seated in our normal two-person desk, his leg bouncing under the table as he worriedly watched the door. His expression melted into relief when he spotted me.

"You didn't come to the table this morning," he whispered, his Old Spice scent surrounding me. The familiar notes comforted me ever so slightly, making the dark storm cloud that rested on my shoulders a little less daunting "I was worried about you. You haven't really messaged much this weekend either. Everything okay, Cali girl?"

My nickname on his lips pushed a new surge of emotions through me, my stress about the future and the strongly ignored, but still growing feelings for the boys raged through me. Nodding, I focused on pulling out my textbook, homework, and other materials for class as I willed the burn of tears away. Soft fingers nudged my jaw, angling my head toward his concerned face. He had scooted closer while I was pulling out my stuff, and for a moment I just looked at him, taking in details of one of my closest friends.

His dark curls had grown out in the last month, the mop becoming a bit unruly as it brushed his ears and forehead. Tanned skin had faded slightly with the quickly changing seasons as summer started to give way to fall. His facial hair was cut short, more five o'clock shadow than stubble, making him look a bit younger. Dark brows continued to pull down over his gorgeous eyes, the honey brown center haloed by a bright, vibrant green. His fingers shifted from my chin to my cheek, the pad of his thumb rubbing against my skin gently.

"Emma?" His baritone voice was subdued as he whispered my name. I tried to give him a reassuring smile, but I wasn't sure if it looked more forced or more like a grimace.

"It's nothing." My cheek pressed into his hand with my sad smile. "I don't want to talk about it right now. Maybe in a few days, okay?" His jaw clenched sharply at my dismissal, but he didn't argue as he gave me a silent nod.

"Where's Jesse at? He wasn't in homeroom," I asked, the worry of not knowing coming to the forefront of my mind.

"He's got some personal stuff he had to deal with, but he'll be back tomorrow," he assured me.

Jesse had skipped school. I could see it in Reid's eyes.

"He's okay, right?" I hedged a guess, knowing Reid was lying to me. Well, maybe not *lying* per say, but not telling me the whole truth.

Then again, I just did that very same thing.

"Don't worry. Okay, Cali girl?" It was my turn to clench my jaw without argument like he had done for me. Miss Ester started class a moment later, but even her vibrant teaching and bubbly personality couldn't hold my attention with the warring thoughts in my head.

Please, let the rest of the day go smoothly.

School went by quickly, and even the school gossips left me be to talk amongst themselves despite their words about Jesse echoing through my mind. Reid and Kingston were going to run to the store and some other errands instead of coming over to study tonight. I took their words for what they were, a hint that they were going to go check on Jesse, but I didn't comment.

The city gave way to Nebraska's corn and soybean fields, the yellow stalks reminding me that it was now October, and Reid brought up going to the pumpkin patch this weekend. Apparently, this pumpkin patch was more than just an actual patch where you picked your orange squash off the ground. If I was honest, I was excited to go and escape the worries that had been plaguing me. Something across the divided highway caught my eye and pulled me out of my thoughts. Looking closer, I felt my jaw drop.

So much for the rest of the day going smoothly.

"What the…" I exhaled sharply pulling my Honda to the shoulder, the rhythmic clicking of my hazards taking over for the music I had been playing. After I had made sure I wasn't going to get run over, I jumped out of the car and sprinted across the four lanes and grass median.

"What are you doing?" I hissed as I finally reached the reason I had run across a highway.

Jesse.

Walking by himself with a bag on his shoulder.

But when he turned to look at me, all irritation at his stupidity was gone. Darkening red marks covered his face, and several of the small gashes were dripping and bubbling with blood. His knuckles were just as abused, cracked and previously bleeding, if the smudged wipes on his jeans were any indication. He favored the left side of his torso, his arm crossed in front of it defensively.

"Holy crap," I breathed, unable to fully process what I was seeing. "What the heck happened to you?" I closed the few feet between us, and his jaw clenched as he leaned away from my gaze. "Is this why you weren't at school? Jesus, Jesse." I ran my fingers through my hair in an anxious attempt to calm myself.

I mean, heck, I'm not the one broken and bleeding and walking on the side of the highway.

"Why are you here?" he bit out, his eyes burning holes in whatever he was glaring at off to the right. I gaped at him.

"Are you freaking kidding me right now?" His head snapped back as he brought a surprised gaze to me at my angry tone. "You weren't in school, and you're on the side of the damned highway!" I hissed quietly. "You're bleeding and obviously injured. Let's go." I hitched a thumb to my car. His eyes turned suspicious as he narrowed his dark brown eyes on me.

"I'm not going with you," he ground out, his shoulders rolling back as he turned to start walking again. I rubbed my face in irritation before sighing.

"Jesse, wait," I called out after he had walked several feet away from me, my tone exhausted as everything built back up within me. "I won't ask questions. I just want to get you cleaned and patched up, okay?" He looked at me for a few tense moments before he nodded ever so slightly, his long legs closing the distance between us. He was an inch shorter than Reid, but he was still at least half a foot taller than me.

We were silent as we went back to my waiting car. The drive was awkward, his attention focused outside the passenger window. I groaned when I saw my mom's SUV in the driveway. Leaning forward, I looked to the front windows of my house finding all of the shades closed.

The one time she actually had to be home was the day I needed her to be away.

"I'm going to open the garage, and I want you to go to my bathroom and wait quietly," I told him, turning off the car and grabbing my bag. "I know I said I wouldn't ask any questions, but if my mom sees you looking like this, she'll raise all sorts of hell. I know you don't exactly like me, but I just want to help, okay?" He watched me briefly before nodding and following me to the garage door. He split off as soon as we entered the basement, his form disappearing behind the bathroom door.

"That you, Emma?" my mom hollered. Taking a steadying breath, I left my bag at the base of the stairs and went up to check in.

"Yup!" I greeted cheerfully, my head popping around the corner into her office where she was typing at her computer. "I'm feeling pretty gross from dance today, so I'm going to go shower. You here for the rest of the night?"

"If no work comes up, then yes, I'll probably just be working for a while before heading to bed. We have an early morning breakfast meeting, so I'll be leaving a bit before you," she informed me, not even bothering to turn away from her work to look at me. I felt a small blooming bubble of hurt at the fact that she couldn't even look at me since it was the first time I had seen her in weeks, but I swallowed it down, my focus on Jesse waiting for me.

"Okay." I gave a quick smile as I inched back down the hall. "I'm going to shower now then probably just hang out in my room; I'm tired." She gave a quick affirmative as I darted down the stairs and into the bathroom. Jesse was leaning against the counter, his shoulders slumped as he saw me, like he was worried I wouldn't be coming back. I held my finger up to my lips as I curled around him, my arm reaching into the shower to turn the knob.

"All right," I whispered, trying to not notice that the bathroom's lack of space was making me brush up against his muscled chest. Swallowing the lump that solidified in my throat when I felt the heat of his body against my chest, I focused on other things to distract myself. The scent of pine and mint surrounded me in a blanket of comfort despite the accidental boob grazes. "Is anything other than your face or your knuckles hurt?"

"No," he whispered harshly, but his eyes darted down too quickly. I waited him out and when he glanced back at me, I raised a brow silently demanding him to answer truthfully. He grumbled quickly but lifted his shirt. Dark skin was stretched tight over chiseled muscles that dipped in sculpted abs and defined pecs. I swallowed the surge of butterflies that took off at his very attractive body and focused on his injuries. There was one cut, but it wasn't deep and barely bled as it sat in a cluster of bruises. I clenched my jaw when I noticed older, more yellow-tinted bruises mixed with too many fresh ones.

My eyes burned, a wall of tears building in my eyes as my fingers brushed against his warm skin. Pulling myself together, I forced the tears away while I dug out the first aid kit under the sink. I busied myself with preparing the antiseptic pads so I could clean his cuts.

"Fuck," he bit out when I pressed the soaked pad to his eyebrow; the cut was the one bleeding the most so I focused on getting it cleaned and bandaged first.

"Sorry." I grimaced, feeling bad that I was making it worse, but I needed the cuts clean before I could bandage them. Working quickly, I washed and cleaned his injuries putting bandages and ointment on the ones that needed it. As I continued to work on him, I started realizing if my mom saw me without wet hair I would have to answer some very unwanted questions. "This might be awkward, but I told my mom I was going to shower, so I'm going to hop in real quick and then we can go to my room." I turned and snatched the robe off the back of my bathroom door before placing it on the hook right outside the curtain.

"I'll, uh, turn around," he murmured before angling himself toward the door and allowing me the privacy to undress. The thundering within my ears drowned out every sound around me as I quickly shed my clothes. I hadn't done anything sexual past a few very awkward fingerings and hand-jobs with Tyler, so being naked with a boy made my skin flush and my heart race. I hopped into the shower and pulled the curtain closed, the water soaking my hair quickly before sticking my face out.

"You can sit down if you want," I offered quietly. Jesse

turned slowly before looking at me and sending my heartbeat ratcheting up another notch. A different kind of fluttering filled my body, the tingling spreading from my stomach to my breasts and to the crest between my thighs. Feeling my skin flare in a bright red flush that had nothing to do with the hot stream of water, I yanked my head back into the shower. Shuffling sounded on the other side of the curtain as I saw Jesse's silhouette move to sit on the toilet lid.

Leaning my head back the hot water cascaded over my heated skin. I couldn't believe Jesse, of all people, was sitting on the other side of a very thin curtain while I showered. That tingling blanketed over me, the heat of the water fueling the strange flame within me. Lathering my shampoo through my dark tresses, I attempted to push the building urge away. I focused on my shower, getting through my different steps until my last step where I soaped up my body, the feeling of the slippery bubbles against my sensitive skin making that flame flare up once more.

Biting my lip, I held my breath and closed my eyes, my fingers trailing against my skin in a burst of sensations. That tingling turned to searing in the wake of my fingers' path as I moved across my breasts. My nipples pebbled against the tips of my fingers, and a surge of need flooded me as I pressed my slick thighs together. Something felt so wrong, so forbidden, about exploring my own body with Jesse right on the other side of the curtain waiting patiently for me, but at the same time it felt so right.

What the heck is happening to me?

With that proverbial splash of cold water, I was brought back to reality. I sped through the rest of my washing before quickly rinsing. Shutting the water off, I snatched the robe off the hook and wrapped it around my skin, the fire burning within my veins still very much apparent. I opened the curtain when the robe was secure, and Jesse's eyes drifted down my body. I felt completely bare even though only my legs were on display since my fluffy robe only went to my mid-thigh. Curling my arms around myself, I stuck my head out the door and listened for any sounds of my mom before grabbing Jesse's shirt and pulling him to my room behind me.

I closed the door quietly. I hadn't realized I still held onto his shirt tightly until his warm hand wrapped around mine. Curious eyes watched me as he squeezed my hand lightly, letting me know that I could let go. When I did, he moved to sit on the end of the bed. I took a steadying breath and pulled out a pair of pajamas and a clean pair of underwear, forgoing a bra like I always did. Before I got dressed, I put on my music and turned it up an extra notch to mask any of our talking.

"Can you, uhm…" I whispered, twisting my finger in a circle to have him turn around. Moving with a sharp turn, he faced the opposite wall, his fingers digging into his denim-clad thighs. I shucked the robe, and the cool air of the room had me shivering as I rushed to get dressed. Once I was, I tapped him lightly on the shoulder so he knew. I sank onto the bed next to him and noticed the incessant vibrating of a phone call.

"Emma?" Reid's voice was frantic. "Have you seen Jesse?"

"Yeah, he's right next to me," I murmured not wanting to speak too loudly. The sound of Reid talking in the background filled the speaker, but it was too far from the phone to understand over my music.

"Holy shit," he muttered, "we've been freaking out for

the last hour trying to find him."

"He was walking on the side of the road. I passed him on my way home and made him come with me." I eyed the boy in question who watched me shamelessly.

"My phone broke," he muttered. "I was walking to Reid's house." My brows furrowed at his admission. Whatever happened to him had put me on high alert, but I had promised not to ask questions, so I clamped down on the urge to assault him with every single one rattling around in my head.

"His phone's broken. He was walking to your house," I relayed.

"This might be a weird question, but how does he look?" Reid's question was hesitant, and after finding Jesse like I had I understood his concern.

Meaning this had happened before.

"Not great, but he's all patched up now," I answered, sullenly staring back at Jesse. His jaw clenched, but he didn't try to stop me. "My mom's home tonight, but she's supposed to leave early, so I'm going to just bring him with me to school tomorrow."

"All right. Thank you, Emma. Seriously, you're perfect." Reid's words had me blushing, my eyes falling to my lap when Jesse's brows drew down at my blush. "Kingston and I have to hit the store still, so we'll text you, okay?"

"Okay," I responded lamely, the emotional baggage of the day catching up to me and frying my brain. "I'll talk to you in a bit."

"Bye, babe." I couldn't be sure, but I'm pretty sure Reid made a kissy sound on the other end, though he had hung up before I could question him.

"Emma!" My mom's voice radiated down the stairs from the kitchen. Despite her being upstairs, I jumped up in a hurry and ran out of the room, making sure to close the door behind me. "You hungry?" she asked, stirring a large pot of mac and cheese. I nodded right as my stomach growled. "I have to get back to work in the office, so if you want to head back downstairs you can."

"All right, I'll do that," I agreed, nodding as I scooped up a normal amount of food, but when she exited the kitchen with her own bowl, I scooped another huge amount into the bowl until it nearly overflowed. As quietly as I could, I grabbed an additional spoon out of the drawer before hurrying down the stairs. The fact that my mom didn't want to eat dinner at the table like she usually did wasn't even on my radar since Jesse being in my room was my main concern.

He wasn't sitting on the bed when I walked in. Panicking slightly, I jogged into the room to find him lying flat on the ground on the far end of my bed. I narrowed my eyes on him as he looked at me and shrugged.

He's so weird.

"I didn't know if she was coming down here, so I hid," he muttered, sitting back on the bed. "What's that?" His head tilted toward the bowl in my hands.

"Dinner, I could only take one bowl, so we'll have to share," I explained sitting next to him on the bed, blatantly ignoring the way my bare knee rubbed against the rough denim of his jeans. "Here." I held out the extra spoon I had grabbed.

"You didn't have to," he started, but I cut him off.

"Don't, Jesse," I sighed, my tone exhausted. "Just don't. You need to eat, so please don't fight me for once." He didn't argue with me, but he didn't move either. His head tilted ever so slightly as he watched me. After a few moments of our staring contest, he took the spoon, the brush of soft fingertips against mine making my heart pitter-patter in my chest under the thin material of my pajama top. We spent the next little while listening to my music and eating boxed mac and cheese, my attention split between making sure he ate enough and texting the other guys.

"I should head out." He started to get up after we had eaten, but my hand on his arm stopped his attempts to get up.

"My mom's going to notice if I have a boy leaving. You're staying here tonight," I ordered softly. He opened his mouth to argue, and I don't know what came over me, but I pressed my fingers against his full lips to silence him.

"Please," I begged, "I don't know why we're constantly fighting, but can you *please* trust me for once. Don't make this weird and just get under the freaking blanket."

"I'm not staying in the bed," he argued, his words soft as he spoke them against my fingers. That wash of tingles flared up my arm and across my torso, making my nipples pebble against my top before spreading to my other limbs.

Please don't be obvious.

"You are and you're not going to fight me on this, Jesse Parker," I ordered more forcefully keeping my voice low to not alert my mom. "Get under the damned blanket so I can turn off the light. And if I find you trying to sneak out in the middle of the night, I'll be so pissed, understood?" He sighed before finally nodding in dejection. I stood and waited to turn off the light as he kicked off his shoes. He paused before looking at me.

"I can't sleep in jeans," he murmured. I rolled my eyes before rolling my hand in the air between us as I talked. My exhaustion was making me cranky.

"So sleep in your underwear, I'll turn around," I

muttered as I faced the door. The rustle of his jeans hitting the carpet sounded before I heard him crawl into the bed. At his signal, I flipped off the light and turned down the music, leaving it playing softly to muffle any whispers between us. My heart pitter-pattered once more with nerves at seeing Jesse wrapped within my bedding and knowing he was only in his boxers. Swallowing my butterflies, I crawled into my bed, his warmth already emanating within the sheets. I was almost asleep when I felt the brush of fingers on my back and heard Jesse's gentle honey voice murmur in the darkness.

"Thank you, Em."

Chapter 9

The sound of the garage opening and closing in my sleepy haze brought me closer to the surface of being awake. I was warm and wrapped in a tight cocoon of mint and pine, unwilling to wake until I realized there was an arm curled around me tightly and a muscled body pressed flush against my back. The breath of whoever was sleeping behind me brushed against my neck as a nose nuzzled deeper into my hair and the person shifted to pull me closer.

What the heck?

My eyes shot open, my phone's clock reading about ten minutes before my alarm would go off. Looking down at my chest, I found a familiar hand was fisting the front of my flannel button-up pajama shirt in a tight grasp. I ignored the fact that Jesse's hand was directly in front of my chest, pressing into my breasts as I turned my head to look back at him. Unfortunately, his face was snuggled into my neck, so I couldn't see him. I stared at the ceiling unsure of what to do. Grabbing my phone, I turned off my alarm and checked my messages, several from Reid who was once again complimenting me for helping Jesse and a couple from Kingston with his sweet 'good morning' texts that had kind of become a regular thing within the last week or two.

"Ugh," a grumble sounded from behind me, "turn that light down." I rolled my eyes but obliged him. He shuffled but didn't move away as he started to wake, his body's natural reaction to the influx in blood flowing through him quite obviously pressing into my hip.

"Jesse," I mumbled, my fingers poking his boxer-covered thigh that had come uncovered in the night. "I need to get up."

"So get up," he muttered irritatedly, his voice thick with sleep. I sighed and finally just rolled onto my back as much as I could to look at him.

"That's hard to do when you're holding on to me like a life preserver," I whispered. I knew as soon as he was awake because his eyes widened sharply as he yanked his hands back. Rolling like I was on fire, he hopped off the bed, and my eyes were inexplicably drawn to the large tent he was sporting in his underwear.

Wow.

That was, uh, very eye popping.

"Sorry," he grouched, yanking on his jeans. I rolled out of bed and came over to him. He stopped his sharp movements at my fingers brushing his arm.

"It's okay." I smiled slightly. "I'm glad you stayed." His chest visibly thudded, betraying his racing heart. "I'm going to go brush my teeth, and I have some extra unopened ones if you want to brush yours. There's towels under the sink in the bathroom if you want to shower," I explained moving toward my dresser and closet to gather my clothes for the day. "My mom's gone, so we can go upstairs and get some food before we head to school." When he didn't respond, I looked back at him. He was staring at me with his head tilted, confusion blatant on his handsome face.

"Why?" He nearly whispered the question. I felt my face scrunch up.

"Why what?" I didn't understand what he was asking me, not sure if it was because I was still partially asleep or if it was because I didn't understand Jesse very well.

"Why would you help me?" My heart cracked at his quiet words. I knew we weren't exactly the closest of friends, but I would have thought he knew me better than that.

"Because you're my friend, Jesse, and I care about what happens to you." I felt my eyes fill with unwanted tears, so I glanced down at my makeup and jewelry taking my time to pick out what I wanted to wear that day. Feeling his eyes on me, I forced myself to look up in the mirror I had on my dresser. He had walked closer when I wasn't paying attention, his shirt now brushing against my back with how close he was standing. For the first time since I moved to the middle of freaking nowhere Nebraska, Jesse finally let his mask slip away. His eyes filled with warmth as he watched me watch him, and his arms slid around my waist to hold me tightly to him.

"Thank you, Em," he mumbled, the words muffled since he had pressed his face into my neck and hair. I wrapped my arms against his, rubbing small circles around his wrists. My heart cracked for an entirely different reason at his emotional hug. My building feelings for Reid, Kingston, and him melted into a large puddle within my chest and sent the butterflies soaring again. "I'm sorry," he whispered.

"For what?" I asked, tilting my head back to rub against his warm forehead in an attempt at a comforting gesture.

"I don't mean to be so..." He trailed off, not knowing how to describe himself. "But I don't dislike you like you think I do." His head came up, a battered cheek pressing into my hair as he looked down at me in the mirror. "I care about you too, Em." I couldn't hold back the wide smile that stretched over my face, my breath catching when Jesse smiled back.

Like really smiled, for the first time.

He's very attractive when he smiles.

"I'm going to go shower quick." He squeezed me to him once more before untangling himself from my body. When the bathroom door closed, I finally breathed shakily.

What the heck just happened?

Shaking my head sharply, I focused on doing my makeup. I went with my usual daytime with a small, black winged eyeliner, mascara, some blush, and a coordinating lip color. Today's was a peachy-nude to match the blouse I was wearing, the gold buttons down the front shining in the lamp light of my room. I had just finished getting ready, making sure to hold off on applying my lipstick so I could brush my teeth, when Jesse came back in. I tried to ignore the paper from my ACT results that was lying on the edge of my dresser near where I kept my backpack and school stuff as I moved out of the room. Its low score taunted me as I walked by.

Curving around Jesse to get to the hallway, I went to brush my teeth, my brain whirling with thoughts. Did this finally get us past whatever barrier we had? Would he be more himself when it was just the four of us? The questions rattled at dizzying speed as I grabbed my bag and shoes from my room to set by the garage door, Jesse right behind me as we snagged something small for breakfast in the kitchen. I wrote a quick note on the paper pad on the counter to let my mom know what we needed from the grocery store since our fridge and cabinets looked a bit empty as I went through them.

"How'd you sleep?" Jesse's question startled me enough that I almost lost the piece of toast I had balanced on my fingers. Thankfully, I caught it before it could go tumbling to the ground. Jesse's lips were thinned as he looked from the toast to me, laughter filling his eyes.

Jerk.

"Pretty well considering I couldn't flip over because *somebody* was being a cuddlebug," I teased. Jesse narrowed his eyes on me as I took a bite.

"Not my fault you're warm and your room is below zero," he challenged, taking a bite of his own food. I couldn't help but laugh at the odd conversation between us. It was like a switch was flipped that made me no longer feel odd or awkward around him. I had just opened my mouth to throw a retort at him when my phone buzzed.

Reid: You guys almost here?
Emma: Haven't left yet, we're eating breakfast. Do you want us there now?
Reid: If it wouldn't be too much trouble. We just want to make sure he's okay.
Emma: We'll leave now then.

"We've been summoned to school so the other two can check on you," I relayed to Jesse who had just finished his breakfast. He huffed but didn't argue as he got up and followed me down the stairs to collect our stuff from by the door.

"Ready?" I quickly asked him after putting on my shoes. "Do you need to get anything from anywhere?"

"I'm good, I have everything in my bag." He finished tying his shoes as he talked. Grabbing our bags, we headed out. The drive to school was much less awkward than it had been the night before when I had picked him up, a tender white flag having been raised to halt whatever stand-off we'd been in before this morning. When we arrived, the parking lot was mostly full, Reid's dirty Jeep parked in his usual spot. I parked as close as I could to the mud covered vehicle and got out. Neither of us spoke, but Jesse wasn't radiating irritation or loathing at me, opting to actually walk next to me instead of just near me.

"Oh, thank god," Reid huffed quietly when we got to the table, his eyes darting around Jesse's face. "You all right?" Jesse didn't speak as he nodded an assent, his shoulders tensing under Reid and Kingston's inspections.

"We'll stop by the store later and get you a new phone," Kingston offered. Jesse didn't look happy at that, but he didn't argue which surprised me.

Guess I didn't know Jesse very much at all.

Standing slightly behind Jesse's shoulder, I stared at Reid and Kingston. When they finally looked back at me, I raised a brow in question, my eyes darting to Jesse quickly before returning to them. They shook their heads ever so slightly signifying they wouldn't answer my questions. My lips thinned, but I didn't argue as the bell rang.

It didn't escape my notice that they both grimaced.

This wasn't over, and next time it happened I wouldn't let it go.

Jesse walked by me as we headed to homeroom, both of us quiet as we were lost in thoughts. I felt the day already wearing on me, and it was only homeroom.

It's going to be a long day.

Yup, very long day.

"Hey, Cali girl." Reid puffed out a hard breath as he flopped into his chair. Mr. Fergusen was away for the day, and we had a substitute with the instructions to let us pair up and study together for our upcoming test on Thursday. "I just wanted to say thank you again."

"Seriously, Reid," I huffed with a small smile. "It was nothing. I didn't do anything…"

"Yes, Emma," he cut me off, "you did. You helped out one of my oldest friends and took care of him even with his more than odd behavior." That certainly was one way to put Jesse's attitude toward me up until today. I laid a hand on his arm to stop him.

"I would do it for any of you," I murmured not wanting to attract attention to our private conversation. I didn't think many people would be paying attention seeing as how everyone was lost in their own conversations, but I wanted to be sure. Reid's gaze was intense as he stared at me, and a warm calloused hand wrapped around mine.

"You're seriously perfect," he whispered, a small smile curling his lips as he squeezed my fingers where they rested on his arm. A blush blossomed on my cheeks, and I was starting to become accustomed to the constant soaring of butterflies that had been reawakened by Jesse this morning.

"Thanks." I tucked my hair behind my ear in an attempt to hide my blush as I side-eyed him. Feeling way too exposed and emotional, I redirected the conversation to focus on studying. The topic of helping Jesse, or Reid complimenting me didn't come up again.

Class and lunch passed quickly and before I knew it, Kingston's hand was pressing into my lower back as we walked to our AP English class. I tried to focus on my surroundings, what the other kids were doing in the halls or what people were wearing, but after all of the emotional buildup today it was no use. His hand was my sole focus as we headed to class. His thumb brushed in soft back and forth strokes that made tingles and shivers want to roll throughout my body, but I held it back. Only when we reached class did Kingston move his hand so he could sit at the desk. Sinking onto my own chair, I busied myself with digging out my class materials.

Book? Check.

Notebook? Check.

Pencil? Well, crap.

The mechanical pencil I had set on the desk fell off, bounced on the carpeted flooring, and rolled under to the other side of Kingston's chair. I sighed, but Kingston bent down to grab it without me having to ask. His coffee brown eyes were warm as he gave me one of his signature laidback smiles. When he held out the pencil I accepted it from him. As cliche as it sounded, our fingertips brushed. A tingling shot down my arm at the contact, making those ever present butterflies—that I was pretty sure were on some kind of drugs based on how active and crazy they were—fluttered and soared in my chest. I was right. Today was a long day, and I learned I couldn't freaking focus with so many emotions and way too many drug addled butterflies.

Awesome.

"Oh!" Lyla shouted, shaking my arm slightly in her excitement. Her gaze was focused on one of those health and beauty stores. This one I knew had a reputation for making bath bombs and other natural beauty products like lotions, shampoos, and conditioners. "Let's go check out what's in there." She dragged me along with her, her red hair flopping around her thin cheeks and forehead with each peppy step. I was happy when Lyla had messaged me at lunch today asking if I wanted to go shopping with her. She had taken the day off and thought going shopping with me would be fun.

I certainly wasn't going to complain.

Getting away from my spiraling out of control emotions for the boys? Count me in.

"I love Lush," I added as we walked into the fragrant store. The aesthetics of the shop were cool and a bit edgy with brightly colored bath bombs in different shapes contrasting sharply against the dark charcoal and black of the containers and labels. "I'm just happy the house we're renting has a tub in my bathroom so I can use them."

Lyla nodded an enthusiastic agreement before focusing her attention back on the products. I followed suit, my attention landing on a few bath bombs that caught my eye. I read the little tags saying what they were made with and what they would be best suited for. Chuckling to myself, I grabbed several meant for relaxation and a couple of their Halloween specific ones. I debated getting some of their lotions, but I still had a large container that I had bought right before we moved. A little pinprick of homesickness bubbled in my chest, reminding me of the local shop I had loved to go to for the lotions and perfumes that were made by a woman who lived one city over.

"Emma!" Lyla calling my name helped me push away

the negative emotion and the signature prickling of tears building in my eyes. "You ready to check out?" I nodded and paid quickly for my things. Lyla hadn't gotten anything, settling on just sniffing all the products while I had browsed.

"So, now where?" I asked, my eyes darting from one store to the next. I hadn't been to this mall before. Since I spent almost all my time outside of school either at work or doing homework with the boys, I never really had the chance to come explore it. We made small talk as we were walking aimlessly through the hallways and window shopping. After our second loop through this wing of the mall, we headed into one of the clothing shops.

"So," she started as she browsed the rack, "tell me about pre-Nebraska Emma. Who was this mysterious Cali girl?" She struck a dramatic pose with her back bowed and hands clasped under her chin. "Was she the popular girl all the boys swooned for? Or..." She tossed on a pair of fake glasses from one of the displays and gave me a dorky smile. "Was she a nerd? A band geek?" She put them back gently onto the plastic stand while I answered, breathless from laughing so hard at her dramatics.

"I guess you could consider me as popular." I shrugged, unsure. "I got good grades and everything, but I wasn't in band or any of the academic clubs. My friends, however, were typically focused on gossip, so I usually ended up dragged into the middle of everything that was being talked about," I explained, fiddling with one of the necklaces on display. "This might sound terrible because they've been my friends since I was in diapers, but since coming to Nebraska I've found more 'real' friendships. You know?"

"I definitely hear you there," Lyla agreed with a nod.

"One thing that also helps is once you're out of high school a lot of that pettiness and gossip doesn't typically mean anything. Granted, I'm working full time with one online college course, so I'm not sure if it's the same in college, but I've found it's a lot better since I graduated."

"When did you graduate?" I asked as I pulled a red plaid scarf off the rack to check the price. Lyla held up a pair of simple hoop earrings and glanced at herself in the mirror.

"This last spring, so it's not like I've been out for a while, but I worked at Coffee Grounds since I turned 16, and as soon as I could I switched to full time."

"Is that what you want to do?" I put the scarf back as I talked, swapping the red out for a gray and white patterned scarf that reminded me of my bedspread.

"I don't know," she hummed. Her eyes narrowed slightly as she tilted her head to think about the question. "I really do love it. Maybe look into promoting to management. I know the owners were looking into expanding to have another shop, so maybe I can get on there."

"That'd be pretty cool," I agreed. We paid quickly for our items, me with the scarf and Lyla with a pair of sleek sunglasses and the small hoop earrings, before heading out to get some food from the food court. Hopping in line, Lyla ordered what she wanted and stepped off to the side while she waited for her food.

"What about you? What does Emma Clark, barista extraordinaire, want to be when she grows up?" I chuckled at her extravagant title before I paid for my slice of pizza.

"I'm not sure." I nibbled on my lip in thought. "I want to get a business degree, but I'm not sure what I want to do with it really. Haven't given it too much thought, was more thinking about getting into the college classes and then kind of picking from there when I see the concentrations and what I fit best with." She nodded sharply before taking a bite of her slice that had just been passed to her.

"That's smart, no use in deciding on something if you don't think you'll like it."

"Exactly." I beamed at her. My slice was passed to me, the hamburger pizza making me smile. *Reid would be so proud,* I chuckled internally, *I'll text him about it later.* We spent the rest of the hour wandering a bit more, the conversation and bond between us having grown tighter during our shopping trip.

Nebraska is definitely not looking so bad.

Chapter 10

OCTOBER 12TH

So... much... homework... hahahelpmehaha
#IsItGraduationYet #NotFunnyFriday

The rest of the week had gone by horrendously slow. The amount of homework I had been assigned had kept me up later than I was used to in an attempt to finish it on time. The mid-term tests in several of my classes on Thursday and Friday had worn me out with the length of studying I had done each night, but now it was officially the weekend, and I only had to study over the course of the next two days for a short quiz on Monday in Civics.

My mom was still working ridiculously crazy hours, but she had finally gone to the store last night and picked up a couple of things, so that was better than nothing. My stomach growled at the thought of food, but I decided to hold off until we were at the haunted house place the boys demanded we go to tonight.

Checking my phone, I felt my jaw clench when my dad hadn't messaged me back at all today. I had spoken to my dad approximately three times since we moved away, each being through text, and only then as a couple of not-so-detailed messages. I was at the point I didn't want to even bother with talking to him if he couldn't give me more than one worded answers. The feeling of loneliness had built to higher levels unless Reid, Kingston, and Jesse were with me. Spending time texting Lyla, Aubrey, and Zoey the last couple weeks helped a bit when I was alone, but the silence of the house was suffocating even with the sound of my music playing.

A text from Reid let me know that they were out front to pick me up, having decided to drop off their bags at Reid's house before getting me since they were all staying at his house tonight. I glanced once more in my mirror to check my outfit; my black fleece jacket was layered on top of my thicker peachy-pink sweater, while my chunky knit gray scarf was wound around my neck. The weather had chilled in the last couple of days, and my California blood wasn't used to the biting wind, so I made sure to also wear knee-high boots and tall socks. Grabbing a pair of gloves and a knit beanie, I stuffed both into my purse on my way out the door.

"Hey, Emma," Kingston greeted as he got out of the passenger seat. His smile made my heart flutter within my chest. In a poor attempt to hide my blush, I fiddled with my hair and bangs, using my hand to hide my cheek.

"Hi, Kingston." I smiled up at him and sank into the front seat. Reid's bright smile flashed my direction as I buckled. "Hi, Reid. Hi, Jesse," I added a bit louder over my shoulder towards the silent boy in the backseat.

"Hey there, Cali girl," Reid responded before pulling out of my driveway. We were fairly quiet, Reid and Kingston the only ones talking on the drive to our destination. I watched the neighborhood and houses give way to fields, the road turning from paved cement to dirt and gravel the farther from town we got. The haunted house we were going to had several attractions like a scary corn maze, haunted castle, and a few other things you could go through as well as bonfires and a couple of food and drink stands. The sun was just starting to set when we pulled into the lot. Tall yellow corn stalks lined the perimeter of the place, and two workers stood under the entrance sign with wristbands and cash boxes.

"Four unlimited please," Reid asked when we reached the gate. He held out enough money for all four of us even though I hadn't given him money for mine. I opened my mouth to say something, and Kingston's hand came to my back, his beard rubbing gently against my hair.

"There's no use arguing, Emma." He chuckled at my pout. "None of us will let you pay when we're taking you out." I was glad it was getting dark and that the main lighting throughout the space was from the bonfires because it helped conceal my blush that once again spread across my cheeks.

"Here you go." The guy who held out the wrist band was about our age. I was pretty sure he went to our school or I had seen him around when I was out with the boys. I pulled up my sleeve so he could secure it on my wrist; his bright blue eyes were focused on my face. "You have fun," he murmured as he winked at me. The action put me on edge, and a wave of sharp tingles ran down my spine as the feeling of hairs standing on end emanated from the back of my neck. Reid must have seen the movement because his arm slipped around my shoulder to comfort me.

"Come on, Cali girl," he whispered, nudging me away from the guy with the intense blue eyes and wavy light brown hair who continued to stare as we walked away. "Sorry, I didn't like how he was looking at you," Reid muttered in my ear as we got farther away from the entrance. I smiled up at him, his face so close to mine I could feel his minty breath on my skin.

"I didn't either, feel free to rescue me whenever you want," I teased.

"You got it." He squeezed me to him. Jesse and Kingston had already gotten in line for food and drinks by the time we joined them. After ordering a hot dog and some hot chocolate, we made our way over to one of the open bonfires and sank onto the hay benches. Reid seemed to know so many people, saying hey or waving at pretty much any teenager who passed us. Kingston knew just as many, but his greetings were usually a nod or a single wave. Like me, Jesse focused on eating and not interacting with anyone else.

I wonder how someone so anti-social ended up with what seems like two of the most well known guys within the city.

"I love Halloween!" Reid practically shouted when he finished his food, his hands clapping in front of his chest. "It's my favorite holiday."

"I like it too, mainly cause all my birthday parties were also costume parties which is super fun," I explained. I tipped up my cup and finished up my hot chocolate. Reid's head whipped to face me at my words. Kingston's coffee brown eyes centered on my face as Jesse slightly angled himself over toward where I was sitting.

"When's your birthday?" Kingston asked before Reid could. I chuckled at the pout Reid sported, his bottom lip curling out in an undeniably adorable way.

I gave them a sly smile. "October 31st."

"Oh, my god! Your birthday is on Halloween? How did we not know? Must plan a party," Reid hollered, although the last statement was more muttered to himself than to anyone in particular.

"How old are you going to be?" Kingston asked nicely, completely ignoring Reid's outburst.

"18. I just realized I have no idea how old any of you are." I turned to them expectantly.

"Kingston's the oldest, he turned 18 at the end of August," Reid explained. "Jesse's the youngest, he'll turn 18 in April. I'm 17, and my birthday is in December."

"I'll need the exact date, so I can get you a present and plan you a party. Kingston, your party will have to wait until next year since I got here late." I gave him a cheeky smile making him laugh. Reid agreed quickly, but only with the stipulation he could throw me a party in return. "I suppose. Nothing super crazy," I shouted after him as he darted to the trash can to throw away our cups.

The next couple hours were spent bouncing between the different 'haunted' attractions which, to be honest, were quite entertaining, and hanging out near the bonfires. We ran into a few different people we knew from school, and by we, I mean Reid, who was sweet enough to introduce me. I had just left the bathroom when I ran into something solid.

"Oh, sorry," I started as hands caught my arms to keep me from falling. My heart rate picked up sharply when I looked up into the worker from the front's bright blue eyes. "Didn't mean to run into you."

"No worries, just glad you didn't get hurt." His tenor voice was smooth, but the way he stared at me still put me on edge. "You didn't get hurt, did you?" I shook my head trying to take a step back, but his hands kept me from going too far.

"I better get back to my friends." I attempted to hedge around him again, but the blue in his eyes seemed to sharpen dangerously as I shifted.

"Emma." Kingston's smooth tone was a blanket of safety as he stepped up next to me. The creep from the front finally dropped his hands and took a step back, his smile friendly as he looked over at Kingston.

"I'm Brad." The worker stuck a hand out to shake. Kingston obliged him, unaware of how edgy Brad was making me.

"Kingston," he said politely. "We best be going back to the rest of our group. Nice to meet you."

"You too." Brad smiled, but when he turned to me, something in his smile made me want to cower. "Try not to run into anyone else, Emma."

"I'll do that." I edged around him and practically yanked Kingston along when I grabbed his jacket.

"Woah, Emma. What's wrong?" He pulled me to a stop after we were away from the creepy worker.

"Something about him was weirding me out. Reid hadn't liked how he was looking at me at the gate earlier either," I whispered, leaning into his chest so I couldn't be overheard. "I don't know how to describe it, but he scares me."

"It's all right," Kingston cooed softly while wrapping his arms around me, his hand rubbing my back in long, soothing strokes. "We'll make sure he stays away from you from now on. He goes to our school, I recognize him from some old classes and parties. Come on, let's go get the others and head out. We've hit all the attractions anyways."

After finding Reid and Jesse, we left. Reid was angry, his normally exuberant attitude nowhere to be seen in his harsh frown and hard eyes. He continued to scan the crowd for the worker, but he wasn't anywhere to be found among the attractions or at the gate when we passed. Jesse looked pissed, similarly to how he did with Veronica, but I worried he would actually punch Brad when he found him. I felt terrible because we had had a great night until this situation.

"Emma," Kingston murmured to me as we got out at my house. The car ride had been completely silent, the tension stifling as we drove home. "Everything's okay, I promise. No one is mad at you, baby doll," he assured me quietly. I felt my eyes well up at the attempt to comfort me. I nodded and headed into the empty house, alone again. The silence emanating through the hollow walls was the last straw, and I crawled into bed and cried, falling asleep to the suffocating silence that was only broken by the quiet sound of my tears.

OCTOBER 13TH

Today, I will think of nothing to do with last night.
No creepers or tense silences with my boys.
#AllTheFizzyBathBombs #SelfCare #StressFreeSaturday

My mom was busy working in her office the next morning with plans for some kind of party at this new hotel for one of their clients and would be staying the night. That meant another night home alone.

Awesome… not.

I had tried to talk to her, but she was too focused on her computer and paperwork to pay attention to me so I gave up after a few measly words. I spent the rest of the morning taking a really hot bath with one of my new bath bombs to try and soothe the jagged edges inside me. It worked, at least a little bit, and soaking in the tub and wearing an exfoliating mask helped to de-puff my face after spending so long crying last night. I felt a bit better this morning since Reid had messaged saying he was sorry he had gotten so upset, that it wasn't at me but at the guy from the haunted house place. I knew that it wasn't my fault and that he wasn't mad at me, but it was still nice to hear it in the light of day. Knowing that any of the guys would say that after they'd had the night to cool down and get some space made me feel much more secure that they truly meant those words.

I alternated between studying, watching some TV, and getting ready for the party that the boys were dragging me to tonight. Studying wasn't too bad since the information was pretty straight forward, and it was just a quiz not a test. After several hours of doing that, my hair was styled in loose curls and my makeup was done a bit more dressy than usual with some eyeshadow, and I had actually painted my nails. Although it was a plain black, it was still more than I usually did.

"I'm heading out, sweetie. I'll see you tomorrow," my mom hollered down, "be good and let me know when you're back from hanging with the boys!"

"All right, bye, Mom. Love you!" I yelled back up as I pulled out my outfit.

"Love you too!" I heard the sound of the door quietly closing and the click of the lock as she left to meet her ride. Turning my attention back to my closet, I tried to decide what I wanted to wear, startling when my phone started to ring fifteen minutes later.

"Hey." I put the phone on speaker, setting it on the bookshelf next to my closet so I could focus on the array of colorful fabric. "What's up?"

"We're heading to your place." Reid's voice was far away but loud enough that I could understand him, meaning he was on speaker. Knowing them, Kingston was holding the phone between them. "You ready?"

"Almost, just trying to figure out what to wear."

Reid chuckled. "So you're a nakey Emma?" he teased, making me roll my eyes.

"No," I lied. Well, it technically wasn't a lie since I was in underwear and a bra. "Is it going to be inside or outside?"

"Both, but there's a large bonfire outside and lots of blankets," he explained, the sound of the radio filling the silence between his words. "Why?"

"Because that'll determine my outfit." I finally made my decision and pulled the hangers out of the closet. "I'll see you in a bit, boys. I need to get dressed."

"You're totally a nakey Emma!" Reid squealed happily.

"We'll see you soon." Kingston laughed as he said goodbye and hung up.

With yet another eye roll at Reid's ridiculousness I made sure I had everything in my crossbody purse before getting dressed. I went with a pair of black tights, black knee-high boots, a camel-colored skirt that had buttons down the left thigh, and a tight, black sweater that had long sleeves. Throwing on a coordinating cheetah print scarf, I grabbed a black jacket and a pair of gloves and a hat in case I needed it, before making my way out to wait for the boys. Within a few minutes of waiting outside for the boys they pulled into the driveway next to my car.

"You look beautiful, baby doll." Kingston wrapped me in a hug as he whispered the compliment. My cheeks only continued to heat when I got in the car, and Reid's eyes widened as his jaw dropped.

"Wow," he breathed staring at my outfit. "You look

amazing." I gave a shy smile and buckled into the seat. "Ready?" Nodding, he pulled himself together and headed to the party at one of the football player's house. We ended up out in the middle of nowhere, cornfields surrounding the large yard and two story house that seemed to be flooded with people.

A large amount of cars were parked in the long gravel driveway and in the overgrown grass leading to the manicured lawn. The house was a farmhouse style with a large wraparound porch that held a swing and an outdoor set of furniture. Students flitted in and out of the open front door and around the back of the house where I saw two large bonfires raging inside their pits. Sticking close to my boys we headed inside. I waved to the people I recognized as we made our way into the living room.

"Emma! Boys!" Zoey and Aubrey greeted cheerfully, their cheeks flushed as they waved their cups at us. Carter, Jason, and Brayden were spread throughout the room talking with different people. Aubrey looked at my outfit, checking out my scarf down to my shoes. "How do you always look so cute? We need to go shopping, so you can help me with my outfits."

"Oo, me too!" Zoey piped in.

Reid leaned over to whisper in my ear. "You thirsty, babe?" I nodded. "All right, we'll be right back. Stay with them, don't go anywhere." My brows furrowed at his serious tone and the way his eyes centered on my face before walking off. Aubrey and Zoey realized we were having a serious moment and turned to talk to each other. "I'm not risking anything happening to you, especially after last night." I nodded again, struck by his intense reaction. Determined not to let him down, I shifted over to Aubrey and Zoey with a tiny smile to Reid who flashed me one of his cheeky smiles before getting lost in the crowd as he followed Kingston and Jesse to the keg.

"How's the party so far?" I asked looking around. There were several kids I didn't recognize who I assumed went to the other school district, Millmer.

"It's fun!" Zoey piped up, her drink muffling her words slightly. "So, now that you've been here for a while, how are you liking Nebraska? It's not California, obviously, but it isn't so bad right?"

I chuckled, my eye catching Reid and Kingston who were joking around with Jesse in the kitchen as they filled cups from the keg. Seeing them interact had warmth spreading through me making me feel giddy, as if I was already a few drinks in. They really were some of the sweetest guys I had ever met. Well, Jesse was a bit iffy most of the time, but my brain was content to ignore that.

"Nah"—I smiled slightly—"it's not so bad. There's some pretty awesome people here. Not sure if it's a Nebraska thing or if it's just I found cool people." I nudged them both letting them know they were included in that group. Both smiled as they did a little dance.

"Good"—Aubrey nodded—"we don't want you to be leaving us for Cali and all its sunshine and beaches." I rolled my eyes at the stereotype.

"I didn't live near a beach." I laughed as Reid, Kingston, and Jesse appeared next to me with an extra cup of whatever alcohol the host had gotten. "I lived by a bunch of wineries and vineyards and snotty people who constantly looked down on everyone else." I finally admitted the one thing I had come to see with blinding reality, not only did my friends focus on who was better than others, so did the adults. Those who were from a higher social class gladly looked down on everyone else, including me, until I moved here and I realized how crappy I had treated people who weren't my friends.

"Well, you're ours now and like I told you before, you're stuck with us forever," Reid teased, pulling me to his chest in a hug. A fake evil laugh filtered out of him catching the attention of people around us, but when they realized it was Reid, they just chuckled and went back to their conversations. Apparently everyone was already used to his antics.

"Oh!" Aubrey hopped up on her toes excitedly. "There's Micah! Come on, I need moral support." She tugged on Zoey's arm, dragging her away while our helpless friend attempted to save her drink.

"Did you know red Solo cups are a common souvenir to bring back from the United States for those who visited? It stems from the fact they're used in so many party scenes in movies," I added after they walked off as we all were taking a drink. Reid chuckled while Kingston smiled down at me. Jesse didn't react, but I was pretty sure that he was smiling behind that cup.

"You're just full of little facts," Reid commented before pepping up. "I have one! If you're allergic to pollen you're allergic to plant sperm." I immediately choked on my sip because anything related to *that* was not what I expected Reid, my clown, to spout out. "Aw, you look so cute when you blush," he teased, his hazel eyes focused on my burning cheeks before looking me in the eye. "It's now my personal goal to see those pink cheeks as much as possible."

He can't be serious.

Reid winked but didn't change his statement, but thankfully Kingston talking cut off any more of that conversation. For now at least.

"I'm going to go check out back and see who's all here," he informed us. "I'll be back." He rubbed my back gently before swerving around people. Right after he left, Jesse ended up in a conversation with another guy I didn't recognize, leaving the music to suddenly fill the space.

"Dance with me," I asked in a slightly demanding tone, tugging on Reid's sleeve as the upbeat music thrummed through my chest making me sway to the song. He smiled down at me and obliged. One of his hands came to my waist as I rested my free hand on his chest, resisting the urge to smooth my fingers over the soft fabric of his t-shirt. The song faded into a pop-country kind of song, and even though I wasn't much of a fan of country, I couldn't deny that the beat was pretty catchy.

"You've never danced to country music properly, have you?" Reid's baritone filled me with fuzzy feelings as he held me closer, my chest brushing his as I slid my hand up to wrap my arm around his neck. I shook my head, the beer in my hand migrating to my lips in an attempt to keep myself from saying something embarrassing. Finishing his own beer, he took both of our empty cups and left them on a side table before coming back to me. "Just let go," he whispered as he started to move.

Before I knew it, we were doing some type of country swing dance I didn't recognize, moving in tandem when he wasn't spinning me out and back. After several songs, I was breathing hard and a layer of perspiration beaded on Reid's forehead. At the end of our fourth dance he decided to end with a flare for the crowd of people who came in to watch us, dipping me so low that I could feel his stubble against my chest. My cheeks flared as everyone clapped, and several whoops and hollers filled the space as Reid pulled me back to standing, his hazel eyes half-lidded when he looked down at me.

"That's how you dance to a country song," he whispered in my ear, lips brushing against my cheek so softly I thought I had imagined it. "Let's go find the other guys." I followed his lead and we filtered out into the chilly backyard.

At this point, I didn't think even the fall air could cool my heated blood.

CHAPTER 11

OCTOBER 13TH

Hard to stress when all you're thinking about is Reid's dancing skill.
#HolyCrap #IThinkImInHeaven #StressFreeSaturday

We found Kingston chatting with a few of the football players and a few girls who I thought were cheerleaders. When we approached, Kingston's hand migrated to my back, rubbing soothing circles into the tight muscles. Several of the girls and a couple of the guys eyed my position under Reid's arm and practically pressed into Kingston's torso with his arm around me, but no one said anything. Scanning the crowd, I found Jesse talking to the same guy from earlier near the other side of the campfire. It was odd seeing him interact with someone other than Reid or Kingston.

Why won't he talk to me like that?

Maybe now he will after our experience the other day.

Pushing the thought away, I turned back to the conversation. Something about state championships coming up as well as all the plans for Halloween. Apparently there was going to be a big costume party either here or at another player's house the weekend before since the actual holiday was on a Wednesday. After about a half hour of talking, I really needed to go pee.

"I'm going to run to the bathroom," I whispered to Reid. "Where is it at?" He gave me instructions before releasing me and telling Kingston where I was headed. I walked into the house, noticing that it had really filled up while I was outside. I waved slyly at Aubrey and Zoey who were flirting with some cute guys I knew they'd had their eyes on, before waving to Brayden who was chatting up some guys I recognized from school.

The bathroom on the main floor was occupied, but a girl from my dance class let me know there was one upstairs as well as one in the basement. Not really wanting to go to the basement alone, I headed up the carpeted steps to the fairly empty upstairs. The only people I saw were couples breaking off into more private areas like spare rooms.

Well, I hoped they were spare rooms.

The bathroom was thankfully empty when I found it. I was washing my hands when someone knocked. Drying them quickly, I unlocked the door and came face to face with the one person I didn't expect or want to see.

Brad.

"Hey, Emma." He smiled down at me from his height of at least 5'11". "Didn't know you were here tonight." The hairs stood up on the back of my neck, something about his words not ringing true. He might not have known I'd be at the party tonight, but he knew I was up here.

Alone.

"Uh, hey Brad," I muttered as I tried to pass him, but his arms came up to the door frame blocking my exit. "Do you need in here?" I pointed behind me as I tried once again to move past it.

"Yeah," he answered, giving me a wolfish smile before smashing his lips to mine and pushing us into the bathroom together. I yanked my head back and hit him in the chest with both fists, the force rattling through the bones in my hands painfully as I shoved him back and out the door, barely managing to break his grip. The cruel, intimidating smile widened at my attempts to keep distance between us. His hands returned to the door frame. This time I had been able to take several steps back to allow a foot of space between us. Regardless of the space though, I could see the cold gleam within his too-bright eyes as they watched me hungrily.

He was the predator and I was the prey.

"Back off," I ground out. He took several steps forward crowding the limited space I had been able to create. Darting to the left I tried to shoot around him, but he was faster. I struggled to wrestle his arms off me, but his grip was like two steel bands around my biceps with his effort to keep me from running away. Wave after wave of adrenaline flooded my system when he didn't move enough for me to escape.

"I don't think I will," he hummed pleasantly, shoving me back into the bathroom, a thud sounding as he kicked the door to close. His predatory smile made my stomach seize.

This is not freaking happening right now.

I screamed loudly as I kicked out and somehow managed to catch him in the shin, but the thumping bass from downstairs and music I heard from the bedrooms blanketed the shrill sound of my yelling. Sprinting toward door I barreled past him, taking advantage of the way my kick had knocked him off balance. I yanked open the door but I was only able to get a few steps away before he grabbed my arms with another tight grasp. Fear flooded my body, and my vision tunneled as I was redirected forcefully toward the bathroom.

"No!" I screeched, flailing in an attempt to loosen his grip as he tried to push me into the bathroom. He had just shoved me through the door frame when suddenly he was yanked back away from me. Stumbling to stay upright, I saw a familiar set of square stud earrings out of the corner of my eye.

Jesse.

When I was finally able to process what was happening, Brad was already sprinting down the stairs with Jesse immediately behind him. Several heads with wide eyes were watching me in the hall from various rooms. I raced after them, Brad's pained screams coming from the yard out back.

Jesse had Brad pinned down to the ground, shouting in his face, "You think it's all right to force yourself on someone?" Spit flew from his lips as he continued to scream while punching Brad in quick succession. His voice was so full of fury that I couldn't keep myself from cowering on the sidelines of the gathering spectators. "You don't get to fuck with any girl who doesn't want it, especially not Emma! I don't ever want to see you near my Emma again, or next time I won't fucking stop!" He straightened after his last statement, but instead of walking away immediately, he kicked Brad in the stomach and lunged back down, as if he couldn't help himself, to punch him one last time in the face. Brad groaned, blood pooling around his head on the grass from the broken nose I was pretty sure he had.

"Hey." I jumped with a startled squeak before realizing it was Kingston who stood behind me. "Let's get out of here." I nodded, the near-immobilizing fear receding and leaving trembling limbs and panic in its wake. The party was silent as everyone stared at us, a bloody-knuckled Jesse stepping in front of our group protectively as Reid flanked my left while Kingston took up position on my right. They formed a protective barrier around me as we made our way out to the front yard and Reid's car.

I didn't want to sit alone, so before Jesse and Kingston could crawl in the back, I sandwiched myself between them in a tight seating arrangement. A haze of white noise blanketed my mind on the drive, my thoughts and brain refusing to work or process what had happened. No one talked on the way back to my house, my trembling catching Kingston's attention, who immediately wrapped me in his arms the best he could in the cramped backseat. When we reached my house, I felt my chest tighten at the thought of being alone, paralyzing me after Kingston got out to allow me space to leave.

"No," I murmured, my voice weak.

"What?" Reid shifted in his seat so he could face me. Despite the anger I saw in his tight expression and burning eyes, his tone was soft. "What do you mean no?"

"Don't want to be alone," I whispered, barely audible in the idle rumble of his Jeep.

"Isn't your mom home?" he asked. Shaking my head sharply, I started to tremble again.

"Won't be home until tomorrow," I told them quietly. Reid's eyes widened before he turned back around and shut the car off. Kingston reached in and guided me out of the car, Jesse following close behind.

"Come on, baby doll." Kingston's smooth voice helped soothe the turbulent emotions burning through my chest. His hand on my back helped ground me, helped remind me that I was home and safe with them, no Brad in sight.

Kingston handed my keys over to Reid who unlocked the front door since he didn't know the code to the garage.

Flicking on the lights, he went to the basement, turned on the TV, and put on something funny. At least I think it was funny, everything was sort of a haze as my mind struggled to focus through the shock that had taken over me. Jesse went into the bathroom, and the noise of the faucet running flowed out into the hallway as he dug out the first aid kit.

Jesse needed help, and somehow in my hazy fog, I made my way into the bathroom and mindlessly started to wash his re-wounded knuckles. Kingston followed me in where he turned on the tub spout and flipped it on hot. I stood like a zombie in the corner, shivering, as soon as the blood was cleared off Jesse's hands.

"Can you get undressed on your own?" Reid's question startled me making me jump. "Do you want someone in here with you? Either way you need to calm and get warm." I looked between the three of them, unable to form a coherent thought. The only thing radiating through me was that they couldn't leave. *I can't be alone.*

I must have said that out loud because Reid responded, "All right, Cali girl, you don't have to be alone. I'm just going to get you to your underwear and bra, and we'll stay in here with you." He and Kingston started slowly removing my shoes, clothes, and my scarf until I stood in front of them in my bikini cut underwear and plain bra. "Do you have any kind of pajamas you want to wear tonight?" I shook my head slightly as Kingston directed me to the tub that had finally filled.

The heat seeped into my frozen, trembling limbs, and the shivering finally stopped after a few minutes of soaking. Jesse finished bandaging his knuckles with Kingston's help while Reid returned from my room with one of my flannel pajama sets. Reid's calloused palm rubbed soothing, gentle circles on my shoulders as he sat on the tile next to the tub. The reality of what happened finally started to process as my brain caught up.

"Aw, Cali girl." Reid's voice was pained as his thumbs gently rubbed my cheeks. "Don't cry. We've got you. You're safe with us. I'll be right back." It was like one of those moments where you get hit or cut unexpectedly—it happens so fast that the pain doesn't seem to register. Yet the moment you look down and see the bruise start to form or the blood begin to well, all the hurt comes crashing down on you. Reid was gone for only a moment but it felt like an eternity. Despite the fact that Kingston and Jesse were still in the bathroom with me, I wanted to call out for Reid, but he came back before I could. It took a moment but finally I recognized Mr. Fritz in his outstretched hands as he offered him to me. I instinctively reached for Mr. Fritz and when I clutched him tightly to my chest, my fears started to subside. Sadly, it would take more than my bear to erase the memory of what happened, but he helped.

Reid sank back down next to me on the other side of the tub, his hands wiping the tears as they started to pour faster and faster. The tracks turned from a tear here and there to a steady stream. Pressing my cheek into Reid's palm, I sniffled.

"I know I am," I finally responded, murmuring as I looked at him. His hazel eyes were bright with emotions, warring between anger and sadness as he watched me. Glancing at Jesse, I felt a wave of gratefulness. "Thank you." He shook his head slightly.

"You don't need to thank me. I didn't do anything special." I sat up straight and looked at him directly, the warmth from the tub finally thawing my shock-numbed brain.

"You stopped him from"—I swallowed the lump that had built in my throat—"that's special to me. I don't want to even think about what could have happened otherwise, so I'm going to thank you," I commanded. He nodded slightly, realizing he wouldn't win this argument. I slouched back down, my tear covered cheeks pressing back into Reid's open and waiting palm.

After the water started to cool, I finally got out. The guys went into the hall and faced away from me, but I couldn't close the door after everything at the party. Dressing quickly in the flannel, I went without a bra as usual before stepping into the hall. I made sure to dry any wet patches off Mr. Fritz before securing him to my chest in a bear hug.

"Are you hungry?" Reid asked me. Shaking my head, I followed them into the basement living room. "All right, come here, Cali girl." He steered me onto the couch, my back reclining against his lean muscled chest, my legs over Kingston's lap with my feet resting on Jesse's thigh. "Did you know, Coke was made before refrigerators, so it was meant to drink warm whereas Pepsi was made after therefore meant to be drank cold? Their recipes have both changed since the original formula, but back then cold Pepsi was supposed to taste like warm Coke." The little factoid Reid read off as we got situated on the couch eased the shock a little more making the shivering recede and blanket of fog over my brain lift.

"Thank you," I murmured cocooning in the blanket they had thrown over me, the heat from the bath and blanket slowly dragging me to sleep safely within their arms. I don't even remember closing my eyes, I only remember being surrounded by the comforting scent of Old Spice, cinnamon, orange, and Mr. Fritz.

OCTOBER 14TH

Going to the pumpkin patch with the guys, time for good thoughts and memories.
#SquashPicking #Fall #SundayFunday

The smell of breakfast cooking pulled me ever so slowly toward consciousness. The tantalizing scent of pancakes, eggs, and bacon filled my nose as I cracked open my eyes. I was lying on the couch in the basement living room, pressed up against something solid. Looking up, I saw Reid's dark curls sprawled out against the cushion, his arm wrapped around my shoulders as I used his chest as a pillow. My right leg was tossed over his legs and hip, his morning wood pressing into my thigh. The early morning light filtered through the patio door, the soft pink and oranges washing over my slowly fading tan.

I shifted slightly wanting to explore who was making breakfast because it couldn't be my mom, otherwise she would have skinned me by this point for sleeping with a boy. Reid grumbled under his breath as he continued to sleep while I untangled myself from him. Thankfully he didn't wake when I finally got up off the couch, but I did notice that somehow Mr. Fritz had migrated over into Reid's arms. The sight of my boy cuddling a teddy bear made me smile and my heart skipped a beat.

Shifting my attention away from Reid and choosing not to change out of my pajamas, I went right upstairs and found Kingston cooking and Jesse sitting at the table with a glass of orange juice, reading a book I recognized from my shelf.

"Morning," I greeted as I entered the room, my voice scratchy from sleep. "When did you guys get up?" I peeked around Kingston's arm; his button-up had been taken off at some point leaving him in a white undershirt making his tan stand out.

"Good morning, baby doll." He lifted the arm I was trying to look around and pulled me into a tight hug. "We've been up for about an hour, but there wasn't enough food for all of us, so we ran to the store for breakfast supplies."

"I'm sorry, I made my mom a list, but she's been super busy and only picked up a few things." I nibbled my lip, feeling bad they had to spend their money to eat at my house because we barely had anything in the cabinets or fridge.

"Don't worry about it." He pulled the bacon off and placed it in the paper towels before flipping the pancake. "Besides, I'm pretty particular on what I like to cook with, so it's a win-win. You guys get fed, and I get to pick the ingredients I like to work with." I chuckled and stole a slice of bacon darting away from his playful attempts to get it back. "Troublemaker," he teased before going back to the food.

"Morning, Jesse," I murmured giving him a small smile as I sat at the table. He dipped his head in greeting, apparently sucked into the book he was reading, so I busied myself with pouring some juice. Staring out the deck door, I watched the early morning sun rise higher in the sky. The house on the other side of us had two younger kids who were out in their yard playing on their swing set. The heaviness of what had happened last night felt like a lead weight in my stomach that not even the brightness of the sun could lift.

"Emma?" Reid's voice radiated up the staircase followed

by his sluggish footsteps. "You up here, babe?"

"Yeah," I responded right as Kingston set a plate of pancakes, bacon, and scrambled eggs in front of me. "Thank you. I could have gotten it, you didn't have to bring it over, you know."

"I know." He smiled down at me and rubbed my shoulder softly. Turning to the cabinets, he grabbed the syrup, butter, and more glasses for him and Reid before dishing up the boys' food. We ate in silence, almost all of us too tired to really converse. When I couldn't fit anything more into my stomach, I groaned and pushed the plate away.

"So full," I whined. "That was delicious, Kingston. Thank you." I gave him a big smile; his food and their company had really helped keep the bad memories at bay. "We still going to the pumpkin patch today?"

"If you want to." Reid finally started to look awake after eating, his sleepy voice giving way to his normal effervescent tone. I nodded, excited to spend the day with them. I wasn't sure what being alone would do to my already worn emotions after last night's events.

"Yeah, I need to shower though. I have extra unopened toothbrushes downstairs if you want to claim your own, and we have enough hot water if you guys need to shower." I stood up, taking the empty plates and dirty silverware from everyone, and started to clean the kitchen. "I'll get this all cleaned up, so you guys can get ready first."

With that, they filed downstairs, Jesse's nose still in the book that he had seemed to nearly finish in the last forty-five minutes we were up here. The clock read almost eight when I finished up cleaning, and the dishwasher's whirring sound filled the silence of the upstairs. When I reached the basement, I found Reid and Jesse on the couch watching TV and Kingston's tall figure standing in the bathroom brushing his teeth.

"I'm almost done." His smooth words were garbled around the toothbrush as I walked in to start the shower. I nodded to let him know I heard him before grabbing my outfit for the day. The weather was even chillier than it had been Friday night, so I stuck with the same style of outfit with lots of layers in case it got warmer throughout the day.

Within a half hour, we were back in Reid's Jeep going toward the countryside in a similar direction to the haunted house we had been at Friday, but we turned off left down a dirt road instead of turning right. I found myself smiling as I watched the corn stalks and Halloween decorations the farmers had put up pass by the window. The sound of Reid and Kingston's conversation washed over me like a comforting blanket, their voices doing their usual job of making me feel cozy, like I was home. A portion of me was sad when we got to the pumpkin patch because I could listen to them talk and watch the world pass by for hours and not get tired of their company.

Maybe they'll take a road trip with me over a holiday break.

I pulled myself out of my thoughts as we reached the parking lot of our destination. The pumpkin patch's sign was large and colorful with the name of the place decorated with cartoon pumpkins and a cute scarecrow. Cars were scattered throughout the dirt lot, but it wasn't overly full since it was still early on a Sunday. Once again, Reid paid for all of our tickets after Kingston handed him a large wad of cash. I rolled my eyes but didn't complain or argue, knowing it wouldn't do any good.

"Thank you." I wrapped my arms around them, my left around Reid and my right around Kingston squeezing as tightly as I could in the odd hug. "So, what do we want to do first?" I asked looking over the large map that was posted inside the entrance. "Holy crap, this place is huge." Kingston snatched up a tri-fold paper that was inside a clear box and handed it to me so I could scan the map and walk around at the same time.

"We can go check out the pig races, shouldn't be too busy right now," Reid suggested looking down at the map. "The next race starts in about five minutes."

"Pig races?" I made a face.

What the heck is that?

"Ugh," he groaned. "Come on, Cali girl. It's time to pop the race cherry!" My cheeks flushed at the statement, my mind immediately going to sex, but none of them seemed to notice as we walked along the dirt paths.

There was so much to see on the way, a large barn that had delicious smells radiating out the open doors, several other food stands, as well as a full blown candy shop where I saw two workers making fresh caramel apples. There were several haunted houses, a corn maze, petting zoo area, and various other attractions I hadn't seen before like a giant teepee and a playground of tractors.

I definitely was not in California anymore.

We came up on the race area where ten rows of wooden benches climbed up the slight incline that looked down on a fenced in dirt track. Sitting down in the third row, I was positioned between Reid and Jesse, the latter content to be quiet as he meandered around with us. Although, earlier he had to shift over to avoid a group of kids and didn't move away from me afterward, so there's that.

Baby steps.

I watched teenagers and parents with younger kids go down a large set of slides before climbing back up the stairs to do it all over again. Right at the top of the hour, a round man in denim overalls walked out with a headset microphone hooked over his ear. I found myself chuckling at his silly pig puns and fake stories fabricated for the little kids who had made their way over with their parents.

It turns out a pig race is a group of pigs that run around the little track, and whoever gets back to the pen first wins. Each time the announcer would pick out five people to come up and take a colored flag that would coordinate with the colored bandana the pig wore. Everyone who participated got a little plastic piggy nose that could be worn over their face, and the winner received a coupon for a free caramel apple. They started with the tiny piggies before moving to larger and bulkier piggies. Reid jumped up at the last race when the farmer guy had asked for people to come up.

"It's her first time," Reid shouted pointing down at me. I hid my face in my hands as everyone whooped and clapped when I got picked. Blushing up a storm at the attention, I made my way down to the fenced barrier and picked the pink flag. I was the oldest; two of the kids looked to be middle schoolers while the other three were little kids, the youngest being a little girl with pigtails.

"I hope my piggy wins!" she told me excitedly. Her two front teeth were missing as she smiled. I knelt next to her to watch the pigs run by, her purple-flagged pig tying with my pink one for first place. "Yay!" She jumped up and down and nudged me in the arm lightly with excitement. "My piggy won, did you see that?"

"I did, that was pretty awesome." She beamed at my words making my heart swell. I stood as the farmer gave us our prizes, but before I could rejoin my boys the little girl tugged on the hem of my sweater.

"Since it was your first time." She held up the coupon for the caramel apple. My brows furrowed as I took the paper from her. Smiling wide, she pointed at her gap." I can't have it anyway since the tooth fairy took my teeth! Bye!" she squealed before running up to her family. Chuckling, I joined up with Reid, Kingston, and Jesse.

"You're so cute with kids, Cali girl." Reid smiled down at me as he wrapped his arm around my shoulder. His tone wasn't teasing, but sweet and complimentary, making my skin flush yet again.

I should just stop wearing blush if this is how it's going to be.

"Thanks, she was pretty adorable. She even gave me her winner coupon since her front teeth had fallen out." I tucked the paper in my jacket pocket so I wouldn't lose it because a caramel apple sounded like a delicious treat for later. "Now where?"

The rest of the day was spent wandering around the attractions, eating deliciously unhealthy food and treats, riding on the hayrack ride, and picking out our pumpkins from the enormous field, before heading home with plans to carve the pumpkins later this week. My mom was actually home when I got back, but I was so exhausted after the crazy weekend that I toppled into my bed and immediately fell asleep without even taking off my coat or shoes.

CHAPTER 12

OCTOBER 15TH

Grow through what you go through. -Unknown
#IAmStrong #IAmResilient #MotivationMonday

Something was wrong.

Reid, Kingston, and Jesse were waiting at the edge of the parking lot when I got to school, frowns and scowls harsh on their faces. My skin prickled as other students, most I didn't even recognize, glared at me with accusing stares. I beelined for the boys, my level of tolerance for the day already nearing zero by the time I reached them.

"All right, what the heck is going on?" I whispered furiously as I got to them. They knew what was going on otherwise they would be inside waiting for me and not out here in the cold.

"Brad's spreading rumors and lies around about what happened on Saturday," Reid started, his anger flowing off him in waves. "Saying how you tried to seduce him and that when you guys were done, you told Jesse some lie about how he forced himself on you so Jesse would beat the shit out of him." My blood froze in my veins, anxiety fizzing painfully in my chest.

"He's telling people we had sex and then saying I lied

about the whole thing?" I clarified. I ground my jaw when they nodded, their eyes filled with both anger at Brad and pity at the situation. "Well, that's a bunch of crap because I'm still a virgin," I hissed. My eyes immediately widened when I realized what I had just said. "I mean, uh..."

"Really?" Reid tilted his head, effectively distracted from my admission. I nodded and continued folding in on myself in embarrassment.

"Didn't want to with Tyler," I muttered, shrugging a shoulder dejectedly.

"Never wanted to with any other boyfriends?" he asked. None of them seemed to look down at the fact I hadn't had sex yet which I wasn't used to. If anything, they seemed weirdly surprised. If my friends in Cali had known, I would have been pestered to do it so I wouldn't be considered 'prudish.'

"I've only had one boyfriend," I added, my brows furrowing at Reid in confusion at his wide eyes.

"Really? I would have thought guys would have lined up for you." My brain finally gave out at that statement and I stared at him.

What is that supposed to mean?

"Well, you're sweet and funny and you're fucking beautiful, Emma." He said it as though that should be obvious to me. Apparently, I had asked that mental question out loud in my stupor. Unable to help myself, I smiled, completely forgetting about the crap that I would have to deal with as soon as the bell rang.

"Thanks." I couldn't stop my smile as Kingston nodded his agreement. Honestly, it was one of the nicest things anyone had ever said to me. Tyler very rarely complimented me, and when he did, it was something crude. I wanted to bask in the warmth of their support, their compliments, but the feeling of eyes on me again pulled me back to the reality of the situation. "What am I going to do?"

"We're going to go in there with our heads held high. None of us did anything wrong, and Jesse stopped Brad from doing something completely unforgivable," Reid hashed out, his tone filled with determination. "If anyone asks, we tell them the truth."

"We?" I questioned, not understanding.

"Yeah, Cali girl, we. You're our girl, and we won't let them talk about you like that. We'll stand by you no matter what people say." Reid curled his arm around me tightly.

"Anyone who believes otherwise isn't worth our time," Kingston agreed, rubbing small circles on my back. Jesse looked about ready to fight someone again, but knowing it was for me made me feel all fuzzy again.

Why do they have to be so sweet?

"Let's just get today over with, and we'll have our study party tonight." I sighed, looking out at the student body and already dreading how the day would go.

Here goes nothing.

I sank into the driver's seat behind the wheel, tears welling up and spilling over despite my best efforts to keep them contained. Today had been about as terrible as I had expected. Sideways glances judged me, a few people straight up came and asked me about it, and finally, several people in the halls and classrooms whispered 'slut' when I walked by. The only people who stuck by me without any wavering were my boys, Aubrey, and Zoey. Carter, Jason, and Brayden stood by us, but it was clear as day in their faces that they weren't sure what to believe.

For the first time since starting at Arbor Ridge, I saw Brad within the halls and cafeteria. It seemed my brain zeroed in on him as soon as he was in my eyesight, not giving me a moment's rest from thinking about what had happened. While it was nice to know when to be aware, I just wanted to go back to being blissfully ignorant and focus on school and not the guy who tried to force me into the bathroom at some stupid party.

The only consolation was that his pale skin was adorned with large, dark bruises and gashes across his brow, nose, and lip. At lunch when I saw him for the third time that day, I leaned over to Jesse to thank him again. When my boys saw Brad watching us, they glared intensely until he finally looked away in fear. Zoey and Aubrey came and sat with us at lunch, the six of us crowded at a four person table, but the show of support was definitely appreciated after everything.

Reid's Jeep was right behind me on the drive home. I could tell from the way they looked in the rearview mirror that the boys had just as hard of a time today as me, especially Jesse who slammed the Jeep door shut when he got in. My tears dried by the time we reached my house, my mom's SUV gone from the garage as per usual. The mood was somber and sullen as we sat around my basement table.

"I'm sorry," I mumbled when the silence became too much for me to handle. A wall of wavering images filled my eyes as the tears reappeared.

"For what?" Reid asked, his hand grabbing mine off the table in a comforting grasp.

"Everything this last weekend and today. I know it's my fault…"

"No," Jesse barked out harshly staring at me. "It's not

your fault. It's Brad's fault for being a fucking rapist."

He sighed, looking tired, before slipping out of his seat and tugging me lightly on my sleeve. Curiosity won out despite his grouchy tone, and I followed him to my room. Standing in the middle of my room, I waited for him to close the door. I wasn't afraid of being alone with him like I had been with Brad. Jesse might be gruff and harsh with his bluntness, but I knew he wouldn't hurt me. He closed the distance between us quickly and wrapped me in his arms. I curled mine around his trim waist and clutched desperately to the back of his t-shirt as everything flooded my system. Sobs wracked my body, soaking his shoulder in a fresh wave of tears. His hand threaded into my hair as he clutched me to him.

"Fuck, Em," he exhaled sharply. A wet drop hit my neck, and I realized he was crying while he held on to me like I was a life preserver and he was drowning. "Reid told me you had gone inside to go to the bathroom. When I went in to make sure you were okay, I thought I saw Brad at the top of the stairs, but I told myself I was imagining things after the night before." His exhale was shaky, his tears falling faster against my skin. "Then I heard you scream, and I couldn't run fast enough. No one moved when you screamed, they all just looked around, but I knew it was you, and when"—he swallowed before taking a steadying breath—"and when I saw him shoving you in the bathroom, I saw red. I was going to kill him, but I knew you needed me more, so I stopped."

"Thank you, Jesse," I murmured, turning my head so it was pressing into his neck. The heat from his body made it feel like I was trapped in a sauna, but I didn't care.

I needed this.

I needed *him*.

I lost track of time of how long we stood there, holding each other like our lives depended on it, but by the time we stepped apart, I felt much better.

OCTOBER 18TH

All I have to say is… my boys rock.
#BestFriends #LoveThem #ThankfulThursday

The thin sheet of paper crinkled in my hands as I made my way to the counselor's office. I had successfully been ignoring the ACT and college situation in the last few days with everything that had happened with Brad and all the stupid rumors, but I was staring it right in the face now. I still hadn't figured out a plan on how to fix my ACT score other than get some study materials and practice until I was used to it.

I pushed the thoughts away as I opened the door. A different student sat behind the desk as I waited for Ms. Rogers to come grab me from the little lobby area. The counselor's upbeat attitude was a nice change of pace from all the glares and stares I had been fielding all week. At least most people were starting to go back to ignoring me whenever the boys were around.

"Emma," she greeted warmly. Smiling, she held an arm out down the hall to have me follow her. Her red cat's eye glasses were still secured with a chain, but this time it was a bright gold, and her blouse was an emerald green instead of red. "How has everything been going? Any more thoughts on career or college?"

"I took a practice ACT test," I divulged, my tone somber.

As if she knew, she started to nod slightly, getting up from her seat to grab a few items off her bookshelves.

"I'm assuming it didn't go well?" I shook my head, feeling the burn of tears build in the back of my eyes, but I was able to hold them in. "These are some study materials for it that you can have and should definitely help. Was it the test itself that was difficult or something else?"

"I get really nervous when I take tests, so I think that didn't help, but I definitely think studying and practicing would be good." I looked through the materials seeing a very thick book as well as a few topic specific ones like for the English essay section.

"I have some techniques that can hopefully help with anxiety, but before we get into that have you considered getting a tutor to help with the test practice?" I shook my head unsure of how I felt about getting a tutor. I should be smart enough to do it on my own.

Right?

"You're friends with Jesse Parker, correct?" My eyes shot to hers, what did Jesse have to do with this conversation? She chuckled, clearly reading my confused expression. "He's a tutor part-time. Maybe you could talk to him about help."

"What?" I couldn't process what she had said.

My Jesse, a tutor?

"He doesn't have any students that he's helping right now, but he is usually the most recommended tutor for the school, so I would suggest speaking with him soon." She pulled another pamphlet out of her acrylic holder on her bookshelf. "If he gets booked, or you would prefer someone else, these are the tutors I would recommend and their contact information." She circled three names on the sheet before handing it to me.

"I'll think about who I'd be more comfortable with and call them." I started looking at the names but I wasn't actually reading any of them, my brain still focused on the fact that Jesse hadn't told me he was a tutor.

"Good. As for the test anxiety, let me show you a couple of techniques."

A little while later our meeting concluded, and I exited the office into a nearly empty hall and cafeteria. There were only a few students sitting around a couple of tables, and some familiar faces stood near the bottom of the stairs. When Carter spotted me over Jason's shoulder, he waved. Jason glanced over and threw a friendly smile, waving his hand to have me come over.

"Hey, Emma," Carter welcomed happily, no longer seeming to be listening to the rumors flooding the student body. His blond mop of curls was trimmed but still unruly as it splayed over his forehead. Jason gave me a nod, his black hair had grown out and now shifted when he moved. I had to look up at both of them; they weren't as tall as Kingston, but at least half a foot taller than me.

"Hey, guys," I greeted. I noticed they had switched out their typical attire of basketball and cargo shorts for jeans and sweats in the wake of the cold fall weather moving in. "What are you guys doing out here?"

"We had a free period. Just got back from getting some coffee. Doing your career counselling stuff?" Carter had a slight accent as he talked, a bit of New York or Boston, but I wasn't sure which since it was so faint. I nodded, readjusting my backpack on my shoulder as it had started to slip. "Cool, cool. Any idea what you're doing after graduation?"

"Go to college, not sure which yet, but I have tours scheduled for after Thanksgiving. You?" I glanced between them. While we weren't the closest of friends, Carter and Jason tending to stick closer to Brayden than anyone else in our group, and the conversation flowed easily between us.

"I'm hoping to get a scholarship for track and field. I want to study sports medicine," Carter responded first. I nodded, it made sense, both of them as well as Aubrey and Zoey were either on the cross-country team or competed on the track and field team.

"Not sure yet, but possibly physical therapy. I thought about sports medicine too. Maybe nutrition," Jason tacked on, glancing at the clock. "Crap, class is about to get out, and my next one is on the other end of the school. I'll see you later, guys!" He waved and took off in a fast-paced walk, hoping to beat the crowd of students that would soon rush the halls. Carter and I said our goodbyes and went on to our next classes. Although the conversation had been nice with them, it didn't distract me enough from my worry about my ACT score or my new mission to find a tutor.

.

Chapter 13

OCTOBER 27TH

Today, I will not think about tutors, tests, crappy thoughts about how I don't know my friends as well as I thought, or about the fact I haven't talked to my dad in ages and my mom is never home.
#EndOfRant #FocusOnWork #DontThinkAboutIt #StressFreeSaturday

The morning rush helped keep my mind busy, the steady stream of customers holding my attention instead of reminding myself that I had yet to talk to Jesse or any tutor for help despite it being over a week later. Something about Jesse or even Reid and Kingston not bringing up that he was a tutor, only referring to his 'part-time work,' stung. I knew it wasn't any of my business, but they knew so much about me and I felt like I didn't know much about any of them. All we tended to focus on was school, what plans we were excited for, or me.

I nibbled my lip as I started making one of the drinks, Lyla's list of orders having grown too long for her to keep up. We were busier than normal since it was right before Halloween and Rick had organized a 'Trunk or Treat' event in the parking lot this morning for parents with younger kids. A lot of the costumes the kids had worn were adorable and had me smiling, but not even happy little smiles could lift my dour mood. Lyla knew something was up, and so she gave me a comforting pat on the back when she went by to grab more syrups from the back.

"Hey, Emma." Kingston's smooth voice pulled me from my zoned out process of working on drinks. His coffee brown eyes darted around my face, his lips falling into a frown the longer he eyed me. "You all right?" I tried to give a smile, but I was pretty sure it looked forced.

"Yeah, I'm good. What can I get you?" I finished up the last drink order before stepping back to the register.

"I have a large order," he warned, still looking concerned, but dropped the subject as he handed me a scrap piece of paper with eight different drinks written on it. I entered the order quietly before shifting to help Lyla. "You're off in a few minutes?" I turned to look at the clock surprised to see that my shift had already come to an end.

"Yeah, at eleven." I turned back to him, his forearms resting on the counter as he looked down at me. "Why?"

"Wondered if you wanted to come help me with something?" Despite the bad mood I had been sporting, he piqued my curiosity. "It's only for a couple hours, so we can hang out afterwards."

"What would we be doing?" My tone conveyed my suspicion as I started on the fifth drink. "Just us or would the other two be there too?"

"Well"—he tilted his head trying to figure out how to respond—"we wouldn't be alone, but Reid and Jesse are busy until later, so it would be me and you." I noted he didn't tell me what we would be doing, but I trusted Kingston, so I agreed.

After clocking out, I changed my shirt and shoes into my usual attire, stuffing the slip-ons and work shirt into my bag. I waved bye to Lyla and took one of the two to-go trays, following Kingston out to his car that was parked in the back of the lot. I ignored the feeling of his gaze on my face as I stared out the window. Kingston pulled off to a gas station parking lot before throwing the car in park and turning to me.

"What's up, baby doll?" He reached out and rubbed my neck in gentle circles, the smooth pads of his fingers warming my skin until the tingles spread across my body. "You seem upset."

"Why didn't you guys tell me Jesse was a tutor?" I murmured, still staring out the window. I couldn't look at him right now knowing I would cry, and I had done enough of that since moving to the middle of freaking nowhere.

"Never really thought about it." He sounded confused, and his hand stilled. "How'd you find out?" I sighed, feeling dumb for being so upset over it. I knew it wasn't a big deal, but something about it had just hurt. It might have been the fact it was after everything we'd dealt with the last couple weeks and their intense insistence that it's a 'we' and not 'me,' or it might just be the fact I was PMSing.

Sometimes being a girl really sucked.

"Need help preparing for the ACT; Ms. Rogers suggested Jesse" I glanced over at Kingston. "It was quite a shock to find out one of my best friends is a tutor. I feel like I barely know any of you or your lives, when you guys know almost everything about me."

"What do you want to know?" His head tilted as he leaned closer, his left elbow resting on the center console, his fingers brushing my left arm in a gentle caress. "Here, I have an idea. How about next time we're together, we'll all write the questions we have on different scraps of paper and put it in a hat. We'll draw them out, and we'll all have to answer them." His massaging fingers were soothing the hurt I had in my chest as he talked. His smile made the butterflies scatter in a wave of nerves when I realized it was just me and him in the car alone. "How's that?"

"Promise?" I whispered, feeling better than I had in the last week. His suggestion sounded fun, and I was happy he came up with it.

I should have just brought up what was bothering me sooner.

Once again, hindsight is 20/20.

"Pinkie promise, baby doll." He held up his pinkie making me chuckle. After returning the promise we started toward wherever he was taking me in a much better mood than before. The drive was only another five minutes, and then Kingston was pulling into a large lot in front of a swanky looking building with the sign that read *Bell and Slate Law Office.*

I guess this would explain why Kingston wants to go to school for law.

There were several cars in the lot lined up in two rows with their trunks facing an open space between them. There weren't any kids and no one was outside, so either this was a 'Trunk or Treat' Kingston brought me to that hasn't started yet or it just finished. Getting out, I took the tray and followed him into the building. The overwhelming scent of paper mixed with the smell of coffee that wafted out of the cups I had clutched in my hand as we walked past the lobby desk and into the hallway. There were five adults and one kid who looked to be middle school aged hanging out in the main office area of the building. Several clusters of desks were positioned around the large area, with offices and conference rooms with open doors on the far wall and two side walls that held large windows. A tall man with the same tanned skin and blond hair as Kingston stood and came over taking the holder from me with a friendly smile before setting it on the table. The younger boy was instructed by a woman who had platinum blonde hair with a petite figure to pass out the drinks.

"Dad," Kingston addressed the tall man. His hair was wavier than Kingston's but cut shorter. Proud, dark brown eyes fell on his son. "This is Emma. Emma, this is my dad, Kaleb Bell."

"It's very nice to finally meet you, Emma. Kingston and the boys have not stopped raving about you since you moved to town." His voice was deeper than Kingston's with a bit of roughness as he reached to shake my hand. I felt my face flare under his admission and glanced quickly at Kingston who, for the first time, also held a pink tinge to his own cheeks.

Reaching out to take his father's hand, I responded politely, "It's a pleasure to meet you too." I wished Kingston would have warned me that I was meeting his dad today. Before either of them could say anything, the younger boy came up to them with two drinks.

"Here's yours, King." He held out a cup for Kingston to take. "I don't know whose this one is." He held out the cup for Kingston to read.

"Oh, that one's Emma's." He took it from who I assumed was the younger brother that I didn't know he had, before handing it to me with a sweet smile. My skin warmed under his gaze, and a wave of tingles washed up my arm when our fingers brushed. "Emma, this is my little brother, Killian. Kill, this is Emma."

"Hi." He waved at me before leaning forward to stare intently at my face. "She's much prettier in person. You did a terrible job at describing her." Their dad chuckled at his son's words as I felt the heat intensify on my cheeks.

"Thanks," I murmured before taking a sip to keep myself from saying anything embarrassing.

"Are you Kingston's girlfriend?" Killian asked, but Kingston's dad saved me from having to answer.

"Killian, that's personal. If they wanted you to know, they would have told you," he chastised, but in a nice way as if he was guiding him instead of berating him. As I watched him and Killian go over and converse with the other people in the room, it became even more obvious that Mr. Bell really loved his kids.

"Sorry I sprung this on you," Kingston whispered in my ear as he curved his body around mine, his chest brushing against my arm. "I didn't know if you would come if you knew, and I really wanted to spend some time with you." At that, my irritation melted along with my heart into an emotional puddle.

"It was quite a surprise, but I'm glad we're here." I smiled. He was standing so close that his beard brushed against my scalp when I tilted back to look up at him. "What exactly are we doing? A 'Trunk or Treat' thing?" He nodded, his eyes falling on the petite woman with platinum blonde hair who had her brows cocked at him.

"You'll introduce her to your father and your brother, but not to your own mother." She shook her head, but her smile contradicted her tone. "I'm Stella Bell, Kingston's mom." She turned her attention to me, the playful reprimand fading until she was smiling warmly. "It's so good to finally meet you." She surprised me by pulling me into a motherly hug. I awkwardly returned the hug, my coffee clutched in the other hand by my hip.

"No Reid or Jesse?" She pulled back to question Kingston. He shook his head.

"They were busy with some stuff today. They plan on

being at the yearly cookout though." He turned to face me. "Remind me to talk to Lyla so you have November 16th off. It's our annual barbecue grill fest." His mom's laugh was tinkling as she shook her head before walking away.

"I could just text her, you know." I pulled my phone out of my pocket to shoot Lyla a quick text. When she responded saying it was marked down, I tucked it back away and followed Kingston to the rest of the people. I tried to remember the names of the three others, Vivian and Brett Slate, the firm's partner and his wife, as well as Zander Morton who was one of the lawyers in the office.

We stood and talked for a while before we had to pop open the trunks in the parking lot. They were already set up with decorations, candy, and games when the first of the kids and their parents showed up. I stood with Kingston at his trunk. It had been set up like a miniature graveyard, and he even had a little fake ghost dangling from the edge of his trunk lid. Slipping on a black hooded robe, he pulled out a plastic scythe and acted as the Grim Reaper watching over his souls. In the spirit of Halloween, Kingston's mom brought over a pair of cat ears and colored the tip of my nose before drawing on cat whiskers. It was a good thing I had decided to go with a black shirt and my black boots tying together the whole costume as she secured the fluffy cat tail to my belt loop.

The next couple of hours passed by quickly, and the event was over before I realized it had been two hours. We got several photos as a group before Stella and Vivian were demanding that Kingston and I get several photos together. After we were finished, Stella told me to keep the costume, saying I could use it for Halloween. I hadn't planned on going to any costume parties, but the way she stared at me had me swallowing my arguments. Kingston's parents and the other adults were polite and made me feel like I was welcome any time. Killian kept trying to ask Kingston and me questions, to which their dad would chase him off. After about the third time it became a game to them making me laugh with each pass.

"So," I began, getting into the car making sure not to smash the kitty tail I was still wearing. Kingston hadn't taken off his robe, the hood resting over his blond hair. "What are we going to do now?" He gave me a sly smile and in a very Reid fashion he zipped his lips and started to drive. Curiosity grew each time I asked him a question and was met with silence, but after a few minutes of driving I recognized my neighborhood. "You couldn't just tell me we were heading to my house?" I teased as he pulled into the driveway.

"Nope." He chuckled and smiled down at me after walking around the car. "I'm the Grim Reaper and all, so I figured being all mysterious was part of the gig."

"Pretty sure he's just scary, not mysterious." I laughed, our footsteps thudding up the concrete steps to the front door. Kingston held the door open for me but headed down the stairs first, and when I reached the bottom, the word 'surprise' was shouted at me. Reid, Jesse, along with our friends, Lyla, and my mom all stood around the basement in costumes. The basement and the backyard had been decorated with an odd mix of Halloween and birthday decorations, but honestly I loved the combination and couldn't stop smiling as I looked around at everything.

"Happy early birthday, sweetie," my mom cheered, coming over to give me a big hug. Squeezing tightly, I willed myself not to cry at their thoughtfulness. Reid immediately scooped me up in a big bear hug after my mom let go which I thought was appropriate since he was wearing a fuzzy bear onesie complete with footies and a hood with ears.

"Happy Birthday, Cali girl!" He nearly cut me in half with the pressure of his hug. Sucking air into my deprived lungs when he let go, I playfully back-handed his stomach.

"Happy Birthday, Em," Jesse murmured in my ear. He was dressed up in what I could best describe as 50s geek in eyeglasses with thick, plastic frames, a short-sleeve dress shirt that had a pocket protector in the front, and jeans rolled at the ankles to show off white socks and saddle shoes. His hug was brief, but his whispered sentiment said everything he wasn't comfortable showing in front of everyone.

I gave Reid and him a warm smile before I was promptly dragged away with Lyla, Zoey, and Aubrey who wanted to get pictures with me and go out and play some of the yard games they had set up. We played cornhole, the ladder toss, as well as beat the crap out of a Halloween pinata with a sparkly stick.

"Time to sing Emma her song!" Lyla shouted cheerfully an hour and a half later as my mom came in with a pitch-black frosted cake with glittering icing that read 'Happy 18th Birthday!' Carter, Jason, and Brayden tried to out-sing the girls which made Reid want to one-up everyone by doing some weird interpretive dance during the song. I could feel my eyes watering with how hard I was laughing, and it was nearly impossible to blow out my candles, but I was able to get all of them out in one breath after getting a hold on the giggling.

After stuffing ourselves full of cake, pizza, and what Nebraskans call puppy chow, Lyla demanded I open her present. Tearing open the coffee cup wrapping paper that made me laugh, I found myself gaping at her present.

A giant basket of bath bombs and other spa type items.

Including a gift certificate to a local spa.

"I know how much of a girly girl you are. Besides, I figured we could go to the spa together," she teased before moving the basket out of my lap so Zoey and Aubrey could bring me their gift which was a gift card to one of my favorite stores. There was a catch, the stipulation that we all go together because they wanted me to help them pick out cute clothes. I, of course, agreed immediately. Carter, Jason, and Brayden all went in to get me a gift card to the bookstore which made me smile.

I might need a second bookshelf at this rate.

"My turn!" Reid shouted as he placed a box in my lap that was wrapped in some of the shiniest wrapping paper I had ever seen. Tearing into it I was cautious as I opened the box in case Reid had something that would explode, like glitter.

Because that's *exactly* something he would do.

When it didn't blow up in my face, I was giddy. There was a beautiful maroon floppy hat and a matching lipstick from M.A.C. I gave him a tight squeeze, excited to wear them the next chance I got. Kingston's present was a pretty, thick-knit scarf and a matching knit beanie hat with a little puff ball on top.

"For your warm Cali self when the winter hits," he teased, giving me a soothing rub on my back. The material of the yarn was fuzzy, soft, and really plush, and as much as I wasn't looking forward to winter and snow, I was looking forward to wearing these. Jesse looked nervous as he bent down to me.

"I'll give you your present in a bit, okay?" he whispered softly, his honeyed tone flowing in tingly waves over the crest of my ear. I nodded and gave him a warm smile, but my curiosity was piqued.

My friends and I spent the next hour hanging out until everyone started heading out since it was getting close to dinner time. The only ones staying behind were Reid, Kingston, and Jesse. The latter pulled me into my room away from the others who were helping my mom clean up the trash and put away any leftovers.

"Here you go, Em." My breath caught when Jesse pulled out a small, velvet box. The soft exterior of the jewelry box brushed against the tips of my fingers as I took it from him. Inside the satin interior sat two square, pink tourmaline earrings. I could barely breathe as the faceted surface of the gems sparkled in the light of my room.

"They're beautiful," I whispered, entranced by the stones. Pulling myself together, I took them out of the box and slipped them into my ears thankful that I had forgone earrings this morning. "Thank you, Jesse." I tucked the box safely into my jewelry stand and turned to him.

"I, uh"—he cleared this throat—"didn't mean to, but that day you brought me home with you I saw your practice ACT score, and don't take this the wrong way, please, but if you want help..." He trailed off looking extremely nervous. I pressed a finger to his lips as he opened them to try and explain again.

"I would love your help, Jesse. I had been trying to work myself up to ask you since my counselor said you were the best tutor." I gave him a soft smile as I told him.

Exhaling sharply, the tension in his body melted away. "Once a week? Maybe on Wednesdays?" he offered against my fingertips. Pulling them away from his soft lips, I nodded and, without prompting, I wrapped my arms around his trim waist.

"That'd be perfect, thank you," I muttered into his shirt inhaling his mint and pine scent. He hugged me back, but soon enough my mom was calling for me out in the living room.

"Yeah?" I came out of my room. The door hadn't been shut, but I knew she wasn't trying to eavesdrop which I appreciated.

"The boys already know this, but for your birthday I figured you guys could have a sleepover out here in the living room area." My brows shot up, my eyes widening. "No going into your room and shutting the door together. Or anywhere else for that matter, and if I find out you've been doing anything you shouldn't..." I cut her off.

"You'll skin me, I know." I chuckled launching myself at her. "Thank you, thank you, thank you. I promise we'll be good." She hugged me back before heading upstairs to get some work in, planning on going to bed early since she had a breakfast meeting with an out-of-town client.

"I can't believe you convinced her to let you stay the night," I whispered, leaning into Reid and knowing he was the one who did it by his smug smile. I couldn't help but giggle at my cute clown in a bear onesie even though I'd been looking at it for the last few hours. "You look so adorable." I reached up and flicked his bear ear.

"Good, because..." He paused dramatically to reach around me, and Kingston's signature scent of cinnamon and orange surrounded me. "You get a onesie too!" Reid cheered holding up a black cat onesie between us. "Pajama party!" He did a little dance, melting my heart even more.

"It can't be a pajama party if only two of the party goers are in pajamas," I teased. Taking the furry outfit, I turned and ran straight into Kingston's chest. My gaze traveled up to land on his face. He was in a panda onesie. I bit my lip to keep from laughing, but when I saw Jesse in a bright orange fox onesie I couldn't hold it in. "Oh, my god."

"Laugh it up, Em." Jesse crossed his arms and shook his head at me. "I'm doing this for you, birthday girl." I finally got control of my laughing, but the tears continued to spill down my cheeks at how cute they all looked.

"I'll be right back." I practically skipped to my room with the pajama outfit clutched in my hands. Stripping out of my outfit, cat ear headband, clip-on cat tail, and bra, I tossed on a pair of shorts and a tight tank top before stepping into the kitty onesie. I quickly wiped the tears off my face, thankful that Stella had used waterproof makeup because the whiskers and the tiny triangle on the tip of my nose worked perfectly. The glint of pink in the mirror caught my attention under the black material. Pulling the hood back down, I admired the earrings Jesse had given me. Butterflies erupted in my chest and stomach as the presents from Reid and Kingston caught my eye from their place on my bed.

They're all so amazing.

Tyler had never done sweet things like this for me. He never worried about me when I seemed upset unless it was at something he had done, and he certainly never bought me such thoughtful birthday presents. His usual go-to was demanding a hand-job or giving me a crappy makeout session.

It was an odd sensation to feel that need, that wanting urge build within me whenever I was super close to one of them or when they brushed up against me. For a long time I thought something had been wrong with me since I never felt sexually attracted to anyone, but these three changed that. Even just thinking about them and what could possibly be hidden under those ridiculously adorable onesies had my breathing picking up.

"Cali girl!" Reid called in a sing-songy voice on the other side of my door bringing my current thoughts to a screeching halt. Taking a deep breath, I mentally prepared to see the three of them after losing myself in thoughts of wandering hands and soft lips.

"How's it look?" I asked softly after coming out of my room, holding my hands up in a wave. I turned in a circle feeling the tail swinging from my lower back. All three of them lit up with smiles, and humor danced in their eyes. "Pajama party!" I randomly shouted before launching onto the couch as they all stood there. Reid recovered first, diving right at me in a playful tackle. "So, what's the plan for our sleepover?"

"Well," Kingston started, turning toward the folding table that had been set up for food. Grabbing a chip out of one of the several bowls left out for us to eat, he picked up something I couldn't see. "I figured we could do that hat thing I suggested earlier." Reid and Jesse both appeared confused, neither having been told what Kingston and I had talked about. I grabbed a stack of printer paper out of the box within my desk as well as a few pens and handed a few out to each of them making sure to save a few for Kingston and myself. Kingston explained what we were going to do but didn't tell them why, which I was grateful for. I didn't want an argument or those negative emotions right now.

I mean, heck, I'm already trying to keep my wandering mind away from dirty thoughts.

We spent the next little while writing down our four questions, figuring it was a good number, before placing the torn and folded pieces of paper into the hat. I tried to keep it fairly 'clean,' but I couldn't help but sneak in one question that was a bit more risque since it was anonymous. I was the second done, Kingston being the first since I'm pretty sure he'd been thinking of questions all day knowing we would have tonight to do this. Jesse tossed his papers into the hat, and surprisingly, Reid was the last to put in his collection. Kingston took the hat and shuffled and shook the questions until they were well mixed. Grabbing the first out, he unfolded it and read it out to the group.

"What do you want to be when you grow up?" He smiled slightly as he looked at the paper. "Lawyer, obviously."

"I'm not sure," Jesse responded. His answer surprised me at first because he was so good on the academics front, but then I realized he'd be able to pick whatever he wanted to do because he seemed to be good in everything.

"Scientist," Reid answered, surprising the crap out of me. I tilted my head at him not realizing he liked science that much, but I didn't say anything as I tucked all of their answers into my memory.

"Something within business or marketing," I answered, "I'm not really sure what, specifically. Maybe owning a business or doing marketing like my mom."

"What are you most afraid of?" Jesse read quietly. We sat in silence, the TV playing at a low volume in the background as we thought of our answers.

"Not being able to live life to its full potential," Jesse answered softly. We had made the decision we would try to refrain from asking questions about our answers and that we were *definitely* not allowed to judge each other.

"Never mattering," Reid added, "to someone or in life in general."

"Being unhappy," I murmured, "in my career, or life, or relationship. Or being the cause of someone else being unhappy."

"Being a disappointment to the people who matter most," Kingston rounded out the group. The sullen silence following our replies was stifling, so I reached for the hat to draw the next question quickly, unable to sit in the suffocating cloud we had created.

"What do you think about before you fall asleep? Do you have something you do every day that helps you sleep? Technically that's two, but I'm not too picky," I added, finding myself smiling as I read the questions. It was sweet and more meaningful than almost everything I had asked. I answered before the others, their expressions thoughtful as they considered what their response would be. "Life, what it holds in the future, and I make little diary entries throughout the day but I don't think they help me sleep." That caught their attention and they all looked over at me.

"You write in a diary?" Kingston asked curiously, but no judgement colored his question.

"Not a traditional one, more like a digital diary. I save them to my phone and email them to myself at the end of each day when I lie in bed. They're just a line or two with a couple of hashtags. I have a theme for each day of the week," I added before realizing how ridiculous that probably sounded to them.

"What are the themes?" Reid asked excitedly, slightly bouncing in his seat. I chuckled and hesitated, but his happy smile pushed me to tell him.

"Motivation Monday, Ticked off Tuesday, Weirdness Wednesday, Thankful Thursday, Funny Friday, Stress-Free Saturday, and Sunday Funday," I muttered quickly. They must have picked up on the fact I was getting embarrassed because Reid nodded while kicking Jesse in the shin to answer the question. Jesse glared at Reid, but ended up answering without any complaint on the fact his best friend just kicked him in the leg.

"The next day." Jesse's somber tone successfully distracted me from the previous topic.

Does this have to do with that time I found him on the side of the road all bruised and bloodied? I pushed the thought away, determined to follow the rules we set, but they didn't stop me from glancing over at Reid and Kingston. Both caught my eye and if I didn't know those two so well, I wouldn't have noticed the minute grimace and averted eyes.

So yes, that did have to do with his bruises.

I ground my teeth and locked down the urge to demand answers from the three of them.

"I daydream," Kingston answered quietly, distracting me from the swirls of questions that danced on the tip of my tongue. "I love that logic and facts come with law, but sometimes I just like to imagine. I don't have anything in particular that helps me sleep though." My heart melted a little more at his answer, his soft tone engraving his answer deep within my chest and my raging emotions.

"What matters most to me." Reid gave a sly smile but didn't give anything else away as to what that was as he grabbed the hat from my lap.

"Best compliment you've ever received that isn't from one of us." He nodded as he read it, his tone respectful at the deep prompt.

"This is some of the best work I've ever seen," Jesse responded proudly. I assumed he was talking about classwork since he was one of the highest recommended tutors within the school.

"You make me proud," Kingston beamed. Remembering

how his parents seemed to constantly be proud of Killian and him during the 'Trunk or Treat' event today, I figured he had to be thinking of his parents or someone else who meant something to him.

"You light up a room." Reid's tone was wistful, his eyes unfocused on the far wall while the tiniest curl of his lip appeared. Shaking himself out of his memory, the boys looked at me, and I wracked my brain for what I could say. Wincing, I thought of one of the nicer things anyone, other than them, had said to me.

"You look hot," I whispered. All of the boys perked up at that looking at me with such intense gazes I wanted to be swallowed up by the couch. None of them questioned me though, remembering the boundaries we had set as Kingston pulled out the next question.

"What do you wear to bed?" He chuckled as he read the question. I held back on my blush as best as I could before responding.

"My flannel pajama sets"—I coughed trying to mask my second portion of my statement—"no bra." The way they all focused on me made my cheeks heat even further.

"Boxers," Reid answered proudly.

"Sweats and a t-shirt," Jesse added, though his tone was normal to Reid's blatant statement.

"Nothing." My brows shot up at Kingston's answer. My blood pounded within me thinking about his tanned, lean body naked and tangled within the sheets of my bed. I prayed for Jesse to take the hat faster to curb my dirty thoughts as they ran rampant.

"What's something you've always wanted to try?" I forced, with great effort, the thought of a naked Kingston out of my mind and focused on the question.

"Skydiving." I smiled, pepping up. "I don't really like

heights."

"Flying," Jesse shared quietly. At my curious gaze, he answered my unspoken question. "I've never been on a planc."

"Well"—I started, placing my hand reassuringly on his arm—"we'll fly somewhere after graduation as a celebration." He cocked a dark brow at me.

"Oh, really?" he playfully challenged. I nodded flashing him a large smile that made him chuckle.

"Diving in the ocean," Reid answered before continuing. "We can fly somewhere on the ocean and go diving!" His tone was excited, and I could see the cogs within his mind moving as he planned silently.

"I've always wanted to go to Hawaii." Kingston looked at Reid who seemed to pick up on his subtle hint. I kept my mouth shut, but I knew exactly what they were doing.

We were going to be flying to Hawaii after we graduated from high school.

"If you could live anywhere, where would you pick?" Reid read after drawing a paper.

"Where I could have my own practice," Kingston responded quickly. I kept thinking of an answer as they others responded.

"I really like it here, but I also like the east coast," Reid supplied. "Don't have a location, but more of where I could get a good job."

"I have no idea." Jesse tilted his head in thought. "I don't think I've ever really thought of it."

"I love California, but I don't know if I would go back," I murmured softly, admitting to something I hadn't wanted to think about, but I wanted to be honest with them. "I've always loved places in Europe, but I don't know if I would live there, so I guess I'm with Jesse." The boys nodded in understanding as Kingston drew a question.

"Have you ever told someone you loved them and didn't mean it?" Silence reigned over the intense question.

"Yes," I whispered knowing they would understand that I hadn't loved Tyler, not really.

"No," Kingston supplied, but didn't add anything to it so I wasn't sure if he meant he loved someone or if he had never said it to someone.

"Yes," Jesse added, "but not in a romantic way, more familial if that makes any sense." I nodded in understanding as did the other two.

"Well," Reid started seeming to struggle with his answer. "All right, I did love them at the time, or at least I thought I did, but now I know I didn't, so I guess yes?" His statement went up at the end making it more of a question, but I knew he was talking about Veronica. I tried to push the jealousy down at the answer, but it was hard.

I mean, it was my question, so you'd think I would have been better prepared than this.

"Perfect way to ask someone out." Jesse chuckled at the question before answering. "I think just being upfront about it." I nodded before putting forth my thoughts.

"I mean, I'll always appreciate the flowers or romance, but I think just being upfront in what you want is best. I have to be honest though, I love cheesy or sweet or silly ways to ask someone out," I admitted looking to Kingston and Reid.

"I'm pretty partial to the make them laugh and find you funny beforehand," Reid joked, but didn't answer anything else.

"I don't know if I really have an answer for this." Kingston scratched his beard lightly. "I've never asked someone out on a date." My brows shot up my forehead.

Handsome, sweet Kingston hadn't asked anyone out? Color me surprised.

"How do you know when you've fallen for someone?" I felt my words go from reading at a normal volume to a whisper by the end of the question, my earlier thoughts flooding my mind. "I think you just know." I shrugged wanting the answer out and away from me. "You care about them, you're willing to work with them to get over hurdles and talk about problems, find yourself craving to be around them more." A pregnant silence happened after my response before nods and agreements went up around the group.

"Something you've always dreamed of." Reid made a humming sound before asking, "Is that too similar to the something you've always wanted to try?" We agreed before moving on to the next question; Reid pulled out another paper. "Something on your bucket list, same thing." He dug around for a third piece of paper. "Biggest deal breaker on a date?"

"Being on your phone the whole time," I added at the same time Reid answered with, "Someone who pays attention to everything except you." We smirked at each other as the others chuckled at us.

"I agree with those." Kingston nodded thoughtfully. Jesse hummed an agreement and signaled Kingston to draw the next question.

"Describe yourself in three words." He tilted his head. "Laidback, friendly, loyal."

"Funny, loyal, caring." Reid looked to Jesse and me, waiting for our answers.

"Stubborn, reserved, loyal," Jesse revealed. Then all three sets of eyes centered on me.

"Caring, lost, loyal," I murmured telling them the truth.

I cared about them and my friends and my life, but I felt lost after everything that had shaken up my life at the beginning of September. Despite all that though, they had stuck by me, and I would do the same.

"How far have you gone sexually?" I felt my face bloom in a wash of red as Jesse read the second to last question.

"Fingering, hand-jobs," I muttered in embarrassment.

"All the way," Reid said quietly, his almost faded tan blooming with pink. "Not exactly my best moment." I rubbed his shoulder reassuringly while keeping my jealousy contained.

"Same," Jesse whispered dipping his head toward Reid. I was honestly surprised he had with how closed off he was, but Kingston's answer surprised me the most.

"Kiss." He wasn't ashamed or quiet in his answer. "I've never had a girlfriend. Never really wanted one." I couldn't help but smile at him. He was seriously the sweetest.

"Biggest turn-on." I groaned as I read the prompt. "I honestly have no idea. Like I said before, I'd never really wanted to do anything in Cali."

"But you have in Nebraska?" Reid teased, his hazel eyes sparking as he looked at me seemingly able to read everything I was trying to hide. I blushed realizing that's exactly what I had implied.

He's not wrong.

"I plead the fifth." I tipped my chin up before zipping my lips closed.

Hey, if they can do it to me, I can do it back.

"Fine, spoilsport." Reid chuckled. "Someone who I can be silly with, someone I'm comfortable around. Although, a nice laugh certainly helps." I couldn't tell if I imagined his glance over at me, but my skin started to tingle.

"I like someone in my clothes," Kingston added. "Seeing

her in my shirt or sweatshirt." Reid nodded adding that he liked that as well.

"Nibbling my neck and ear." Jesse rubbed his nose to try and cover up his words, but we heard him. Reid and Kingston looked at him in appreciation while I felt my skin erupt in flames. Thinking about doing that, feeling his warm skin under my lips, the beating of his heart pressing against my chest, all had me shifting on the couch to relieve some of the discomfort between my thighs. The embers in my body grew sharply to flames as my mind wandered to him or the others doing that same thing to me. I made sure to press my legs together discreetly.

Holy crap. I felt a slickness rubbing against me from my underwear. Apparently, nibbling was a turn-on for me too.

Who knew.

The guys had started to talk, but I couldn't focus on what they were saying; tingles and sensations seared through me as we transitioned from our game and on to the couch to watch a movie. Situating myself the way we had a couple weeks ago, I found myself unable to focus on the TV with all three of them touching me. I shoved the thoughts away and ended up drifting into a dreamless sleep still in their arms.

CHAPTER 14

The parking lot was filling quickly when I parked, and the chill in the air had me shivering. The weather was getting to the point I wasn't used to, the app on my phone saying it was low 40s with a chilly breeze. I yanked down my hat and adjusted the scarf Kingston had gotten me for my birthday, my lips adorned with the lipstick courtesy of Reid, and to round out the group, Jesse's earrings sparkled in my ears. Speaking of Jesse, I had picked him up this morning early enough for our first study session. It had gone well as we fueled up on caffeine over at Coffee Grounds.

"Cold?" Jesse noticed my tightly wrapped arms holding my jacket closed. I nodded, shivering slightly. Without further exchange, he wrapped his arm over my shoulder in a very Reid fashion and pulled me into his heated torso, the warmth curbing my shivering. "Better?" I nodded gratefully soaking in the heat that radiated from his body.

How on Earth is he so warm in just a t-shirt?

We walked into school, and the eyes of my fellow

classmates *finally* didn't dart to me in harsh judgement. It only took almost three weeks, but I was glad I could walk through the student body without feeling every set of eyes on me. Reid greeted me with his usual smile as Kingston rubbed my back once Jesse's arm fell away.

"Good morning!" Reid cheered, pulling both Jesse and me into a tight hug, one of us in each arm. "The stupid bell is about to ring, isn't it?" I started to chuckle, which made Reid laugh, and I heard Kingston chuckling as he stood right behind me. Finally, Jesse joined in, unable to not be sucked into the laughing fest. His laugh was just as honeyed as his words.

"Yes, Reid." I pressed my face into his soft t-shirt to try and stop laughing, but unfortunately it turned to butterflies and tingling at being wrapped up by my three boys.

"Lame," he huffed when the bell rang. "I'll see you next period, babe. I'll see you guys later." Reid made a goofy kissy face at me before waving to Kingston and Jesse and splitting off toward his homeroom.

"See you soon, baby doll." Kingston's hand rubbed against my lower back, nudging me into his tall body. I wrapped my arms around his trim torso and squeezed lightly before stepping back to stand next to Jesse. "See you at lunch." He clapped Jesse on the back before following the crowd of people.

"Come on"—I tugged on his sleeve—"I don't want to be late."

"Hey, Emma." Brayden nudged my arm. "How's it going?" I swerved around the people going the opposite direction of us.

"Not bad, have tonight off work. How're you?" I felt my arm brushing against Jesse's lightly, and a blush bloomed on my cheeks at the contact.

"Pretty good. Going camping this weekend." He gave me a quick rundown of his plans before eyeing us with an expression I couldn't make out as he walked down the hall to his homeroom.

I'll have to deal with that set of rumors soon, I'm sure.

Yup, knew it.

"So," Ashley started, but I cut her off, already tired of whatever questions they wanted to field my direction.

"No, Jesse and I weren't cuddling or making out in the hall or cafeteria." I couldn't keep my tone flat, the irritation blatant in my words. She smirked at me.

"Are you and Reid dating? Because that's what his ex-girlfriend told me." She sat patiently waiting for my answer.

This is going to come back to bite me.

"Yes," I huffed, unsure of what else to say since Reid had played it off that way. "We are. Which Veronica already knew when we told her almost two months ago."

"How does Reid feel about you walking in with Jesse's arm around your shoulder or you hugging Kingston?" Right Twin questioned haughtily. I internally groaned, my fuse shortening until it was almost non-existent.

"He doesn't care because he isn't jealous. Jesse and Kingston are our best friends; we're not going to stay away from them just because we're together," I reasoned, my heart squeezing with the fact that I had to pick one of them, but this finally had me staring what I had been ignoring right in the face.

I like all three of them.

As in like *like all three of them.*

I'm so screwed.

As soon as the bell rang, I tried to keep myself from bolting out of the classroom in a frantic urge to make it to Reid. The hallways were crowded, and while it normally didn't bother me with how long it took to get anywhere, today was different. I didn't want Reid to be blindsided or upset with the entire school thinking we were together. My skin was flushed when I finally got to the classroom. Reid's curly head was tilted down as he reviewed the information in front of him for the test we had coming up next week.

"Reid," I whispered sinking into my seat before I leaned into him. "Okay, so Ashley and the creepy carbon copy twins were pestering me today in nutrition asking about Jesse and all that normal crap," I rushed to explain, my words blurring together as they came tumbling out of my mouth. "Then they brought up Veronica and how she was talking about how we were dating, and they were asking me about that and so I told them that we were dating. I'm sorry, I probably should have talked to you first or something. I'm not sure if this will be weird or not…"

"Woah, woah, woah. Hold up, Emma," he whispered, pressing his fingers to my lips lightly, effectively silencing me. "All right, let me get this straight. Ashley has been talking to my ex about us?" I nodded, his fingers rocking against my lips at the movement. "You told them we were dating?" I nodded again feeling my chest tighten painfully. "I'm going to ask you some personal stuff, all right? Do you want to have a boyfriend?" My brows furrowed, but I couldn't stop my head from answering yes. "Do you like me like that?" Again, I nodded. "You also like Kingston and Jesse, correct?" I closed my eyes unable to look at him as I dipped my head in agreement. He was silent for a moment, and my heart pounded deafeningly in my ears.

This is it, he's not going to want to be my friend anymore.

"Emma." At my name I opened my eyes; his hazel eyes were soft as he looked at me. "It's okay. I'm not blind, I've known for a while." He didn't sound mad or upset, but that didn't mean he wasn't. Tyler had been the best at sounding normal when he really wanted to just blow up. It made it hard to trust if people's tones were true.

"I'm sorry," I whispered against his fingers that shifted to my cheek. His palm cupped my face, the years of lacrosse callouses a rough pressure against my skin.

"You don't have to be sorry." He smiled at me, humor lighting up his eyes. "I like you too, by the way." I blushed at his admission. "As do Kingston and Jesse." My cheeks practically radiated heat as I felt the flush deepen.

"So, where does that leave us?" I could hear the worry and fear wavering within my question.

"How did you feel when we talked about all taking you to the dance?" Scrunching my brows, I didn't understand where that question came from or why he was bringing it up. "We do everything together"—he shrugged—"why can't we see where we go together?"

"Like, date all of you?" My brain must have fizzled out of commission because that could *not* have been what he was suggesting. He nodded, his thumb brushing against my cheek.

"Think about it for a while, and we can talk about it at lunch or some other time if you're not ready. All right, Cali girl?" I felt my heart crack at his handsome smile; it was one of the rare times Reid was serious, yet his smile was still warm as he looked at me before turning to the front of the class.

I couldn't focus on what Mr. Fergusen was talking about despite liking his teaching methods and class in general. Could it really be that easy? Date all of them? I liked them all, but I couldn't just date three people. Would they date other girls? Heck no, I couldn't handle that. My jealousy surged within my chest at just the thought. Did Jesse even like me like that? *He bought you jewelry*, I reminded myself.

The questions swirled in my mind so loud I didn't even notice the bell had rung and students were shuffling to go to lunch. Reid's fingers brushed my arm pulling my attention back to around me instead of getting lost in all the worries and fears. What would people think about us? How would my mom take this? I shoved the stupid questions down, realizing there was no point in worrying if they wouldn't even go for it.

"You all right, babe?" Reid questioned, his arm dropping around my shoulders same as usual. "I didn't mean to upset you with everything."

"You didn't," I said with conviction. As scared as I was, I was glad we were finally going to address everything we'd been tip-toeing around. "I'm just lost in my own head." We didn't talk as we grabbed food and headed to the table; Jesse and Kingston were already seated when we arrived.

"So," Reid started as soon as he sat down. "I talked to Emma about everything." My brows shot up my forehead. They had talked about this without me?

Rude.

"When did you talk about this?" I asked, irritation building that I had spent all class worrying when they had already talked about it.

"After Lyla brought up taking you to the dance." Kingston

was unfazed by my attitude. "We didn't bring it up because we weren't sure how you would react." I took a deep breath trying to calm myself.

They had a point.

"Even you?" I turned to Jesse who was staring at his tray until I questioned him. He looked at me and shrugged.

"I didn't know you liked me until a little while ago," he said defensively. I rolled my eyes.

What a cop-out.

"You're the one who barely talked to me for the last two months," I hissed. It wasn't my fault he didn't try until the last couple weeks. "You guys had this conversation over a month ago, and I've been over here worrying. Were you guys even planning on talking to me?"

"Hey," Reid tried to redirect our attention, but I was too emotional. I dropped my food on my tray and moved to standing. "Emma, wait." I shook off his hand when he tried to rest it on my arm, knowing it'd be that much harder to leave if I let him make that contact.

"I can't talk about this right now," I ground out. "I'm too upset. Maybe later." With that, I walked off. Dumping my tray, I went straight to the library hoping diving into school work would calm my turbulent emotions.

Stupid drama.

I found myself standing in the lobby of the counselor's office waiting for Ms. Rogers to come get me. The upholstered chairs against the wall were stiff and uncomfortable, and my phone buzzed lightly in my pocket for what seemed like the hundredth time. As I reached to grab it, Ms. Rogers appeared, not allowing me time to check it. Her familiar cat's eye glasses and friendly smile shined in the drab office. I sank into my usual seat already ready for this meeting to be over. Now that I had calmed down, I wanted to talk with the boys.

"Any progress or updates since our last meeting, Emma?" She grabbed my file off the stack and turned to the notes page, her pen poised over the lined paper.

"Jesse and I had our first study session this morning, and I got visits scheduled for UNL and UNO set for next month. Jesse, Reid, and Kingston are all going to go with me." I felt proud because of Ms. Rogers' brightening expression.

"Very good!" she praised, jotting down the information. "I figured we could set another practice ACT for mid-December and see how you're doing, that way we can schedule the actual ACT for January. Then the scores will come back before deadlines for the universities." I nodded as she talked, making a mental note to remember this. She opened her mouth to continue speaking, when a knock sounded on the door. Brows furrowing, she stood and opened it. Someone I didn't recognize was standing on the other side, but based on his outfit I thought he probably worked at the school.

"Ms. Rogers," the man greeted. His tone was polite, but his voice was grating and set my teeth on edge. He was a burly man with a buzz cut, his brunette hair fading to gray on the temples. He was wearing black slacks and a gray dress shirt, and his shined boots thudded on the floor as he walked into the office. "Miss Clark, do you know who I am?"

I shook my head. "I'm afraid I don't, I'm bad with faces and names." The thinning of his lips told me he wasn't happy with my answer, and his intense gaze burned my face as he stared down his nose at me.

"I'm the Assistant Principal Mr. Derosa." He cocked a

brow as if that was supposed to make me remember. I nodded respectfully and waited for him to continue. Ms. Rogers stood by her seat eyeing the man with disdain, her normal smile traded out for thinned lips and crossed arms.

"Mr. Derosa," she reprimanded, "I was in the middle of a meeting with Miss Clark. If you need to discuss something with me, you can do so after we are finished here."

"I'm here to have a talk with Miss Clark, not you," he snapped. His broad shoulders seem to have expanded, puffing up as she chided him. I tried not to cower, but he was intimidating, and based on his hard set jaw and pulled back shoulders, he was on a warpath. His shrewd light brown eyes centered on me. "Now, Miss Clark, I was wondering what a sweet girl like you would be doing to tarnish your reputation."

"What?" I felt my blood turn cold at his statement. Whatever he was talking about confused me, but I didn't miss the hint of judgment in his words.

"I have been made aware about an incident with another student, Brad Warland." He raised a brow in question. "About the lies going around at what happened." I couldn't tell if he was saying the rumors were lies or what I had experienced was a lie.

"Mr. Derosa," Ms. Rogers started, but a glare from the Assistant Principal silenced her.

"We here at Arbor Ridge don't want unsubstantiated claims against another student to go around." I ground my teeth knowing he was taking Brad's side. "A sweet girl like you could damage a student like Brad's future beyond repair with these types of rumors."

"They aren't lies. He forced me into the bathroom at that party with bad intentions," I bit out, practically shouting at him. "I didn't 'seduce' him. I didn't lead him on, and we certainly didn't do anything."

"Well," he started, "it doesn't look good for you to be dating someone like Jesse Parker especially after what he did to Brad." I was panting with anger, the fury building within my chest burned my veins.

"Mr. Parker is the senior class valedictorian, Mr. Derosa. It is unbecoming to reference him in such an inferior manner," Ms. Rogers snapped, her cheeks reddened with anger. I felt my brows raise at the fact that Jesse was valedictorian.

"Just because he can fake his way through classes doesn't make him a good student or person," he snapped back. "He's a hellion bent on causing trouble, skipping school, and fighting. As I was saying"—his attention turned back to me—"I suggest you keep your inaccurate accounts of what happened to yourself, Miss Clark, otherwise Brad will most likely have the police charge Mr. Parker with assault and you with being an accessory." With that, he stormed out of the open office door. I saw several of the other counselors staring wide-eyed at us from the hall and lobby. Ms. Rogers firmly shut the door to her office with a huff.

"I would like to apologize for his…" She struggled with the proper word, her voice filled with rage as she stared at the closed door. "…inappropriate behavior. He should not be demanding such things from you, slandering a student's reputation, or silencing your experiences."

"Thank you," I whispered, my limbs trembling after the confrontation.

"Do you want to share what happened?" she asked softly. I shook my head violently.

I would some day, but not right now.

Too soon.

"All right, you don't have to share anything with me that you don't want to, but know that you can talk to me whenever you're ready. I'm going to give you a pass to excuse you for the rest of the day." She glanced at the clock which read a half hour before school ended. "You shouldn't have to power through class after his brutish accusations." She wrote out the slip and took it to the front desk in the main office after walking me out of the counselors' area. I beelined for the door and straight to my car, my vision filled with watery shapes. Try as I might, the wayward tears slipped down my cheeks as I pulled out of the lot, intent on getting as far away from the school as fast as I can.

"Cali girl?" Reid's voice was muffled through the comforter I had pulled up over my head. "Do you want to be alone?" I sniffled again trying to contain the tears, but his soft, caring voice pushed me over that edge, and the tears poured down my cheeks. Shoving the blanket down, I jumped off the bed and barreled into his chest. His arms wrapped around my shoulders as I fisted the back of his t-shirt. "What happened?"

I spent the next ten minutes alternating between crying and explaining what had gone down in the counselor's office today. A familiar hand rubbed circles into my lower back letting me know it wasn't just Reid who had come over. I couldn't see or hear Jesse, but I knew he was here as well. After a few minutes of their soothing words, I got the crying under control enough for us to move out into the living room. I hadn't realized how grateful I was until now that my mom's crazy work schedule allowed us to talk in private.

"Fuck that asshole," Jesse ground out, his gaze staring holes out the patio door as he leaned back against the table. "I seriously can't believe him."

"I can't either and I was sitting right there," I murmured, curling into the blanket I had snatched off the back of the couch. "I'm sorry about earlier, I was just really overwhelmed, and I took it out on you guys."

"It's all right, Emma," Kingston soothed, rubbing the knee that I had tucked in front of my chest. "Are you up for talking about it now?" I nodded not trusting myself to talk.

"Have you thought about what we talked about?" Reid questioned from his position on the coffee table. I nodded again, feeling my heart squeeze within my chest.

"I'd like to try," I whispered. "I wouldn't be able to pick between the three of you." Reid lit up as Jesse's head whipped around to face us.

"Really?" he murmured as if he couldn't believe my answer. Holding his gaze, I nodded. Kingston's hand gripped my knee softly pulling my eyes over to him. His tanned face was bright with a broad, happy smile.

"But we have to talk about what, if anything, is bothering us," I stipulated. "I can't handle the keeping things to yourself and letting it fester for days on end."

"Deal," Reid practically shouted, his hands clapping excitedly. I couldn't help but smile at him and his cheerful disposition. A bubble of happiness bloomed within my chest despite all the crap that had happened today.

"Not to be a downer," I started, "but what are we going to do about Mr. Derosa and Brad?"

"We're not doing anything wrong. We're telling the truth, so if he wants to play that route, we'll fight back," Reid directed. "He might be able to charge Jesse, but we could just as easily go after him for attempted rape."

"Exactly. If it gets to that, I'll talk to my dad and see what we should do," Kingston added.

"We might want to fill him in now anyway." Jesse's words were somber. "I have a feeling they aren't going to back off, and we need to be ready." I nodded—I didn't want them to take advantage of the situation and not be prepared. Kingston and Reid also voiced their agreement.

"So," I hummed looking between the three of us. "How is this going to work? Like, are you guys going to be seeing other girls?" All three shook their head violently.

"Just you for us." Kingston surprised me by being the one to respond. "And us for you."

"But"—I tilted my head in confusion—"how is that fair to you? Wouldn't you three get jealous?" They all looked at each other before Reid shifted forward quickly, his calloused palms cupping my cheeks. His lips were warm and soft on mine in a hesitant kiss. My breath knocked from my chest as he pressed them harder against me. Without thinking, I kissed back. My body moved forward at the feeling of his tongue brushing my bottom lip, but before I could respond, he pulled away. My rattling heart pitter-pattered into my throat at his gaze, his hazel irises blazing and centered on my face. Our breaths were heavy pants as we stared at each other for a brief moment until my mind suddenly reminded me there were two others in the room. Pulling back, I felt blood rush to my face in a bright red flush. I glanced over at the other two in the room to gauge their reactions, pleasantly surprised to find no harsh expressions.

"I don't feel jealous," Kingston answered with a slight shrug. "Especially knowing I get to do it too. Jesse?" We all looked at him. His body was tense, but it had been all day.

"I feel fine," he responded, his tone soft. "I don't feel jealous, but I would if it was someone other than us." I nodded. A weight I hadn't realized was crushing my chest lifted leaving me light and excited.

"We're really doing this?" I couldn't stop the anticipation lacing my question or my smile as I looked around us. They all nodded, and three happy smiles faced me.

Three boyfriends.

Nebraska *definitely* wasn't so bad.

CHAPTER 15

NOVEMBER 5TH

"We must not allow other people's limited perceptions to define us." - Virginia Satir
#BeBrave #WhoNeedsBlushWithThreeBoyfriends
#MotivationMonday

Good morning, babe," Reid greeted me in the parking lot alone, Kingston having driven Jesse and himself. Reid's arm curled around my shoulders before pulling me into his warm chest that was covered in a Nebraska Cornhusker sweatshirt. I wrapped my arms around his waist as best I could with his backpack on one of his shoulders. Standing on my tiptoes, I gave him a quick kiss.

"Morning," I whispered smiling up at him as I dropped back down to the cement. I kept my left arm around his waist while we walked side by side into the building.

"How'd my girlfriend sleep?" His question was laced with humor, a cocksure smile curling his lips. I rolled my eyes, but felt my heart warm at the reminder.

"Not bad. These three guys kept me up late last night with an in-depth argument on whether it's pop or soda," I playfully reprimanded. His scruff was scratchy against my scalp as he pressed his cheek into my head.

"Tell me who these three hooligans are and I'll tell them off." He chuckled unable to say his statement without laughing. I felt eyes on me when we walked through the front doors. Looking around, I saw several curious gazes as well as a few not-so-friendly ones.

"So, how is this going to work?" I asked as quietly as I could in the crowded room, the sound of everyone's conversations a dull roar in the all tile space. "Like the four of us? I didn't figure Jesse would be very open with his affections, but are we going to try and keep it on the down low or... what?"

"Uh..." He pursed his lips and tilted his head back and forth as he thought. "I hadn't even considered that. I don't really care if people know, they don't matter to me, but we can ask the other two." I nodded. We stayed silent with me tucked under his arm as we neared the table. Kingston was talking to Jesse while the rest of our friends were deep in a conversation about the upcoming holiday break for Thanksgiving. "Hey." Reid slipped away from me to greet the other two boys.

"Morning." Kingston patted Reid on the back once before wrapping me up in his arms, his thumbs rubbing soft circles on my lower back. "How are you, baby doll?"

"Better now." I gave him a cheeky smile before stepping back. Jesse nudged my hand slightly with his knuckles, shuffling closer to me so he could intertwine our fingers.

"Hey, Em," he murmured softly giving me a very tiny smile. Reid's body angled toward our group closing up the circle.

"So, Cali girl brought up a good point on our way in. Do we want to try and keep us a secret or just do our own thing and say screw everyone else? I'm all for the second option, but it isn't just about me," Reid put forth quietly.

"I'm good with option two," Kingston agreed, nodding. Jesse nodded his head as well signifying he was good with option two as well. Before I realized it, I had three sets of eyes on me.

"I'm not ashamed of you guys, so why would I hide it?" I smiled shyly, and their tense body postures melted at my answer before Reid converged and grouped all of us in his arms. The bell rang during our cramped hug, and we all split toward our respective classrooms. Jesse kept ahold of my right hand which Brayden's brows shot up at. Knowing there was going to be rumors, I decided to give them something to talk about. I leaned over and pressed a quick kiss to Jesse's cheek. It was warm, but soft, the scratchy scruff having been shaved this morning leaving it smooth. Jesse's dark brown eyes centered on me with a smirk. He knew what I was doing. I could feel Brayden's eyes dissecting everything Jesse and I did as we curved down our hallway.

"Putting on a show, Em?" he teased quietly as we sank into our seats. I couldn't help but chuckle because that's exactly what I had been doing. Eyes continued to drift in our direction at our soft conversation mainly because Jesse and I hadn't talked in homeroom even after we waved our tender white flag a few weeks ago. "I'll see you in chem." He gave me a soft kiss on my cheek before heading to his first class. I floated on cloud nine all the way to history.

He kissed me.

Jesse. Brooding and stubborn Jesse.

Cue the internal girly squealing.

"Hey, babe." Reid sank into his seat next to me with a kiss dropped on the top of my head as he did. He narrowed his eyes on me when he looked at me, leaning in close to me as he examined the expression on my face. "Someone looks happy." He gave me a cocky smirk. "Jesse kissed you, didn't he?"

"On the cheek." I jutted my chin out proudly. "So..." I stuck my tongue out maturely. He leaned into my ear to whisper.

"Be careful with that tongue, Cali girl. I might not tease so nicely." I flushed at his heated words as I discreetly squeezed my thighs together at the building heat between my legs.

"What would you do?" I found myself whispering back, my cheek brushing against the scruff on his jaw when I angled my face toward his ear.

"Wouldn't you like to know?" he taunted as he pulled back with a smirk. I huffed but couldn't hold back my giggle. Mr. Fergusen started class before we could continue our conversation, but I felt Reid's thigh pressing up against mine under the desk warming my body and sending a wave of tingles over my skin. Reid walked with me under his arm to my next class where Kingston was waiting for us at the door.

"Hi, Kingston." I felt myself blushing as he directed me into the classroom, my skin practically burning under his touch with the amount of attention I was putting into his hand against my back.

"How's my baby doll?" he asked, sinking into his chair. I couldn't stop the giddy giggle that bubbled out of me. "That was adorable."

"Oh, shut up." I rolled my eyes. My face was bright red, but not because of embarrassment. "I can't help it, you're too sweet." He beamed at me, his fingers brushing against my thigh under the desk until class started. After class was over, Kingston walked me to nutrition. I mentally prepared for the onslaught of questions I was about to get from the school gossips. Steeling myself, I pressed a quick kiss to Kingston's beard covered jaw before heading into the classroom.

"I thought you were dating Reid?" Left Twin questioned with a brow raised, her shrewd gaze was locked on my face as I walked to my desk.

"I am," I answered while pulling all my materials out of my bag.

"So, why were you kissing Kingston?" Right Twin took over for her sister in the 'interrogate Emma' questions.

"I'm dating him too." I ignored the silence that followed my statement as I flipped to the right page in my notebook.

"What about Jesse? Rumor has it you were holding hands and kissing this morning," Ashley finally chimed in, but for once her voice was hesitant and confused. Looking at her, I smiled making sure to keep it friendly despite wanting to throw something at her.

"Yup, him too." I couldn't help the slight smug tone that laced my words. Her mouth opened as her brows furrowed in confusion, but I cut her off. "Yes, I am dating all three of them, and yes, they all know. We made the decision together, but last I checked, our personal lives aren't any of your business." I couldn't help the harsh note my statement ended on. I may have come in ready for the interrogation, but that didn't mean I was all right with their incessant prying.

"Seriously?" That was all she said; her one question made her unspoken question clear—you're not pranking me?

"Yeah, seriously. Any other questions before you go tell the entire school?" I cocked a brow. She reeled back, surprised by my directness, but she shook her head, turned around, and left me alone for the rest of class.

Despite the gossips having just left with 'their scoop' to dish out, I felt eyes wandering toward me as I made my way back up to my homeroom classroom for civics. Brayden was just as much of a gossip as Ashley and the twins. I held my head high as I walked into class. What I had told my boys was true, I wasn't ashamed of them, and I wouldn't cower because of it.

"The school gossips officially know"—I smiled over at Reid—"so, everyone else should know by the end of the day."

"You just straight out told them, didn't you?" He chuckled and grabbed my hand so he could intertwine our fingers. I couldn't help but laugh with him.

They knew me so well.

"If they were going to talk about it, I'd rather have them spread the truth." I shrugged, tingles spreading as he rubbed circles on the back of my hand. "Does that bother you?" I realized while we talked about it not being secret, I might have been a bit too quick for their liking.

"Of course not, Cali girl." He gave me a heart melting smile. "I'm not ashamed of us. I don't give a shit who knows about us. We aren't hurting anyone."

"Good." I leaned forward. Reid seemed to read my mind because he met me halfway for a quick kiss. Someone in the back of the room whooped and clapped at us making me laugh as a blush rushed to my cheeks.

Good thing I didn't put on blush today.

The smell of coffee was soothing as I changed into my work shirt. I had picked up an extra shift when Rick had called this weekend saying there was an event going on at the business next door and we would be busy later in the evening. My mood was brighter today than it had been in a long time despite all of the rumors going around about me and the boys. Lyla was manning the front, her red hair freshly cut in her stylish long bob and straight across bangs. Rick was, as per usual, trapped under a mound of paperwork he was filing for last month after finishing his input into the computer system. I hopped right on in taking and filling orders, the flow of work comforting.

"Emma." Rick poked his head out of the hallway door a few hours later when the after school rush was finished. "You want to come help me in the back storage room? Just got a new shipment in today that needs to be put away." I nodded before heading back. His red hair was bright under the fluorescent lighting of the stock room. Shelves lined all three walls, the wall that the door was propped open against held several large cardboard shipping boxes stacked together.

"All right, so just open the box and put it on the shelf?" I asked looking to Rick who had just grabbed the box cutter off the wall hook. "I'm assuming pulling the older stuff forward so it gets used first?" He nodded with a happy smile.

"Perfect, this is just cups, sleeves, and lids and then two boxes of syrups. We got beans delivered yesterday," he explained cutting open the first box. We spent the next little while working our way through the supplies until we were left with flattened cardboard boxes to go out in the recycling. "I'll take one side of the stack if you want to take the other." Rick pointed to the half he wanted me to lift. Together we walked the thick pile out to the bin.

"That all?" I asked him as we stepped back into the employee area. I felt comfortable around Rick having worked with him for a while, but not as comfortable as Lyla since she and I talked constantly even when we weren't working. Rick was a good boss, fair in his expectations, and he never yelled if one of us messed up, only explaining what needed to be done to fix it as he helped us.

"Yup"—he nodded looking around the hall—"if you want to go take your fifteen minute break, I'll go let Lyla know." I nodded and headed to the break room. I had just sent a message to the boys when my phone started to ring. Without looking, I answered the call expecting Reid or Kingston.

"Hey." I smiled, but as soon as the other person started speaking it turned down into a frown.

"Hey, Emma." Tyler's voice surprised me as I pulled the phone back to look at the number. It was indeed his, but I had deleted the contact after finally telling him to stop calling and texting me. "How's everything going in Nebraska?"

"It's good," I answered hesitantly. "Why are you calling me, Tyler?"

"I just missed talking to you. I figured we could talk for a bit, you know, like old times," he explained. His tone was respectful and polite, but it still threw me off.

"I only have a tiny bit before I have to go back to work," I lied knowing I still had almost the full fifteen minutes.

"Where are you working now?"

I felt my brows furrow. *Why does it matter?*

"Local coffee shop." I kept my answer short.

"So…" He hesitated and I braced myself knowing the entire reason he was calling was about to be revealed. "You seeing anyone?"

Nosy jerk.

"Yes, actually, I am," I answered brusquely.

"Emma, I miss you. Would you consider giving me another chance?" he pleaded. "Please?"

"No, Tyler." I rubbed my forehead feeling a headache coming on. "I'm not getting back together with you. If you decide you can settle for being friends, and friends only, I will consider that, but we're not getting back together. I'm happy with my boyfriends." My phone beeped telling me there was another call, and without looking I said goodbye to Tyler, despite his protests.

"Hey, sweetie." Now it was my dad's voice on the other end surprising me. This was the first time I had talked to him in two months that wasn't through a couple very short texts. "How's everything going? I'm sorry I haven't called recently, we're working on expanding the vineyard to include a brewery, and we've been traveling like crazy to plan for that."

"It's surprisingly not bad. I'm on break at the coffee shop I work at." I felt my throat close up in the wave of emotions that flooded me, my eyes prickling with the build of tears. "When is the addition supposed to be done?"

"Spring next year is when we're going to be opening." There were several hollers in the background that I didn't recognize calling for my dad's attention. "I'm sorry, Emma. I have to go. I'll call you soon, love you."

"Love you too," I whispered before hearing the click of the line, my heart cracking painfully in my chest. I might not miss much about California, but I missed my dad.

Even though it seemed he was too busy for me.

When technology could put us in contact at a moment's notice.

Heck, I still didn't even know why my parents had gotten divorced.

I went back to work drowning in wave after wave of loneliness while a cracked heart stuttered painfully in my chest. With those bearing down on me, I made my way home after my shift had ended. I came home, unsurprisingly, to my mom still out working. I found myself curled in bed surrounded by the sound of my tears. The only consolation in the hollow walls of my house were the warm texts my boys sent me.

At least I'm not completely alone.

CHAPTER 16

I've proceeded to have 3 sit down dinners at the table with my mom since we've moved... What happened to my mom from Cali?
#IMissMyMom #WeirdnessWednesday

M orning," I murmured to Jesse who had just sank into the car. Pulling away from his house, I made sure he buckled his seatbelt. The house I picked him up in front of was run down and small. It couldn't be bigger than two bedrooms, if that. One of the windows was boarded up, and the yard was full of junk. Both times I had picked him up, Jesse practically ran to the car and slid in urging me to drive as soon as he had closed the door.

"Morning, Em." Jesse's hand came over the console to gently rub against my jean-covered thigh. The drive to Coffee Grounds was quiet but not uncomfortable, and his fingers traced a figure eight on top of my leg until I was parked. Our silence continued as we walked into the shop, my hand nestled in his tightly as we dropped our bags at one of the two person tables.

"What do you want, babe?" I asked quietly leaning over Jesse's shoulder. My arms slid around his toned chest, and he gripped them lightly hugging them to himself before giving me his order. His dark eyes focused on my face next to his when he looked over.

My heart stuttered to a stop when he closed the tiny distance between us, and smooth lips tasting of mint met mine. The kiss lasted for only a moment, but seemed to go on forever. Jesse felt perfect wrapped up in my arms with his soft lips against mine. I felt my blood start to flood with an unknown fire, an ember sparking between my legs. Pulling back, I squeezed once before letting go and stepping up to the counter where Lyla was giving me a huge smile and thumbs up. My face flushed as I realized we had just kissed in front of everyone within the shop, my body burning in a room full of strangers.

"Oh, girl"—she leaned forward, her eyes sparkling— "please tell me you two are dating." I blushed, leaning in to close the distance between us.

"I'm dating all three of them," I whispered, and her face paused in stunned silence before she started hopping up and down excitedly. Her uncontrolled squeal caught the attention of the couple customers within the store, but she didn't seem to care.

"I knew you'd end up with them." She grabbed ahold of my arm closest to her and shook it encouragingly. "I'm so happy for you."

"Thanks." I smiled pulling back to stand properly. Once she calmed, I gave her our orders. As soon as they were finished, I sank back into my seat across from Jesse who had arranged our materials. "Here you go." I handed him is small black coffee, his fingers brushing against mine making me tingle again.

"Thanks, Em." His smile was dazzling enough that I felt my brain fizzle out of commission, so when he kept talking I didn't understand a word he said. "Where do you want to start?"

"Hm?" I hummed, mentally shaking myself in an attempt to focus. "What?"

"Emma," he huffed, but his smile contradicted his stern tone. "Focus. What do you want to start with? I was thinking we could work the first section and continue down the line from there." I nodded flipping to the proper part of the study booklet. After about twenty minutes of studying, a familiar face I absolutely did *not* want to see stepped through the shop's door.

Mr. Derosa.

He ordered quickly, his tone harsh and short as he stared down Lyla who worked as quickly as she could on the other side of the counter. My heart rate picked up when he turned to scan the shop. Feeling his eyes on me, I kept my head turned down looking at my work page without actually seeing any of it.

"Miss Clark," he practically sneered my name as he walked up to us. "Mr. Parker." He definitely sneered Jesse's name which made Jesse clutch his pen tightly within his grasp.

"Mr. Derosa," I responded coolly. Nerves worked their way through my body as my stomach clenched painfully. My hand shifted, reaching for Jesse's under the table. My resolve steeled as I felt his tender squeeze.

"What are you two doing?" Mr. Derosa demanded.

It is way too early for this.

"Studying." I waved to the paper, my tone making it sound like it should have been obvious.

Which it was.

"Hm." His judgmental hum was cut off by Lyla calling out his order saving us from any further confrontation. When he walked away to grab his drink, Jesse squeezed my hand once more before letting go. Unfortunately, Mr. Derose caught the motion, and a smug smirk curled his lips. A sense of dread washed over me. I glanced at Jesse whose thinned out lips indicated he saw the facial expression.

"Come on, Em." He tried to give me an encouraging smile, one that looked more like a grimace than a smile. "Let's get back to work."

The day was almost over, and I was swapping out my books for the ones I needed for homework before my last class so I could immediately leave after dance. Jesse had just left to go to his class, which was AP calculus, when three sets of feet entered my vision; my eyes were angled toward the floor as I double checked my backpack. Looking up, I found Ashley and the twins staring at me.

"Can I help you?" I snapped when they didn't say anything. I didn't want to be late to my last class and I still had to change into my dance outfit. "I'm kind of in a hurry."

"What really happened that night at the party? With Brad," Ashley straight up asked, her tone hesitant. "I know we don't get along, but you haven't tried to hide or lie to me about what's been going on, and there's a *lot* of rumors going around about it still."

"I had gone upstairs to go to the bathroom since the main level one was occupied. He had tried to corner me the night before at the haunted house place he worked at, so when I saw him on the other side of the door, I tried to get away from him by going around. He blocked me in and then kissed me without permission," I ground out. I explained the rest of what happened as briefly as I could; the memory of the feeling of Brad's lips and hands on me made my skin crawl. "If you could spread around the *truth* of what happened, I'd be very grateful."

"You got it." She nodded, for once looking sincere. The three turned and walked away without further questions or banter. They might be the school gossips and struggle with asking things nicely, but I came to the realization they weren't so bad.

Maybe they could get the rest of the students to believe the truth.

I'm not going to hold my breath though.

"Are you kidding me?" I muttered to myself looking through the cabinets and refrigerator.

Nothing.

All empty except for some moldy bread and curdled milk.

Can I just say ew?

I checked the cash I had in my purse. I was saving all of my paychecks except for the cost of gas, so I had some to spare for food. Sighing, I grabbed the list I had left my mom four days before and tossed it into my purse as I headed out the door. The local grocery store was only a five minute drive from my house and the lot was fairly empty since most people were still at work. I grabbed a cart and started walking down the aisles being sure to grab only what we needed because I only had fifty dollars with me.

"Cali girl?" I heard Reid's effervescent voice call out from down the aisle, and I turned toward it. He was wearing a pair of black pants, a t-shirt with the store's logo on it, and a name tag. I had completely forgotten Reid said he worked part time at the grocery store.

"Hey," I greeted, trying to add some pep into my voice. The day had worn on me, the lack of food in our house just the icing on the cake at this point making me tired and irritable. "How's work?"

"Not bad, just stocking the shelves. What all are you picking up?" He tried to look into my cart, but a woman's voice caught his attention.

"There's my little Reid." She was shorter than me by an inch or two, with dark brown hair that was pulled into a messy bun on the back of her head. The man standing next to her was tall, at least 6'4", with black curly hair that was cut a bit shorter than Reid's. "Ah, you must be Emma!" the woman exclaimed. Her hand shot out to shake mine; her nails were short and well maintained in a layer of nude polish. "I'm Reid's mom, Faith. This is my husband, Micah. It's so nice to finally meet you." Her hand was warm and soft against mine.

"Nice to me you too," I responded genuinely, my attention darting to Reid who was smiling at me. The look in his eyes had me flushing. I couldn't figure out why or what emotion was deep within his hazel eyes, but whatever it was, it was intense and wormed its way into my chest.

"How's work, dear?" She focused on her son, and his cheeks tinged a slight wash of pink. "We should let you get back to it." She changed topics quickly without waiting for his response and before I knew it, they were making their way to another aisle.

"Sorry, I didn't realize they'd be coming to the store today, but it makes sense since they always make a store run before work." He stepped a bit closer, but not close enough to be inappropriate at work.

"What do they do?" I couldn't be mad at Reid, his parents were cute. Well, his mom was, his dad hadn't said anything the entire time, content to let his wife do all the talking.

"My mom's a flight attendant, and my dad is a pilot. They work for the same airline and take the same flights. They have a red-eye flight tonight to Hawaii, so they'll be gone until Friday." He started to stock the shelf again, finishing up the box he had been working on.

"I'll let you work, babe." I brushed my fingers against his forearm as I walked by. His hazel eyes sparkled at the nickname.

"Bye, Cali girl," he murmured before I got too far. Glancing back, I gave him a flirty smile and turned the corner, his laugh following me.

The total had come to $49.89. Counting my lucky stars, I loaded up the car and headed home. I refused to take more than one trip, so by the time I had all the bags on the counter, my hands were throbbing from the weight of the food. Shaking out the tingling that radiated in my palms, I unloaded and put everything away.

I had just lay down a couple hours later when a small knock sounded from the back door. Hesitant, I peeked out my door to look through the basement. Reid's curly head and bright smile met me as he waved animatedly. Crossing the basement, I opened the door with my finger in front of my lips to signal him to be quiet. He nodded and followed me to my room.

"What are you doing here?" I whispered. My mom was up in her office having come home twenty minutes earlier with plans to go to bed soon. I could hear her rummaging around organizing files from her work day. He finished shutting the door, taking the couple of steps to close the distance between us. Staring down at me, he wrapped me tightly in his arms.

"I could tell something was bothering you at the store," he whispered softly in my ear. Laying my head against his soft sweatshirt, I enjoyed the feel of his stubbled jaw pressed into my scalp. "I wanted to make sure you were all right. I also missed you, we've all been really busy the last few days."

"I'm better now." I couldn't hold back the tears that leaked from my eyes onto his shirt. "How long are you staying for?" My voice cracked when I asked which had Reid pulling away to look down at me. The rough pad of his thumb swiped at my cheek to clear the trickle of unwanted tears.

"Do you want me to say tonight?" He surprised me with his question, but looking into his hazel eyes I knew it wasn't just for me.

Reid didn't want to be alone tonight either.

Nodding, I popped up on my toes. His lips were covered in a thin layer of chapstick that tasted like berries. I shifted to bring my hands to the back of his neck, his soft curls teasing my fingers. A shiver ran through me as he smoothed his palms slowly down my back to wrap around my waist, my chest pressing against his tightly. Everything else faded away, my room, the troubles from today, the worry about my future, everything as he ran his tongue light as a feather against the seam of my lips. I opened my mouth, tentatively exploring. Tyler was the only person I'd ever kissed like this, and my heart rate galloped when I brushed the tip of my tongue against his. I couldn't believe I was making out with Reid.

My cute clown, Reid.

The sound of footsteps upstairs brought us to a screeching halt. I didn't move away from Reid's warm embrace, but I pulled my head back. The berry scent of his chapstick washed over me as I listened to make sure my mom wasn't going to come down here. When her steps faded into her room, I let go of the breath I had been holding in.

"Emma's going to get in trouble," Reid teased in a soft whisper.

"Shush." I giggled. Having Jesse here after finding him walking alone on the side of the road was one thing, but having Reid stay the night just because was a whole other ballgame. My heart pounded loudly in my ears as I looked up at him; his hazel eyes were soft and half-lidded. Unable to help myself, I rubbed my fingertips and nails up and down his neck, the dark curls shifting under my movements. His eyes sparked and before I realized what I was doing, I felt him hardening against my hip.

"Careful, Cali girl," he mumbled shifting his hips so he was no longer stabbing me in the side. "You're too pretty for your own good."

"Says the guy who's too attractive and funny for *his* own good," I teased back trying to calm my racing heart. "Let's go to bed, babe." I tugged the ends of his hair lightly before pulling away. I was already in my pajamas, but Reid had to strip down to his boxers before crawling under the covers. Shifting slightly, he pulled me to him until I was using his chest as a pillow, my arm draped over his muscled torso. It was like how we'd slept on the couch after the party from hell, except he was wearing much less clothing. I inhaled his Old Spice scent, willing my heart to slow and my body to calm, but that ember sparked once more.

"Goodnight, Cali girl," he murmured softly in the dark room, his warmth radiating around me. It took a long time before I finally dozed off, Reid's steady breaths lulling me into a peaceful sleep.

CHAPTER 17

NOVEMBER 16TH

Should I tell Reid that last night he was barking in his sleep? #MySecret #IgnoranceIsBliss #Cuddlebug #SoCute #Funny-Friday

Nebraska had a cold front move through last week bringing it down to freezing temperatures, so I was thankful it had moved on and it was back to upper 40s otherwise this cookout at Kingston's house would be miserable. Securing the knit hat he'd bought me for my birthday over my hair, I yelled a quick goodbye to my mom who was packing her suitcase for an all weekend business trip, and headed out. Reid and Jesse were waiting on the street to pick me up. Reid's Jeep was cleaned and washed for once since the weather warmed back up, the black paint shiny in the fall sun.

Kingston's house was large with two stories. The siding was a light gray with dark gray trim, the door a bright red that stood out against the monochromatic face. Cars littered the wide driveway and both sides of the street. I couldn't stop my eyes from taking in the area around the house. It seemed like a new development at first glance, with the large space between houses, but on closer inspection I realized it was just the yards for each house voice was filled with laughter as he hollered from outside the playset. Standing up right as the kids converged on me, I tossed the ball to Kingston who was waiting with his arms up. When they realized I no longer had the ball, they all went down the slide in a fit of giggles and chased Kingston who was purposely running slow. They tackled him and he went down in a wave of dramatics quoting the *Wizard of Oz* when the Wicked Witch was melting. Finally leaving the clubhouse, I chuckled as I slid down, and nostalgia of being little flooded me.

"Hey there, Cali girl." Reid stood at the bottom of the slide, his calloused palms going out for me to grab. "Didn't mean to throw you into the fire there, but I needed reinforcements." He chuckled, enveloping me in his arms. I couldn't help but melt in his embrace, the feeling of warmth and comfort washing over me.

"Don't think I'll forget that," I teased pulling back. His arm looped around my shoulders as Stella started hollering over the deck railing saying the food was done. Jesse was helping Kingston up as we approached. Once he was up and dusted off from rolling around in the dried grass, we went inside. Killian was gathering the food from the grill outside that Kaleb had been manning and moving it to the counter. People started to line up to weave around the kitchen buffet style.

The longer the get together went on, the more at ease I was around everyone. No one gave judging looks when Reid wrapped his arms around me or when Jesse held my hand. I wasn't sure if it was because they truly didn't care or if Kingston's parents already knew about the four of us. I pushed away the thought and focused on the sense of belonging. I tried to remember any time back in California I felt like this but came up blank. My family wasn't big.

were huge. There was a trail that looped between a few of the homes on the street that seemed to lead to one wide path spanning as far as I could see on both sides behind Kingston's house. I felt a little smile curl my lips when I noticed a couple of little kids playing on a playground in the small park area that the path went by.

I ended my perusal of the area as we neared the bright front door which opened as soon as we hit the steps. Stella was on the other side in a pair of stylish jeans, knee-high boots, and a long-sleeve sweater with some collegiate regalia on the front.

"Come in you three." She stepped to the side leaving the door open. Reid and Jesse hung back making sure I went first. Immediately after stepping over the threshold, I was wrapped up in a hug, her sultry floral perfume tickling my nose. "It's good to see you, Emma." Her smile was warm as she looked from me to Reid and Jesse. "Come here you two." Her arms opened, hands waving them over to her expectant hug.

"Hi, Stella." Reid had to duck down to hug her with her petite stature. Her platinum blonde hair was shiny as the sun peeked out through some of the clouds, the black ponytail holder a sharp contrast in her light tresses.

"Hello, Mrs. Bell," Jesse greeted, looking awkward in her embrace. He patted her back lightly and I had to squish my lips together to keep from chuckling at his stiff movements.

"Jesse Eric Parker, how many times do I have to tell you? Call me Stella," she enunciated while pulling away from him. Her hands waved animatedly in the space between them. "You make me sound like Kingston's grandmother with that Mrs. stuff."

"Stell"—Kingston's dad, Kaleb, materialized at the end of

the entryway—"you going to hog them all day?"

"Oh, shush," she teased, her tinkling laugh filling the air as we walked down to meet him. "Kingston is out back, you three, if you want to go out there." Now that I was no longer distracted by Kingston's mom's jovial personality, I glanced around. The house had flowing hardwoods, an open kitchen with white cabinets and marble counters, a very long dining table that had at least twenty chairs, and a bright and airy living room with a sectional and several overstuffed armchairs. The fireplace caught my attention, the stacked stone flowing from the hearth all the way to the second floor ceiling. A thick wooden beam acted as the mantel and was tastefully decorated in a very chic, timeless style.

"Come on, Em." Jesse nudged my arm with his elbow. I jumped slightly, his honeyed words startling me. I had been so taken in with the extravagance of the house that I hadn't realized he stood next to me. "Sorry, didn't mean to scare you."

"You didn't, I just wasn't paying attention." Flashing him a small smile, I followed Reid out to the yard. Nerves immediately bubbled within my chest when I saw several unknown faces amongst the crowd of people I did in fact recognize. The same people were here from the 'Trunk or Treat' at the law office, Vivian and her husband Brett as well as Zander, but there were a lot more children running around.

"That'd be Kingston's family. Aunts, uncles, cousins. That woman there is the other lawyer that works at the firm. Her name's Brit." Reid seemed to notice my hesitation to join the crowd in the yard, opting to stay standing on the raised deck. I quietly counted—seventeen—there were seventeen people here that didn't include my boys or me.

My nerves settled as we made our way to the yard and no eyes darted in our direction. I wasn't exactly sure why I was nervous other than it was a lot of new people, a lot of small talk and introductions, and I didn't want to be the center of attention being Kingston's girlfriend.

"Hey, baby doll." Kingston met us at the bottom of the stairs. Soothing circles from his hand on my lower back melted the last of my nerves. "Aunt Natalie," he called out catching the attention of a woman who looked almost exactly like Stella, only her hair was shorter and down. "This is my girlfriend, Emma. Baby doll, this is my mom's sister Natalie, and her husband Nathan. Their kids are those two"—he pointed to a boy and a girl, both with light blond hair—"Sara and Charlie." I shook their hands, committing their names to memory. Nathan was pale, fairly short, although a few inches taller than his petite wife, with light brunette hair and a clean shaven face. Kingston ushered me on to the next set of people allowing Natalie and Nathan to head inside.

"Uncle Chris." Kingston's voice snagged the attention of a man who was lean with the familiar platinum blond hair. He was holding hands with another man who had jet black hair, bright blue eyes, and was bulky in the amount of muscles stacked on his body. "Emma, this is my mom's brother, Chris, and his husband, Demetri. The twins, Zoey and Zain"—he pointed out two little kids who looked about five with olive skin, black hair, and captivating green eyes—"are theirs." I felt my mind start to spin with the amount of names and faces that were being thrown my way as Kingston started moving me to the last two adults.

"Emma, this is the other lawyer from the firm, Brit. She wasn't at the Halloween thing." I shook her hand. Her graying hair was pulled back in a severe bun, but the smile and crow's feet softened her harsh look. "This is my dad's sister, Kaycee, and her daughter, Kae. She's a sophomore over at Millmer East."

"It's nice to meet you." I repeated the same line for the third time since arriving. My hand tingled from all of the handshakes. Names and faces blurred in my mind, meaning I would need help remembering who was who.

Who knew Kingston had such a large family?

Not me.

"You go to Arbor Ridge?" Kaycee asked. She was probably one of the easiest to remember, looking like a female copy of Kaleb. I nodded, leaning slightly into Kingston's warm torso, already overwhelmed with questions and the party had just started. "Senior like the boys?" I nodded again.

"Cali girl, save me!" Reid's loud shout from farther down the lawn saved me from making any more small talk. Reid was surrounded by little kids, all of which were trying to get the ball he held above his head. One of the twins was hanging off his other arm in an attempt to climb him like a tree. "Here!" He chucked the ball the remaining distance to me. I fumbled but caught it, and immediately four sets of eyes zoomed in on me.

Oh, boy.

I broke away from Kingston and my silent Jesse who stood on his other side, taking off across the yard as fast as I could. Little kid shouts and laughs followed me, my face breaking into a bright smile when I spotted a small playset with a pair of swings and a slide attached to a little clubhouse. Darting up the slide, I crawled into the wooden clubhouse. Little footsteps sounded on the slide and on the rungs of the ladder.

"Throw it here, baby doll!" Kingston's normally laid back

Both of my parents were only children, and my friends were always more focused on typical 'teenager' things. Sitting around the large table, I really felt that family dynamic even though several of the people here weren't even family. Kingston's fingers gently brushed my thigh under the table pulling me from my internal musings.

"Want to come help me get dessert?" he asked. "It's in the garage refrigerator." I nodded and followed him through the main level and out into the cold garage. He paused before opening the appliance door, his hands wringing in front of him.

"You all right?" I murmured, his nervousness putting me on edge. It wasn't like Kingston, who was very go with the flow, to be nervous.

"I was just wondering"—he cleared his throat as his voice cracked—"if maybe you'd want to go out on a date with me? Just you and me," he whispered looking down at me. His coffee brown eyes darted around my face waiting for my answer.

"I would love to go on a date with you." Wrapping my arms around his shoulders, I had to stand on my tiptoes to reach. A girly squeal echoed through my head as I mentally did a little happy dance.

He just asked me on a date!

My sweet Kingston.

"Good." His smile made my heart pitter-patter, his thumbs rubbing gently through my sweater. There was a split second hesitation, but Kingston's eyes melted in warmth as his head came down. His kiss was different than Reid's or Jesse's, hesitant and soft, just a brush against mine. Feeling him pull back, I leaned further into him to bring our lips together. He realized I didn't want the kiss to end and gripped me tighter, his hands splaying out against my lower back.

"You guys get lost? Oh..." Reid's voice filtered into the garage. My head whipped to him, worried about how he'd react. His brows shot up when he saw us entangled in each other's arms but instead of appearing upset, his lips curled into a smirk. "My bad"—he started to turn away from us—"continue your make-out session."

"Shut up, dude, and come help us." Kingston laughed, his lips brushing my forehead in a quick peck. My skin tingled under his lips, my face flushing as Reid made his way over, wrapping me under his arm.

"Didn't mean to interrupt your kissing time, Cali girl," he teased, playfully punching Kingston in the arm. "You should have shut the door, King."

"Emma didn't seem to mind, did you, baby doll?" I melted under his gaze, the heat in his coffee brown eyes stoking the embers growing between my thighs. I tried to keep my face calm as I smiled, but based on their chuckles and pink cheeks, I didn't hide squeezing my legs together as well as I thought. Reid pulled back as Kingston opened the fridge and we loaded up our arms and headed inside. There were cupcakes, brownies, ice cream, as well as a bunch of candy that Stella had set out while we were in the garage.

Once everyone was filled on food and sugar, people hung out and relaxed, filtering out one group at a time until it was just us and Kingston's immediate family. When I attempted to help Stella and Kaleb clean, they waved me off with the demand that we go relax since it was the beginning of our weekend. Killian plopped down in front of the TV and started playing a video game which we watched and played for a while with him, but after about thirty minutes there was a knock on the door.

"Can I help you, officers?" Kaleb answered, his voice cool and polite as he addressed the two police officers on the other side of the threshold.

"Is Jesse Parker here, Mr Bell?" the younger officer asked in a stern voice. My heart started to pound painfully in my chest as I sat forward. Jesse's eyes narrowed; his hands clenched into fists when the officers looked around Kaleb into the house.

"Can I ask what this is about?" Kaleb addressed the older of the two officers, the one who had an expression of empathy etched into his middle-aged face.

"We have a warrant for Mr. Parker's arrest," the younger officer demanded roughly, practically pushing past Kaleb as his steps thudded across the distance between him and his target.

Jesse didn't fight or argue as he stood. Turning around he held his hands behind his back. My eyes blurred with unshed tears as the officer read him his rights. My mind fuzzed over. *This can't be happening.* I couldn't believe my eyes.

"I'm sorry about this, Kaleb," the older officer murmured as Jesse was taken out to the cruiser. "They just sprung this warrant on us, or I would have warned you ahead of time."

"What's it for?" Kaleb held out his hand, taking the folded piece of paper. His eyes scanned while the other officer, whose badge read Mulligan, summarized the warrant.

"Assault against that kid, Brad Warland." Officer Mulligan's tone was harsh when he brought up Brad. His clenched jaw and hard eyes made it clear as day that he didn't like him. "Jesse'll be up for bail once they finish processing him, if you want to meet us at the station."

Kaleb nodded his head looking over to us. Officer Mulligan dipped his head politely toward the rest of us, a pitying grimace passing over his face when he spotted me. Turning, he exited quickly leaving us in a stunned silence. I hadn't realized I was squeezing the living daylights out of Reid's and Kingston's hands until that moment. I loosened my grip and took a shuddering breath, thankful that my tears hadn't poured yet.

"Their warrant is solid," Kaleb told us, his tone low. "I'm going to go get him; it might be a while depending on how long they take to process him. The Warlands are fairly influential, so it might be several hours. Kingston already told me what happened, but Emma"—his eyes centered on me—"if this is how the Warland's want to play, I'll need to sit down with you to go over everything. Your recount of what happened might be the only thing keeping Jesse from doing jail time." Dread crushed my chest, but I nodded knowing I would do whatever it took to keep Jesse from that. Kaleb left quickly after a kiss to Stella who had watched on with worried eyes.

"Killian, go on and head to your room for a bit. I need to talk with them privately." When Killian started to protest, Stella gave him her 'mom glare.' He quieted and left without further argument. "Reid, Emma, you're more than welcome to stay tonight. I know it'll help to be around each other." Her eyes turned to me, and she pulled me gently into a tight hug before whispering, "It's going to be a long night. If you need anything, let me know, all right?"

I felt the burn of a fresh wave of tears fill my eyes, my arms squeezing her back. The love radiating within her arms only added to the ache in my chest, not just from the Jesse situation but from the fact that my mom had barely spoken to me in over two months. Pushing those problems away, I focused on what was most important.

Jesse.

Nodding, I silently let her know I would do just that. Kingston and Reid didn't talk as they led me to Kingston's room on the second floor. It was large, with a king-size bed and plush tan carpeting. The walls were painted a light blue, his comforter a gray and black plaid with matching blue sheets. A guitar sat in the corner along with black and white photography canvases that covered the walls. Normally, I might have been intrigued, or even remotely interested, but given the circumstances I was numb and going through the motions like a zombie.

"Emma." Reid's words were soft, his baritone soothing the jagged emotions warring in my chest: fear, anger, anxiety. "Cali girl"—his more forceful tone held my focus—"do you need to ask your mom if you're all right to stay?" I shook my head.

"She was going to be gone for the weekend on a work trip," I whispered. Kingston reappeared from behind a door with a handful of comfy clothes.

I hadn't even realized he'd walked out of the room.

"These will be big on you, but they should be comfortable enough for sleep." He held out a t-shirt and a pair of sweats. When I took them, Kingston went back into what I assumed was the closet and shut the door, and Reid exited with the mumble that he was going to the bathroom. I changed quickly, but the sweats were too big even with the tie, so I decided to just forgo them. My underwear was no smaller than my swimsuit bottoms and Kingston's shirt covered everything anyway.

"Baby doll?" Kingston's smooth voice radiated out of the cracked closet door. "All done?"

"Yeah." I had just finished folding my clothes, when he

loosed a sharp exhale.

"I thought you said you were done," he murmured, unable to pull his eyes off my exposed legs. I flushed, fiddling with the ends of his borrowed shirt.

"The pants were too big," I explained quietly, shrugging slightly. "Are we all sleeping in the bed?" Reid's curly head had just poked around the door when I finished my question. Exhaustion beat down on me despite the worry and fear coursing through my body, and my eyes barely stayed open as Kingston who was wearing a pair of sweats, and Reid who was in his boxers, led me over to the bed. Crawling into the middle of the large, plushy mattress, I was sandwiched between the two. My head and arm draped over Reid as Kingston curled around my back. It wasn't long before my body and mind gave up and slipped into blissful sleep, all worries silenced.

For now.

NOVEMBER 17TH

Screw Brad.
#StressFreeSaturday #YeahRight #NotTodaySatan

I sat, bleary-eyed and fidgety, at the breakfast bar in the kitchen. The sun had just peeked over the horizon, my eyes unfocused on the wash of vibrant colors welcoming the day. I lost track of how long I had been awake, at least for an hour, if my numb legs from sitting on this uncushioned stool were any indication. A shuffling sounded from the hall, but I was too zoned out to pay attention or particularly care.

Stella was in a pair of pajama pants, a plain t-shirt, and a fuzzy robe that went down to her knees. She went about her morning routine of making coffee and emptying the dishwasher, then she started pulling ingredients out of the double door stainless steel fridge. Silence reigned through the space, both of us caught up in our own thoughts. Before I knew it, the smell of bacon, eggs, and pancakes filled my senses. A steaming cup of coffee appeared in front of me, Stella's concerned eyes focused on my face.

"Emma, honey, you need to eat and drink something"— she nudged the cup of black liquid closer to me—"do you need creamer or sugar or anything?" I shook my head. The numbness had continued through night, and my heart felt like a solid chunk of granite.

I sipped the drink mindlessly, back to unseeing around me. More steps sounded down the stairs and through the hallways, Kingston's messy blond hair and Reid's crazy curls appearing in the corner of my eyesight. They had been passed out when I had woken up from a nightmare. Tangled in their limbs, I thought I was going to wake them as I got out of the warm comfort of their embrace, but they didn't, both in a deep sleep.

"Good morning, Cali girl," Reid mumbled pressing a quick kiss to my temple. Kingston rubbed my back, but with the numbness, I didn't really feel it. His kiss landed gently on top of my head before he moved over to the coffee pot to pour a cup.

"All right, kiddos"—Stella turned to us—"everything is done. Come get it." Reid and Kingston started through the piles of food. I couldn't bring myself to move; my stomach rolled at the thought of food, my one concern focused on Jesse. Stella plopped a plate down in front of me with her 'mom glare' when I didn't get up to eat. I had just stabbed the first piece of food when the front door opened.

My head whipped around. Kaleb's tired face came through the door first with Jesse's right behind him. I surged forward, everything finally flooding my system. I didn't slow down as I barreled into his open arms. Sobs I couldn't hold back any longer wracked my body and soaked his shirt. Once more, we found ourselves clutching to each other as if our lives depended on it.

Maybe it did.

Old Spice, cinnamon, and orange surrounded me, mixing with Jesse's pine and mint smell. Two bodies pressed into either side of us when they encircled us in one giant bear hug. I finally took in the sounds around me as the numbness receded fully; they had been murmuring and cooing soothing words to me until my cries silenced.

"I'm so glad you're home." My voice cracked under my emotion, palpable relief in my voice. Kingston and Reid stepped back just enough for me to look up at Jesse. His eyes were glassy, and tear tracks coated his dark chocolate skin. He kissed me hard, clutching my shoulders tightly in his fingers before pulling back.

"I hate to be the bearer of bad news." Kaleb's deep voice caught everyone's attention, all of our eyes drifting to focus on him. "This is far from over. Brad and his dad are in for the long haul. This is going to get ugly before it gets better. I fully believe we'll be all right, but it'll be rough on you, Emma. Are you sure you're up for this?" I felt my blood run cold at his warning, but being surrounded by my boys filled me with hope and strength.

Jesse needed me.

"Heck yeah, I am," I vowed, Jesse's hand squeezing mine tightly. "He deserves this. I'm not going to let him get away with what he did."

I'm not alone in this fight.
We totally got this.

MISTERS & MOCHAS

BOOK 2 OF THE HIGH SCHOOL CLOWNS & COFFEE GROUNDS SERIES

COMING NOVEMBER 2019

ACKNOWLEDGEMENTS

Jake, my amazing husband, who supported me and cheered me on even when I doubted myself!

My PA Katie and closest friend Jare for keeping me sane when things got overwhelming!

My beta readers-Michelle, Jessica, and Cassie—you guys are awesome and are the best, forever #AJsAlphabets!

Finally, for all of my readers, this wouldn't be possible without you.

ALSO BY A.J. MACEY

Best Wishes Series:
Book 1: Smoke and Wishes
Book 2: Smoke and Survival
Supplemental Point-of-View Stories: Smoke and Wishes:
Between the Wishes

The Aces Series:
Book 1: Rival

About Author

A.J. Macey has a B.S. in Criminology and Criminal Justice, and previous coursework in Forensic Science, Behavioral Psychology, and Cybersecurity. Before becoming an author, A.J. worked as a Correctional Officer in a jail where she met her husband. She has a daughter and two cats named Thor and Loki, and an addiction to coffee and swearing. Sucks at adulting and talking to people, so she'll frequently be lost in a book or running away with her imagination.

Stay Connected

Join the Readers' Group for exclusive content, teasers and sneaks, giveaways, and more at A.J. Macey's Minions on Facebook

Made in the USA
Columbia, SC
15 June 2019